"I care about you, Lily. I have feelings for you."

"Feelings?" Lily's heart beat fast and she had to stop herself from jumping to conclusions. There was a chance he didn't see her the way she saw him. Best she just hear him out.

"Yeah, feelings." Simon stared at her. "And they're not platonic."

Oh, thank God. "What a coincidence. I've been having those same kinds of feelings."

"Midpregnancy sex drive?"

She liked the sexy glint in his eye. "Maybe, but I don't think it's only that. I care about you, too, Simon. I have strong feelings for you."

"Well, then. I guess I can kiss you."

How long had she been waiting to hear those words? "Please do."

His kiss was everything she wanted it to be. They were breathing hard when she felt a series of kicks that startled her. Her hand went to her stomach. "Sorry, they've never kicked so hard before." Could it be her babies approved?

Dear Reader,

I love to do hands-on research for my stories. I've ridden in fire trucks, I've interviewed FBI and secret service agents and had someone teach me how to create a rolling chassis for a book featuring a race-car-driver hero. This time around, I *borrowed* a baby for a day. A former student of mine has a little boy who, at the time I wrote *Be My Babies*, was eight months old. Little Patrick Hoff visited me so I could recall what having a baby was like. (My own *babies* are twenty-six and twenty-three.)

We had a wonderful time. You'll see Patrick's actions in this book: his babbling, his ability to hold his bottle, how he pumped his arms when I fed him, how he tugged his socks off, along with other details of an infant's life. I'd forgotten how satisfying it was to hold a baby, sing him to sleep, or even brush my hand down his wispy hair. You're in for a treat here and do check my Web site for pictures.

And you'll also love reading about Simon and Lily. They're great with kids, and great with each other, even if it does take them the whole book to realize it. I admired Lily for her courage and loyalty, and Simon for his steadfastness and integrity. It was heartwarming to see their romance unfold.

Let me know what you think at kshayweb@rochester.rr.com, or P.O. Box 24288, Rochester, NY 14624 and be sure to visit my Web site at www.kathrynshay.com and catch up with me on my blog at the site.

Happy reading,

Kathryn Shay

BE MY BABIES
Kathryn Shay

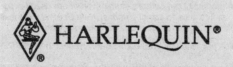

HARLEQUIN®

TORONTO • NEW YORK • LONDON
AMSTERDAM • PARIS • SYDNEY • HAMBURG
STOCKHOLM • ATHENS • TOKYO • MILAN • MADRID
PRAGUE • WARSAW • BUDAPEST • AUCKLAND

ISBN-13: 978-0-373-71479-7
ISBN-10:   0-373-71479-3

BE MY BABIES

ABOUT THE AUTHOR

Best parenting advice ever received? Pick your battles and don't sweat the small stuff. I really do this, and it works. Messy rooms are ignored in my house when I compare them to the real trouble kids can get into. **Mrs. Brady or Mrs. Cleaver?** Oh, Lord, I hope neither. **Cloth or disposable?** You've got to be kidding. Do people really use cloth these days? **Favorite bedtime story?** *Goodnight Moon* and *I'll Love You Forever* are the best books. My kids delighted in my reading the latter, because I always cried. **If you could've kept your child at a specific age, what would that be?** About three. **Most poignant moment with your own bundle of joy?** Definitely when my daughter was born. I was awestruck by her existence. I couldn't believe she was mine. **What makes a mom?** Unconditional love. I think it's the most important thing you can give a child.

Books by Kathryn Shay

To Patrick Hoff.
May you grow up to be
the kind of hero in this book.

CHAPTER ONE

STANDING OUTSIDE the *Sentinel*, Lily Wakefield slid the crumpled yellowed article from her purse and held it up in front of the old brick edifice. The newspaper office looked more or less the same as it had when her mother, Cameron, clipped the picture just before she left Fairview, New York, carrying a suitcase containing practical clothes, serviceable shoes and one hundred dollars. Now, Lily stood before the building in her Prada sandals, DKNY slacks and tailored jacket, with about the same amount of cash in her wallet. The Louis Vuitton bag at her side held a few more outfits, but only as many as she could carry.

Someone bumped into her, said, "Excuse me," and kept going.

Lily nodded and stayed where she was.

About five feet away, the man turned back. "Are you all right?"

"What? Oh, yes."

Glancing up at the sky, he frowned. "Looks like we're in for one of those April showers." His comment was underscored by a draft of wind that lifted and swirled her dark chin-length hair around her face. He pointed to the office. "There's a pot of coffee in there and some homemade cookies that Mrs. Billings made. Want to come in?"

"Um, yes, I guess I do. Thanks."

Bending down, he picked up her suitcase before she could take hold of it and walked alongside her toward the front doors.

It's a beautiful place. It used to be an old home, and then it was converted into the newspaper offices. In the front reception and waiting area, there's a fireplace, a comfortable couch and chairs, and a worn desk like the kind you'd see in reruns of the old TV show, Superman. *I used to love to go there after school and wait for Daddy to be done with work.*

What Lily's mother hadn't told her, and what she only figured out years later, was that Cameron would have done anything to delay going home to her own mother.

Once they were inside, the man motioned to the couch. "Please, sit down." When she'd seated herself, he added, "I'm Simon McCarthy."

"Lily Wakefield."

"Nice to meet you." Again, he smiled. His hazel eyes did, too. "Would you like some coffee?"

"I—I can't have that."

"Oh." When Lily said no more, he asked, "How about tea?"

"Decaffeinated would be okay. Lovely, really, but don't fuss."

"No problem." He went into the back room, and while he was gone Lily studied her surroundings. The windows let in the afternoon breeze, along with the chirping of the birds in the leafy maple trees outside. Engraved plaques hung on the wall before her, citing the *Sentinel* and its editor for various good works. Pictures were interspersed with the awards describing the accomplishments of the paper and its reporters. A few minutes later, Simon returned with a steaming mug. Lily took the cup and sniffed. Mmm. Cinnamon. "Thank you so much." It had been a long time since a man had waited on her.

When she said nothing more, he sat down on a chair opposite her. "Is there a reason you were out there just staring at the building?" He nodded to the suitcase. "With that?"

Her stomach churned. She prayed she wouldn't get sick

all over this total stranger. "Yes." She glanced up at one of the pictures she'd noticed earlier. Its headline read, Gardner Garners The Gold—Best Of Small-town Newspapers. From other photos she'd seen, she recognized the man. "I'm looking for him, Gil Gardner."

Simon tracked her gaze. "I'm not quite sure where he is today."

"Is he out on a story?"

"No, he doesn't cover the news anymore." Sandy eyebrows were raised. They matched his short, dark blond hair, which had a bit of curl. "He's at the office sometimes, but he doesn't do much reporting."

"Doesn't he own the paper?"

"Yeah, he's still the owner. But I run the place. I'm editor in chief." He chuckled self-effacingly. "And a lot of other things. Our staff is small and the tasks are many."

Because she still wasn't ready to explain herself to him, she dodged his question about why she was here and said only, "I'm sure newspaper work is taxing."

His gaze narrowed on her. "Do you know Gil?"

"I've never met him, no." Her hands began to tremble. Steaming tea sloshed over onto her fingers.

"Here." He handed her a handkerchief pulled from his pocket.

"Thanks."

"Why are you shaking?"

"I'm fine. Listen, could you call my…call Gil? I need to see him."

"I guess I could."

She noticed he had Gil's number on speed dial. Who would be in Lily's top five these days? A paltry few. But it was her own fault for letting her life unfold as it had. And now when she needed help, she was going to have to turn to strangers. The thought scared her to death.

Simon was frowning as he spoke into the phone. "Yeah, Gil, it's me, Simon. I need you to come to the office as soon as you get this message. I'll explain why then." He clicked off.

"Thank you, Mr. McCarthy."

"A lot of cloak-and-dagger," he said easily.

"I suppose. But I have my reasons."

"What are they?"

"I'd rather not say." Lily was a private person by nature, and she was particularly embarrassed by her present circumstances. And though he seemed nice enough, who knew what this man's relationship was with Gil?

The bell over the door sounded and Simon and Lily looked toward it. A teenager stepped inside. "Dad?"

Even if the girl hadn't uttered the word, Lily would have known immediately that she was Simon's daughter. Same tawny hair, although hers hung almost to her waist. Same hazel eyes. Nose, a feminine version of his. She had an aura about her, too, making Lily want to sketch her.

"Hi, honey." He introduced her to Lily.

"Grandpa Gil's coming in behind me. Katie and I were walking home and he picked us up. It's starting to drizzle."

The cup jerked and tea sloshed again. "Grandpa?" Lily asked.

Jenna smiled. "Not my *real* grandpa, but he's like one."

Lily got the drift. In other words, Gil had found a replacement. Well, why not? So had Derek.

Again, the door opened, and in walked a tall, lanky man with a full head of salt-and-pepper hair and blue eyes just like Lily's mother's. And her own. Lily felt her heart thump in her chest at finally seeing Gil in person.

"Hi, everyone." He focused on Lily. "Who's our gu—" Before he could finish his statement, Gil's complexion paled and he grabbed on to the high table just inside the door.

Jumping up from his chair, Simon rushed over to him. "Gil, is it your heart again?"

"Grandpa?" Jenna sounded afraid, too.

Gil's mouth was slack-jawed as he stared at Lily. Finally, he said, "Not like you mean."

"What, Gil?"

"It's my heart, but not like you mean." Letting go of Simon, he crossed the room. "Who are you? You look just like my daughter, Cameron."

"I know I do. I'm *her* daughter, Lily."

SIMON WATCHED IN AWE—and with a little bit of horror—as tears filled Gil's eyes. In the almost thirty years he'd known the man, he'd never once seen him cry. "Gil, are you all right?"

"Grandpa?" Jenna's tone was even more worried.

"You're Cami's girl?"

Lily stood. She couldn't tear her gaze from him, either. "Yes, I am. I'm sorry to spring myself on you unannounced."

His face was still ashen. "I know... I know Cami died. We found out through a lawyer. But...she had a *daughter?* The only thing she ever wrote to us was that she hadn't gone through with her pregnancy."

Now, Lily Wakefield's face paled and she reseated herself. "That's new information to me." She bit her lip. "I realize this is a shock, Mr. Gardner."

After a moment, Gil, also, took a chair. Simon followed suit, while Jenna sat on the opposite end of the couch from Lily. "I—I didn't know," Gil repeated.

Lily glanced nervously at Simon. "Is there somewhere we can go to talk privately?"

"What? Oh, no need for that. Simon and Jenna are like family. I want them to hear what you have to say."

Frown lines around the woman's mouth told Simon that she wasn't pleased by Gil's answer. Who cared? No way was he leaving Gil alone with this stranger who claimed to be his granddaughter. She could be anybody.

Sighing, she drew a sheaf of papers from her purse. "I have documentation to verify who I am."

When Gil didn't take what she offered, but just stared at her, Simon snatched the papers from her hand. Birth certificate for Liliana Clarkson. Mother, Cameron Gardner Clarkson. Father unknown. There were also pictures. Photocopied drivers' licenses, social security cards for Lily and her mother, a passport. And a picture of a young girl with Gil in his youth. "They seem in order." Simon would have his sister, Sara, a lawyer in town, check them out, though. Documents could be forged and stories made up. He'd arrange a background check on this woman, at least.

"Do you have any idea what a gift you've brought me?" Gil finally asked her.

"Have I?" Lily's gaze hardened almost imperceptibly. "You didn't stay in touch with your own daughter."

Jenna gasped, and Gil's face reddened. "It sounds horrible. It *is* horrible."

Simon sat forward. "Gil, you know what happened with Cameron wasn't all your fault."

"It *was* all my fault. No one will ever convince me otherwise."

Simon was not only wary now, but anger bubbled inside him. If what this woman said was true, she'd surely resent what had happened to her mother, and rightfully so. But given that, her motive for coming to Fairview couldn't be good. Who could possibly forgive that kind of abandonment? "Is this why you came here—to make accusations at Gil? To hurt him with them?"

Lily focused on her grandfather. "I don't want to hurt you. That's not why I'm here."

"Why, then?" Simon knew his tone was too harsh, but he worried about Gil—especially after his heart attack a few years ago. He'd protect Gil from Lily Wakefield, even if Gil wouldn't protect himself.

"Dad?"

"Simon…" Gil admonished.

But Lily held up her hand. "I'll answer his question."

She looked around. "But privately. I don't feel comfortable baring my soul in front of strangers."

Gil stood. "Then come with me. My house isn't far." To Simon he said, "I'll call you later."

Simon watched them go out the door. He had a feeling this wasn't going to be good, and he hated it when he couldn't keep the people he loved safe.

"Dad, is Grandpa Gil gonna be okay?"

"I hope so, honey. I hope so."

TAKING IN A DEEP BREATH, Gil faced his granddaughter over the kitchen table in the home where her mother had grown up. No, that was wrong. Cami hadn't finished growing up here. Alice hadn't given her the chance to, and part of the whole ugly chain of events involved the fact that Gil himself had allowed his wife to have her way regarding their daughter. As he'd told Simon, his role in what happened was something for which he'd never forgive himself.

"Are you comfortable, Lily? In that straight chair?"

"Yes. My back feels better in one of these." She sipped the tea he'd fixed her, while he made strong coffee for himself.

"Then talk to me. Tell me why you've come here."

Shaking back her hair, Lily held his gaze. "I'm here because I'm pregnant and I have nowhere else to go."

Gil froze. *Oh, my God, just like Cameron.* For a few moments, he couldn't speak. Finally, he recovered his equilibrium. "What about the baby's father?"

"Babies."

"Excuse me?"

Her smile was as broad and generous as his daughter's had been before things went bad. "I'm having twins."

"Twins? That's great." What to say? "Are you feeling well?"

"I am." She placed her hand on her abdomen. "The first trimester was hard, but it's been better this past month."

He felt awkward talking about this but he forged ahead. "How far into the pregnancy are you?"

"Four months."

She didn't look it. She was thin, and her complexion was pale. Her makeup was perfect, however, and her dark hair was stylishly cut. Yet, despite the sophisticated exterior, there was a vulnerability about her that tugged at his heart.

"Twins don't always go full-term, but I'm going to make sure mine do."

"You didn't answer my question about the father."

"He's in no condition to help us now." She drew in a deep breath. "So I came to you."

Why she'd even ask him after what he did—or didn't do—for her mother was beyond Gil. But maybe, in some convoluted way, Lily Wakefield showing up here was a chance for Gil to make up for having let his daughter down when *she* was having a child. "I can and I will," he said instinctively. "I'll do whatever you want. Is it money?"

"No! I didn't come for a handout."

He recoiled. "I didn't mean it that way."

"I'm sorry. I shouldn't snap at you."

He drank his coffee and measured his words. She should be doing more than snapping at him. "Then what *do* you need from me, Lily? What can I do for you?"

"For now, a place to live, until I can find a job. I'd like to look for one in Fairview, if you wouldn't mind my staying in town."

"I'd love to have you in Fairview—and in my home, for as long as you want. But should you be working?"

"Pregnant women have been working for centuries."

Stalling for time, he got up and poured himself more coffee, let its strong scent waft up to him. "I don't want to rush you. I'm in foreign waters here. You'll have to tell me what's best for you."

"That's a switch."

He pivoted to face her. "What?"

"In the situation I came from, nobody cared much about what I wanted."

"Do you want to tell me about that first?"

Her slate-blue eyes grew shadowed. "No, not yet."

"All right. Will you tell me about Cami and your life together? I never knew how she fared."

"Nobody called her Cami."

"No? I guess it was only my pet name for her."

Lily shook her head. "You talk about her so...warmly, but I know she was kicked out of her home when she got pregnant."

"That's not exactly what happened."

"It's what she told me."

"We sent her away to have the baby at a place for unmarried girls who were pregnant."

"She saw that as the same thing. In any case, she didn't blame *you*—just her mother. She talked about you in a kind way, too, which is why I felt I could come here."

"Where did she go when she left Fairview?"

Lily fidgeted. Shifted in her seat. "Downstate. I grew up in New York City. She worked there as a waitress. She died in a bus accident."

With his newsman's instinct, Gil read Lily easily. Either what she said wasn't true or it wasn't the whole story. "I have no information at all on her life after she left us."

"She wanted it that way." Lily yawned. "I'm sorry—it's been a long day. Would you mind if I rested a bit?"

"The house has several bedrooms. You can take your pick."

Now those eyes, so much like his daughter's that it made his heart ache, clouded over. "Would the one where my mother stayed be okay?"

"More than okay." He smiled, but he felt as if somebody had kicked him in the gut. "It's been redone." Alice had said it was better that way. "But I saved Cami's things."

"I—I didn't expect that." She yawned again. "Oh, excuse me."

Standing, he set his empty mug in the sink and rinsed it. "Give me a minute to go tidy up the room. Put on sheets, air it out a bit."

"I can do that myself."

"Please, Lily. Let me."

"All right." Gil had crossed to the doorway, when she said, "I don't know what to call you."

Grandpa. Please, call me Grandpa. He smiled over his shoulder. "Whatever's comfortable for you."

She nodded. "Thanks for not pushing—about that or what's happened to me."

"You're welcome. I meant what I said about being given a gift."

This time around, he planned to embrace it.

"WHY'S SHE HERE, DAD?"

Ah, the sixty-four-thousand-dollar question. "I don't know, honey, except for what Gil told me when he called."

At the long counter, Jenna was tearing lettuce to make a salad while Simon put rigatoni into boiling water at the stove. The scent of the meat sauce his daughter had made over the weekend spiced up the whole sunny kitchen.

Jenna's thick braid swung back and forth as she shook her head. "It must be scary, being pregnant and having no place to go." She frowned. "Why didn't Grandpa Gil ever know about Lily?"

Though she was still young and innocent by today's standards for a teenage girl, Jenna was sixteen. Old enough to know the truth and learn about the foibles of people she loved and admired. He was chagrined to think that she didn't know about his own. Turning the heat down on the pasta, he crossed to the bar that jutted out from the counter. "Sit a minute, honey."

They took stools opposite each other. "Gil's daughter left home when she was sixteen."

"No way. Dad, that's my age."

"I know. What's more, she was pregnant."

"With Lily? Then, why didn't Grandpa know about her?"

He explained about Alice and Gil's decision. "Actually, Cameron never went to the home. She ran away."

"Grandpa Gil did *that?*"

"It was more his wife's decision. You didn't know Alice."

"Did you?"

"Only after Cameron left. She was a stern woman—a strong believer in propriety and paying for your sins."

"She sent her own kid away to punish her?" Jenna said the words as if she couldn't quite grasp the concept. As her father, Simon was glad Jenna found the behavior incomprehensible.

"I've always thought so. And to avoid scandal. Her parents, the Caldwells, were well-known in Fairview. You know the term *pillars of the community?*"

Jenna nodded.

"That's what her family was."

"Yours, too, Dad. Everybody in town still talks about how great your mom and dad were."

Simon smiled. He'd adored his mother, Catherine, who'd been a teacher, and his guidance counselor father, Patrick, had been his best friend. When they were killed in a boating accident, Simon had been twenty and he'd walked around in a daze for months, mourned them for years. He'd always vowed to be as good a father as his own had been.

"My parents were well loved, but they didn't have the clout of the Caldwells. They had a lot of money. They owned the *Sentinel,* as well as some stores in the area. Gil said Alice was trying to avoid embarrassing the family, so they told everybody Cameron was going away to a private school."

"What happened when she never came back?"

"The real story seeped out. People got wind of the pregnancy. Ironically, it wasn't a big deal to anyone but Alice, and gossip died quickly. Her parents survived just fine. But Alice went a little crazy."

"She doesn't sound like the kind of person Grandpa Gil would marry."

"She had her good traits. She did a lot of charitable work in her church. But she grew more severe as she got older."

"Huh."

"Between trying to run the paper and deal with his wife, Gil was a wreck."

Jenna's brows furrowed. "He should have stood up for his daughter, Dad. It sucks that he didn't."

"I think it's best not to judge people, Jen." Especially not their marriages. "We know the broad strokes, but not all of what happened."

His daughter studied him.

Simon took her hand. "You know, don't you, that you could never do anything that would make me send you away?"

Her eyes twinkled. "Even if I dated that motorcycle guy who just moved here from the city?"

"What motorcycle..." He stopped. "You're teasing."

"Yep. You're an easy mark, Dad. You need a life."

They both stood, and from behind he got her in a headlock. Kissed her hair. "You, little girl, can be a brat."

"I love you, Daddy. Now come on, let's eat."

The meal was satisfying, and Simon enjoyed his daughter's company. Even if she didn't know all his foibles, what his life had really been like before Marian died. He wondered briefly if she'd ever be old enough to handle *those* details?

LILY'S GRANDFATHER looked over at her when she came to the doorway of the kitchen. He was stirring something at the stove and it smelled heavenly. "Did you rest?" he asked.

"Yes, I fell asleep right away, but I've been up for a bit. I went through a few of the boxes you left on the dresser." She couldn't resist a glance into her mother's past.

"Ah." He adjusted the heat on the burner. "Ready for some supper?"

He seemed more uncomfortable than he'd been before she went upstairs. Nervous. Maybe he had had too much time to think about the history between them.

Dropping down into a kitchen chair, she watched him. "Do you mind talking about those boxes for a minute?"

"No. Of course not." He leaned against the counter.

"I found a christening gown in the one marked baby things." It had smelled musty, but it was beautifully preserved.

"Your great-grandmother made it. You can have it for one of your twins, if you want."

"Maybe. Whose handwriting was in the baby book?"

"My wife, Alice's. Your grandmother."

Well, at least there had been some good times. Loving comments had been recorded about Cameron's early development. As if he read her thoughts, Gil said aloud, "Those were happy years for us all."

There was a second carton, marked Cameron's School Days. It included pictures, drawings, some done with finger paint. A few notes from teachers. Report cards. Lily's mother had been smart and well liked by her fifth grade class. Somebody had saved all that, too.

Lily held up a diary. "This was in the last box from my mother's high school years. Along with a faded corsage, pictures with a few girls, things like that."

Gil pushed off from the counter and got plates out of the cupboard. "Alice read it, looking for a clue to where Cami might have gone when she never showed up at the Sisters of Mercy home."

"There's not much in here."

He retrieved silverware and set everything on the table. She sniffed when he set a bowl on the table. "Spaghetti?"

"Mmm. Jenna made it yesterday for me." Gil sat at the table. "What were you looking for in the diary, Lily?"

"Information about my father."

"I'm afraid we never knew who he was. Cami refused to tell us. That pregnancy capped off several bad years. Did you ever ask your mother about him?"

"Yes, but she didn't tell me much."

He was a boy I met in a bar outside of town, where I used a fake ID. He wasn't interested in either you or me after I got pregnant and he left the area. I never heard from him again.

I'm sorry, Lily, but you should know the truth. Men— they're not reliable. I hope you have better luck than I had, but there it is.

"I'm sorry," Gil said. "I wish I could tell you more."

Maybe that was for the best. Discussion of a father who didn't want her made Lily realize she was depending on a man who'd left his own child fatherless.

Placing the diary on the oak table, Lily shook her head. "Guess we'll never know who he was."

"Does it matter now?"

She stared at him for a long time. "Fathers always matter."

It was too bad that Gil Gardner hadn't learned that sooner.

A SMALL READING LAMP illuminated the darkness as Simon sat at the desk in his den refiguring his finances. He'd awakened at 4:00 a.m. after a vivid nightmare. He'd dreamed that Lily Wakefield had taken ownership of the *Sentinel* and kicked him and Jenna out on the street. Not that he'd ever be destitute. Despite the fact that he was slowly buying up the paper's shares and now owned a whopping thirty percent, he'd made sure he and Jenna had their nest egg. If he did lose the paper, he'd only have lost his dream and not his ability to take care of his daughter.

Still, here he was before dawn, adding up the numbers again. He shook his head. There was no way he could expedite this process. He'd just worked himself out of debt from Marian's accident and Jenna's medical bills. He tried to tell himself that was okay, that Gil had assured him there was no hurry. After his heart attack, Gil had even put it in his will that Simon had the option to buy the remaining stock if anything happened to him. He'd wanted to leave the paper outright to Simon and Jenna, but Simon had balked. As it was, Gil's plan would guarantee that no one else could take over the *Sentinel,* especially a larger chain such as the Heard Corporation, which had already approached them about a buyout.

Now, the appearance of Lily Wakefield put a whole new spin on Simon taking ownership. Finally, he admitted that to himself. Though he was mostly worried about Gil, this possibility had been buzzing around in his subconscious since he'd met Lily yesterday.

He leaned back and sipped his coffee. Damn it, wasn't even a single part of his life going to go easily?

Think about your priorities.

Jenna. She meant everything to him. Guilt, dark and ugly, reared its head. His daughter had been the most important person in the world to him since the day she'd been born, but he still hadn't managed to protect her completely. Instead, when Marian had wrapped her car around that pole and hurt Jenna in the process, Simon had blamed himself. It was one of the reasons Simon understood Gil and his situation with Cameron so well.

But this time, when Simon had the chance to protect someone he loved, he was going to make damn sure he did it. And if Lily Wakefield got caught in the cross fire, so be it.

CHAPTER TWO

LILY LAY BACK against the pillows and watched the morning sun stream in through her bedroom windows. The birds had awakened her at dawn, but she'd dozed off again. She couldn't believe she was sleeping so much, or that she'd been so lazy all week since she'd arrived in Fairview. At home, in Westchester, having Derek to tend to, and, worse, his parents' constant visits had kept her on edge and unable to relax or sleep well. She hadn't realized how the anxiety of her life had affected her physically until she'd begun to feel better here, in the cocoon of her grandfather's house.

There was a knock on her door, a light tapping, in case she was still asleep. This had become a morning routine—one she was beginning to cherish.

"I'm awake, Gil."

Entering with a tray, he smiled. "Good morning. You look rested."

"Completely." She looked askance at what he carried. "I wish you wouldn't do this."

"You gave me a week to pamper you, and I'm thoroughly enjoying myself."

At times like these, Lily couldn't imagine Gil allowing her mother to leave his house and certainly never kicking her out. It just didn't make sense. But yesterday he'd come clean with the fact that he had, indeed, let Alice send Cameron to the home for unwed mothers. He took full blame for it, which had eased somewhat her resentment of what he'd done. As did his confession that his daughter's disappearance had caused him long-standing guilt and grief. He'd also tried to undo it, but ultimately he couldn't find her. Though Lily would never understand what he'd done, she was coming to terms with his actions.

Now, he beamed as he approached the bed. "This is the last day I'll spoil you."

She glanced at the tray after he set it down and inhaled the scents of cinnamon and warm bread. "Oh, Lord, I love French toast."

Gil cleared his throat. "So did your mother. We used to make it Saturday mornings before I went to work."

Picking up a glass, she sipped the tart orange juice. "You worked Saturdays?"

"And Sundays." He took a seat near the window. "In those days, I was a workaholic, Lily."

"That's what you implied yesterday." She didn't want the resurrection of the topic to ruin the morning, so instead she nodded to the tray. "I see you brought the paper."

"Yeah, it looks great this week."

"Simon's a good editor?"

His eyes sparkled. "He learned from the best."

"I'll bet." She settled her hand on the newsprint. "I'm going to look for a job today, Gil."

"I wish you wouldn't. There's no need."

"I can't just laze in bed forever."

"Why?"

"It isn't right."

"It might be right for the babies."

"I won't overdo it. I have to start taking control of my life."

He checked his watch. "Jake is coming in an hour to pick me up for our bowling league. I've got time, if you want to tell me about that. About Derek."

Lily had yet to reveal the reason she'd run away from her husband or tell Gil what really happened to her and Cameron all those years ago. Now might be the time to explain about Derek. But she didn't know if she'd ever tell him the latter. Some things were better kept from a father.

She bit into the toast. It was delicious. "A shortened version, maybe. After I eat."

When she finished her meal, Gil took the tray and put it on the dresser. Sitting back down, he said, "I'm listening." He'd brought a mug of coffee for himself and he sipped from it as she talked.

"I met Derek after college. His family business was a big customer of the agency I worked for and Derek was at the firm a lot."

"What business is he in?"

"Wakefield Enterprises."

"Wow, I didn't make the connection. Huge conglomerate."

"They're rich." And spoiled and arrogant.

"So why do you need a job, Lily?"

"Because it's the Wakefields' money. When I left the house in Westchester, I took some clothes and my jewelry, but not even my car. I only took the jewelry because I needed a security blanket, and because I intend to pay my own medical bills when I have the babies."

"What on earth brought you to this point?"

"Derek swept me off my feet. He was so charismatic, I didn't stand a chance." She could still remember a young black-haired, blue-eyed Derek wining and dining her, catering to her every whim, professing his undying love. She didn't know until after they were married that this wasn't the real Derek Wakefield, this wasn't his true personality. She explained all this to her grandfather.

"Once we were together, he couldn't keep up the facade. But by then it was too late, because I was crazy about him. I thought I could handle the negligence and self-centeredness." She shook her head. "It wasn't until we tried to have a child that things became unbearable."

"You had problems...in that area?"

"Yes. Derek wouldn't get tested, but there were no

physical issues with me." She shrugged. "Still, maybe I was too tense."

"How did he feel when you told him you finally were pregnant?"

She waited a long time before she answered. "I didn't."

In her mind, she could still see their last scene together. She'd come home from her doctor's appointment elated, having waited to tell Derek about the pregnancy until she was past the miscarriage stage. That day, she'd rushed to his downstairs office, knocked and entered without waiting for a reply. And there he was...

"What are you *doing?*" she'd asked, horrified.

The traces of white powder still visible beneath his nose, and the paraphernalia on the desk answered her question.

"Get out of here. This is my business."

"Derek, you can't—"

"I said get the hell out." He came around the desk as fast as a jaguar. When she didn't move, he yelled, "I said, get out!"

"Derek, please."

The slap came fast and it was hard enough to knock her back against the door. And for the first time Lily was afraid he'd hurt her and the babies.

She told Gil everything, except the part about Derek hitting her. For some reason, she couldn't share that with him. "So I left."

"Oh, Lily, I'm sorry."

"Me, too. I'm going to file for a legal separation, but I need to get back on my feet again first, in case he isn't agreeable."

"Do you still care about him?"

"Derek was my first love, and I think I'll always care about him. But now I have two children to protect."

His eyes widened beneath bushy brows. "You're not going to tell him about them?"

"I'm afraid for them, and truthfully, I'm afraid his

parents might try to take them from me. I just don't have everything figured out yet, Gil."

"You're not alone anymore. I'm here for you." His eyes were sad. "I know I wasn't there for your mother, but I learned what's important."

She wanted to believe that, but Lily had a hard time trusting men these days.

The doorbell rang. Rising, her grandfather said, "That's Jake. I've got to go."

"Tell him I made an appointment with Dr. Rabin." *Jake* was Doc Jacobs, an established physician in town and Gil's best friend. He had a young partner who was slowly taking over his practice. "The last time he came here, he insisted. I do need checkups."

"I'll tell him." Leaning over, he kissed Lily's head. It was the first time he'd done that. "I'll be back this afternoon."

"Enjoy bowling and lunch."

After Gil left, Lily was feeling discomfited, probably because she still had some conflicted feelings about Gil's role in her mother's life. And because she'd talked about Derek. She'd tried to downplay that last encounter to Gil, but in reality the scene had been a nightmare. Getting out of the house unnoticed. Covering her tracks. Derek wouldn't be able to trace her to Fairview because when she met him she'd been using the Clarkson name—which her mother had taken to protect her identity—and he'd never known Lily's connection with the Gardners.

To dispel her anxiety, Lily opened the *Sentinel* to search for the classifieds. She'd feel better if she was doing something with her time.

The paper did look good, though with her art and advertising background, she couldn't help thinking of improvements that could be made to the layout and design. The classifieds, especially, needed revamping. She began circling jobs that she could do and not be on her feet all day. There weren't many. She was halfway through the ads when the phone rang, and she answered the extension by her bed. "Gardner residence."

A hesitation. "Lily? This is Simon McCarthy. Is Gil there?"

"Ah, no. He just left to go bowling and have lunch with Doc Jacobs."

"Damn."

"Is something wrong?"

"Our receptionist called in sick and we're fielding a lot of local ads today." He sighed. "Never mind, I'll try Sammy's mother. She might be able to pitch in."

Sammy Johnston was the photographer on staff. From the looks of the paper, she was a good one.

"What about me?"

"You?"

"I can answer phones. Take ad copy."

"No, that's okay."

"Really, Simon. I was just looking at the classifieds for myself."

"You're staying in town?" His tone of voice was odd.

"For a while. I need to earn my keep."

"I see."

"Give me a half hour to shower and get over there."

"I don't think…"

"I insist I be allowed to help out. See you then."

Lily hung up, wondering why Simon McCarthy didn't want her at the *Sentinel*. She allowed a spark of anger to surface. She was on her way to becoming the woman she'd been pre-Derek and here was *another* man who seemed to want to hold her back. Well, not again. She'd be damned if she let Simon McCarthy interfere in her life.

SIMON DIDN'T WANT HER HERE. When she walked through the door, he felt trouble sidle in along with her. She looked rested today. Her cheeks were rosy from the walk here and the warm April wind had played havoc with her hair, tumbling it into wavy masses. The light blue top she wore with a navy skirt accented the color of her eyes. "Hi. I told you that you didn't have to come."

At that moment, Sammy poked her head out from the newsroom. "Simon, we need you back here." She smiled. "Hi, Lily. Feeling okay?"

"Yes. Thanks."

Just then, the phone rang.

Lily crossed to the desk. "Go back. I'll get that."

"Suit yourself." He disappeared into the newsroom, cursing the curtness of his voice.

After he'd made the decision about which photo to use for the upcoming fair in town, he went back out front.

Lily was sitting at the desk, taking notes. "Why, yes, Mr. Martini, I think that copy reads well. Might I suggest a little tweak?"

Simon stood behind her and watched. She smiled into the phone and listened to the caller. "Perhaps replace *cute* with *adorable*." She paused. "All right, good. Do we usually bill you? What? Well, news travels fast. Uh-huh, I'm his granddaughter. Why, thank you so much. I'm glad to be here."

When she hung up, she swiveled the desk chair around and saw Simon. "Lots of ads coming in today. That's the third since you went back."

"I know. It picks up on Friday. You've made yourself at home."

Her eyes narrowed. The mirth had gone out of them. "I hope I'm helping."

Running a hand through his hair, he said, "Sorry. You are."

"Is there a reason you don't want me here, Simon?"

About a thousand. He could never reveal his worry that she might make a claim to the paper, but eventually he was going to warn her not to hurt Gil. "Gil said you were exhausted. I don't want to answer to him if you get tired out."

Her hand went to her abdomen. "Didn't your wife work when she was pregnant with Jenna?"

"No. She was sick a lot, throughout the first and second trimesters." He glanced at his watch. "I've got an appointment with the mayor in ten minutes. I have to go. I hate to leave..."

"Don't worry, I won't run off with the company savings."

His heart knocked against his chest.

"Kidding. I can hold down the fort."

"Our advertising guy is out soliciting ads and Sammy's only here in the mornings, but Evan, the other reporter, is in back."

"Fine."

"We usually close at lunchtime."

Her expression was amused. "Really?"

"Uh-huh. Fairview's pretty much a reincarnation of Mayberry, only bigger."

"It's a nice town. I like it."

"You can go home at twelve. I'll be back by one."

"Trying to get rid of me?"

"Of course not." He snapped the words at her, then started out.

"Simon, wait." He turned back. "Have I done something to offend you?"

Just exist. "No, I'm sorry. I'm swamped, is all."

"Then go unswamp yourself." The phone rang and she picked it up. "The *Sentinel.* Lily speaking. Why yes, yes, I'm taking the information today." She arched a brow at him. "Mr. Martini said what? Oh, how nice, Mrs. Conklin. Yes, I'll help you with the phrasing."

Simon scowled as he left the office. He'd never expected her to fit in here. Didn't want her to. As he stepped outside into the bright sunlight, he felt a sense of things slipping right through his fingers. And Lily Wakefield was the cause.

AT NOON, AFTER LOCKING the front door as Evan had told her to do when he left for lunch, Lily had taken a twenty-minute nap on the couch and then she'd fixed herself some soup she'd found in the small kitchen out back. She'd just returned to the reception area with her sketch pad and tea, when she heard a knock at the door. Rising, Lily crossed to it. Jenna was there, wearing a light yellow top and capris to match and looking like sunshine herself. She let the girl in. "Hi, Jenna."

"Hi, Lily. Is Dad here?"

"No, he's gone out."

"Darn. I wanted to have lunch with him."

"I had some soup." She nodded out back. "There's more in the cupboard, if you want to eat and wait for him. I'll make it for you."

Her face was a lot friendlier than her father's. "Cool. But I can fix it."

Lily went back to the couch and began to sketch the wall where framed editions of old newspapers were. She'd learned this was Simon's collection. As she drew, she thought about his daughter. Jenna had such an interesting face. A study of innocence on the verge of adulthood. Maybe she'd try drawing the girl today.

Jenna returned with a cup of soup and some crackers and sat on the chair. "Mmm, this is great." She cocked her head. "What are you doing here?"

Lily told her.

"Poor Dad. He needs more staff, but I guess he can't get it. I usually help out during summer vacations." She nodded to the pad on Lily's lap. "What are you doing?"

"Drawing."

"What?"

"The wall of old newspapers."

"Dad's collection. He loves those things, but they're expensive as all get out."

"I'd like to draw you sometime, Jenna."

The girl's eyes lit up, accented by the sun coming in from the window. "Now?"

"How long do you have?"

"Lunch is forty-five minutes. Sometimes I stay here for the next class session. I have it free. The school doesn't mind."

"Then, now it is."

They talked as Lily flipped the pages and began to sketch Jenna. "Tell me about yourself."

"Well, my best friend's name is Katie Welsh. We're tight and we always hang together."

"It's nice to have friends. What do you take at school?"

"Same old, same old. I like English best."

"You do? Why?"

"I dig reading. Dad's read to me since I was little and I've never stopped. And my English teacher, Miss Jameson, is the bomb. She lets us pick a lot of independent stuff."

"What are you reading now?"

"*Ordinary People.* I love the book, and we're seeing the movie next week."

"I loved that book, too. It's sad, though."

"You read?"

"Not much lately."

Jenna waited a beat. "Are you in trouble, Lily?"

"Not like you mean." How much should she tell this girl? "I left my old life because I didn't feel safe there."

"Why?"

She looked up and almost succumbed to the sincere expression on Jenna's face. Amazing how, after only one week, she had to remind herself she didn't know any of these people all that well. "Some of it's private."

Unselfconsciously the girl rolled her eyes. "Dad says I ask too many questions."

"No, you don't. Just so long as you can accept it when people don't want to answer them."

"I can. No worries."

"What else do you do?"

"I'm in the plays here. Katie, too. We do one a year, and then there's a summer production. Last fall, I was the second lead in *No, No, Nanette.*"

"I'm impressed. I saw a revival of that on Broadway."

"I'm *dying* to go and see shows on Broadway." She added, "I love to babysit, too. Hey, maybe Katie and I can babysit the twins when they get here."

Lily's pulse sped up. "I'm, um, not sure I'll be in Fairview then."

"Where would you go?"

She gripped the pencil tighter and had to stop drawing for a minute. "I honestly don't know."

"You should stay. Grandpa Gil loves having you here."

She knew that, but she wondered how Jenna had figured it out. She asked the girl.

"He just acts it. He always talks about you and smiles a lot more than before you came. Dad says it's good to see him happy."

"That's nice."

After fifteen minutes, Lily studied the sketch. "It's okay. Could use more detail. But there's not much time left before the paper's open again."

"Can I see it?"

"Sure."

Jenna plopped down close to Lily on the couch. "Wow. This is sweet."

"Think so?"

"Yeah. You even got me holding a book." She smiled at the picture. "Can I have it?"

"I'd rather finish... Oh!" Lily's hand went to her abdomen. "Oh."

"What? Are you okay?"

Tears came to Lily's eyes.

"Lily, should I call somebody?"

"No, no, honey. I just felt a kick for the first time."

"Get out!" She stared at Lily's stomach. "What did it feel like?"

"A pressure pushing against my tummy. Oh, there's another."

"Maybe it's the other baby."

"Maybe."

Jenna was silent. Then, she asked, "Lily, can I feel it?"

"Well…of course." Not exactly how Lily planned sharing the first flutters of the babies—with a teenage girl she barely knew—but what the heck? At least someone was with her to appreciate this milestone. She took Jenna's hand and moved it to where she'd felt the first kick. Nothing. "Come on, sweetie. Kick again for Jenna."

In a few moments, there was another gentle nudge. "Man, Lily, that's the best." She moved her hand a bit and waited. "Oh, I felt that, too."

"Looks like one isn't going to be outdone by the other."

The bell over the door sounded again and in walked Simon. He stopped short when he saw his daughter close to Lily on the couch. "Jenna, what are you doing here?"

"I came for lunch. You weren't around, so I had soup with Lily."

He checked his watch. "I see. You'd better get going."

"Dad, she drew me. And then I felt the babies kick. It was so awesome."

His face softened. "Which? The drawing or the kicking?"

"Both. Come look."

Crossing to the couch, he stood behind them. He was so close, the scent of him practically surrounded Lily. Aftershave? Soap? "Hmm. Very nice. You're good, Lily. What's your background?"

"I was an art and design major in college."

"Not much call for that in Mayberry."

"I…"

The phone rang and Lily rose from the couch. "I'll get it."

"No, I will. You can go home now."

"Dad?" Jenna had obviously caught the rudeness, too. "Are you okay?"

"Yeah, sure." He answered the phone. "Hello? Oh, yes, Mrs. Billings. She's here. I guess it's all right if you talk to her." He held out the receiver. "You're drumming up quite a fan club."

Lily shrugged and ruffled Jenna's hair. "I hope to see you soon."

"I loved feeling the babies move. Do you know what they are?"

She took the phone, but before she spoke into it she grinned at Jenna. "Yep, one of each."

"Isn't that great, Daddy?" Jenna said.

"Great," Simon said, staring at Lily. "Just great."

DEREK WAKEFIELD rolled over in bed and reached for Liliana. When he came up with only a handful of silk duvet, he grunted. Gradually, he came awake to the smell of stale booze. There was a putrid taste in his mouth.

"Aw, shit," he said, burying his face in his pillow. As awareness dawned, he began to crave another drink. Slowly, he opened one eye and stared at the clock until it came into focus. Noon. What day was it?

Sighing, he turned onto his back, and his stomach pitched. The bright sun slanted in from the skylight and hurt his eyes. Liliana liked spring afternoons—maybe he'd take her to the park. She looked so cute in that straw sun hat he'd bought her in the Caribbean.

Then he remembered. Liliana wasn't here. She'd left in the middle of the night a week ago. Why had she done that? He had a vague recollection of something…her walking in…something happened. His head began to pound when he thought about it too hard.

The phone rang and he dragged a pillow over his head to block out the sound. When it persisted, he picked up the bedroom extension. "'ello."

"Derek, it's me."

"Hello, Mother."

"Are you all right?"

Sighing, he hoisted himself up and stuffed a pillow behind him. "I'm fine."

"You missed a meeting with vendors this morning."

"I did?"

"Listen, darling, I know you're upset that Liliana left, though I think it might be for the best. But your father isn't happy about your not showing up."

"I'm sorry, Mother." For a lot of things. Not the least of which was the wreckage he came face-to-face with when he looked around the bedroom. The desk chair was on its side. A lamp lay broken on the floor. A wastebasket was tipped over, its contents tumbling out onto the floor.

And several pictures of him and Liliana were smashed into pieces. He must have lost it last night. Damn, why did she have to leave him? He couldn't function without her.

You couldn't function with her, either.

He swore vilely.

"Derek!"

"Sorry, Mother. I stubbed my toe. What were you saying?"

"Would you like me to come over there? I could cancel my nail appointment. I know Liliana didn't appreciate my visits, but now that she's gone…"

He rubbed a hand over his jaw. God—days of growth. He could smell himself, too, and it wasn't pleasant. "No, Mother. I'm going to shower and head over to the office."

"Placate your father, dear."

"All right. I'll talk to you later."

He hung up and surveyed the room again.

No wonder Liliana had left him.

CHAPTER THREE

"OH, MR. MARTINI, they're beautiful." Simon watched Lily gush as she knelt on the floor of the reception area and picked up a furry black creature. She looked cute in a dark pink-and-red skirt and pink blouse. Not for the first time, he noticed how attractive she was. "He's so little. And soft."

"I like the one with white on his face." Jenna scooped another kitten out of the box, and Simon watched as she held it the same way Lily held hers. For a minute, he worried. His daughter mimicked Lily Wakefield a lot these days. Then, with less effort than last week, he let it go. He believed in the old adage that you could tell a person's true character by how he or she treated children, older people and animals.

In the three weeks she'd been in Fairview, Lily had earned gold stars in all categories. She even had the cranky O'Malley brothers behaving. They owned the local pub and usually made everybody miserable. It was odd how people in small towns were so trusting. But Simon vowed he'd keep a clear head about her. He would try not to jump to conclusions.

"Any takers on the ads?" Lily asked Mr. Martini, as she scratched the kitten's neck. Her nails were painted pink to match her blouse.

The seventy-year-old man smiled at Lily. "All but these two." He stretched out a stiff leg, and winked at Simon. "Don't know what I'm gonna do with the last of them."

Jenna's eyes widened. She looked heartbreakingly

young in overall shorts and a T-shirt, with her long hair pulled back in a ponytail. "Oh, Dad, can we?"

He stuck his hands in the pockets of his jeans. "Who'd take care of it?"

"Me. I'm not a baby. Lily says I'm very mature for my age." She lifted a chin in a haughty manner. She'd learned that from Lily, too. "I can do it."

"Well, if Lily said so." The woman already had spent an inordinate amount of time with Jenna. She was even taking his daughter along to her next prenatal checkup after Jenna had begged to hear the babies' heartbeats.

Lily looked over at Simon. Her smile was genuine and it did beautiful things to her eyes. Her face, fuller now, was alight with that pregnancy glow. He wondered about her life before she came here and why it had been stressful enough to make her thin and pale, as she'd been when she arrived. Gil hadn't told him and he hadn't asked. "They make wonderful pets, Simon."

"I'll think about it."

After a minute, Lily stood and stretched, placing her hands on the small of her back.

"Your back hurt, Lily?" Jenna asked.

"A bit. I can't figure out why. I'm not quite five months along. I haven't gained that much weight. I'm not even in maternity clothes."

"Cells are dividing in your lower back, stretching your muscles to accommodate the babies. Probably more than normal with twins."

She stared at Simon, as if he were speaking Greek. "How do you know that?"

Simon brushed his hand down Jenna's hair. "I learned everything I could about my baby girl, even before she was born."

Mr. Martini harrumphed. "In my day, we didn't take much interest." He went on to tell Lily about his wife, who'd been dead ten years, and his four kids, all of whom had moved away to bigger cities.

Seating herself across from the older man, Lily listened intently, petting the kitten the whole time. Simon watched that soft rhythmic stroke, mesmerized. It stirred something inside him; something he hadn't felt in a long time.

Eventually, Mr. Martini struggled to his feet. "So, should I take them back with me?"

"Dad?"

"All right. You can have one."

Mr. Martini zeroed in on Lily. "What about you, young lady?"

"Me? Oh, no, I can't have a kitten." Her expression was sad.

"Why not?"

"What if I don't stay?" Her voice trailed off, reminding Simon of the damage she could do to Gil and Jenna if—when—she left Fairview. Lately, that had been even more of a concern to him than her laying claim to the paper.

Then, she surprised them all by saying, "You know what? Yes, I'm going to take him."

"Yay!" Jenna threw her arms around Lily. "They can visit each other for company."

Lily laughed, Jenna laughed, and Mr. Martini forgot for a minute to maintain his gruff exterior and smiled broadly.

The front door opened, and Mr. Martini said under his breath, "Here comes Her Ladyship."

"Hush," Lily told him, then turned to the visitor. "Miss Jameson, how nice to see you." She nodded to the woman's outfit. "That green dress goes great with your hair and eyes."

"Thank you, dear." She held up a basket. "I brought you some muffins."

A lot of people in town had been trying to feed her over the past month. "Oh, dear. I'm going to be a blimp by the time the babies come."

The woman glanced at her stomach. "Are they doing well?"

"Yes. Kicking up a storm."

"It must be a nice feeling." Miss Jameson had been Simon's high school English teacher, as well as Jenna's now, and as far as he knew, she had never married or had a child. There was an aura of mystery to her, too, since she came from the big city and had settled here, all chic and sophisticated, like Lily. Miss Jameson glanced at Mr. Martini, who was heading for the door. "No need to go on my account, Marco."

"Job's done here, Loretta." He tipped his summer hat. "Goodbye, ladies. Simon. Don't work our girl too hard."

As if he'd had any choice. "I won't."

Leaving the women to coo over babies and kittens, Simon went back to his office just off the newsroom and sat down at his desk. The mock-up of the classifieds was finished. He shook his head, wondering how life had changed so significantly in less than a month.

Lily had been working at the paper since that day Simon couldn't reach Gil and she'd pitched in to help out. When Gil had found her at the office, he'd come up with the idea himself.

"This is perfect for you, Lily. You can sit down and take phone calls."

"I can do more," she'd said excitedly. She glanced at Simon, who knew his displeasure at the idea showed on his face. "I have some suggestions for the layout of the ads."

"Already?" he asked.

"If it's okay with you."

She was always so hesitant, so self-effacing, that it had been hard to hang on to his doubts. Besides, Simon was sensible, if nothing else. "Sure. Truthfully, I've thought they needed an overhaul, but Tom Barker's way too busy just getting the ad accounts."

"Great." The smile on Gil's face had also made it hard for Simon to cling to his reservations.

Since that day, Simon's negative feelings about Lily had dwindled even more. He stared at his latest editorial on global warming, thinking about how Lily was winning everybody over, including him. She'd been enthusiastic about these weekly columns, too, offering insights and effusive praise.

She came back to the office a half hour later.

"Where's the kitten?"

"Jenna took both of them home. Miss Jameson was going to drive her, and get some food and kitty litter for them on the way. I hope that's all right."

"Yeah, as you said, she's a big girl."

"I can stop by and get Blackie on my way home."

"Blackie? Very original."

"Hers is Whiteface."

"Clever."

She regarded him with a knowing smile.

"What?"

"You're a good father, Simon."

"Am I?"

Perching on the edge of a chair, Lily crossed her legs. The gesture distracted him. She hadn't worn stockings, so her legs were bare, and through her open-toed sandals he could see her pink toenails. "You know you are. Jenna's a wonderful girl. You've raised her well."

He leaned back and felt the familiar tightness in his chest. "When she got hurt, I thought I'd die."

"Jenna was hurt? Gil didn't tell me."

"Her, um, mother died in a car accident when Jenna was five. Jenna was in the backseat."

"Oh, no." Was that moisture in her eyes? "How badly hurt was she?"

"A broken arm and leg. She had to have a pin put in her femur. And then there were years of therapy, to get her to walk without a limp."

"You'd never know. She's so graceful now."

"Thank God."

Giving him a watery smile, Lily shook her head. "You've had a difficult life."

"You, too, I'm guessing."

She averted her gaze over his shoulder.

"You don't have to tell me. I know I've been unpleasant to you."

Looking back at him, she asked, "Why, Simon? I can tell it's not in your nature to be unkind."

"The truth?"

"Of course. Always."

"At first I worried about your motives. That you came here to..." He struggled for the right word. "Milk Gil, I guess."

"I'd never do such a thing."

"I see that now. If he buys you any kind of gift, even chocolates, you balk."

Her hands curled on her lap. "I guess you were right to worry. I just showed up out of the blue. I could have been anybody, wanting anything." When he didn't say more, she asked, "You said at first? What about now?"

"I'm not worried about *that* anymore."

"What are you worried about?"

"When you go away, Jenna and Gil will be hurt. Every day, they invest more in you."

No response.

"I caught what you said out there about not taking the kitten. Because you didn't know if you'd be staying here."

"My life's a mess, Simon. I don't want to hurt anybody while I'm trying to straighten it out."

"Are you? Straightening it out?"

"Yes, I think so. I've contacted a lawyer. He's sending my husband legal separation papers."

"Ah." Simon knew only that she'd left her husband for what Gil considered good reasons. And now, the fact that she was asking the guy for a separation made Simon glad. It must be because it meant she was moving on with her life and wasn't planning to go back to her old one. For Gil and Jenna, of course. "Will he sign them?"

"I hope so." He could see the sadness in her eyes. This was hard for her.

"If I knew the situation," he found himself saying, "I might be less wary."

"I'm ashamed to talk about it."

"For what it's worth, I'm ashamed of some things about my past, too."

Lily laughed, a bright sound that filled the office. He liked it. A lot. "Are you kidding? Gil, Jenna, the whole town think you walk on water."

"I've gone under a time or two." He shrugged. "But I don't like to talk about those things, so I really shouldn't ask you about your private life."

She bit her lip. Her vulnerability struck a chord in him. She was determined and strong, too, a combination that was far too appealing to him as a man.

"I'll tell you about it, Simon. But I'd appreciate it if you didn't share this with Jenna. It's not pretty."

"All right, I won't." He watched her. "And I won't judge, Lily. I promise."

"Thanks."

And then she told him her story.

THE MINUTE LILY WALKED into Simon's house she felt a sense of well-being. Her modern three-story back in Westchester County, with its soaring pillars, high ceilings and acres of windows, was a showplace, but it had never, ever felt like a home, as this one did.

The floors and trim around the doorways were done in warm wood in the foyer and in the rooms on either side. Off to the right, a fireplace stood guard in a living room filled with comfortably upholstered earth-toned furniture. Splashes of whimsy were everywhere, in colorful pillows and throws and frames. So different from her expensive, hard-edged modern furniture, these sofas and chairs beckoned you to curl up on them. On the other side of the entrance was a dining room, again with light oak furniture and padded chairs. The aroma of beef coming from the kitchen completed the homey picture.

"Lily!" A rumble on the stairs followed the shouted greeting. "You're here."

Gil had let them in unannounced.

"Hi, sweetie." They hugged, and Lily held on to the girl an extra second. Her hair was damp, as if she'd just washed it with rose-scented shampoo.

"Hey, what am I, Princess? Chopped liver?" Gil accepted a second hug warmly.

"Oh, Grandpa Gil. You know I love you."

"Mmm. Me, too." As Jenna took their raincoats and hung them up, he asked, "What's that I smell?"

"Your favorite. Pot roast. Dad says you can have some, but not a lot. 'Cuz of your heart."

"Did you make dinner?"

"Mostly." This from Simon, who walked down the hallway, wearing an apron that read, Kiss The Cook.

When Lily's first thought was that that sounded like a great idea, she chided herself. But he looked so good wearing a red shirt beneath the apron and jeans that fit his butt like a glove. She admonished herself for the wayward thoughts and the perusal.

"Welcome to our home, Lily."

He was looking at her differently, too. Ever since she had told him last week about Derek, he'd been nicer. Kinder. Sweet, really. She'd begun to like Simon McCarthy, and she thought she was making headway in getting him to like her, too. Though something niggled at her.

He was concerned about Gil and Jenna, if she left town abruptly, but there was something else that was bothering him, too. Usually, she got the feeling at the paper, when she wanted to try something new. He'd shut down and become cold or distant. Not now, though. He was smiling with genuine warmth.

"You have a lovely house."

"Daddy did a lot of the work on it."

"Really?"

"Uh-huh. My pride and joy."

"Marco Martini and I helped," Gil put in. "Then, we all worked on my kitchen. The old codger's wanted to buy my house from under me for as long as I can remember, so he was trying to rack up some points."

"And you're not selling, of course." Simon started down the hall. "Come back and sit."

They followed him to the back.

The family room flowed into the kitchen and was demarcated by a rug that bumped up against the ceramic tile. A bank of windows faced the wooded backyard. Off the kitchen was an enclosed porch, its screens open, despite the rain outside. "This is gorgeous."

"Thanks. We like it." He took the wine they'd brought with them. "Want a glass?" he asked Gil.

"If Lily doesn't mind."

"I made you tea, Lily," Jenna said. "The kind you brew with a ball."

"Go ahead, have the wine. I'll help."

Gil said, "I'm going to beat Jenna at cards."

Lily followed Simon into the kitchen while Gil and Jenna went into the family room.

"Can I have some wine, Dad?" Jenna called out from there.

"I'll pour you a sip or two."

Curious about the indulgence, Lily cocked her head as Simon got her a mug and took wineglasses out of the cupboard.

"It takes the mystery out of drinking," he explained quietly. "Hopefully, as a result, she won't feel the need to experiment outside of the house."

Lily's hand went to her midsection, which was just rounding a bit as her fifth month got into full swing. "I wonder if I'll ever know what to do with these babies."

He gave her the mug. "You will. A lot of it's instinct, but I read child-rearing books, too." He poured wine for the rest of them.

As Lily got her tea, she said, "Thanks for having us for dinner. Too bad your sister couldn't make it."

"She's a busy lawyer. There's only Sara and Mac Madison in the firm, and they have clients from all the neighboring towns."

Lily knew Mac. On Gil's advice, she'd met with him a few weeks after she'd arrived. He'd filed for her legal separation.

"I'd like to meet Sara. In any case, I appreciate your having us for dinner."

A silence. Then, "We have Gil over all the time."

Oh, no. She'd never thought of this. "You haven't had Gil to dinner since I've been here. It's been more than five weeks."

"He's been busy with you."

"I'm sorry I interfered. Did you mind?"

"The truth?"

That's what he'd said at the paper that day last week. She nodded.

"Yeah, I minded some. But Gil needed time with you."

"It won't happen again, Simon. I won't come between you and Gil."

His face shadowed, and there it was—that feeling Lily got, that her words, or sometimes her actions, meant more to him than what she'd intended.

They joined Gil and Jenna in the living room. "What are you playing?" Lily asked.

Simon shook his head. "Poker."

"Yeah, Grandpa Gil taught me how."

Gil arched his brows at Lily. He looked younger when he teased. "You know how to play?"

"I'm afraid not." Bridge had been big in her circles. She'd never liked it, but Derek had insisted she join a club.

"Maybe we can teach you some seven-card stud after dinner."

"You're on, for whatever that is."

When Lily went to take a seat, she noticed something hanging on the wall opposite the couch. "Oh, my."

Jenna looked over. "It's all right, isn't it?"

"Why, yes, of course." She stared at the matted and framed picture she'd drawn of Jenna. "At least I got to finish it."

"You're very talented, Lily," Gil said.

"Thank you. My mother started me young."

A silence invaded the room like an unwanted guest. She had yet to tell Gil the details of what had happened to Cameron and whenever something like this came up, it was awkward.

"She continued to draw? She was really good in high school."

"Yes, I know. I found some of her work in the boxes you left out."

Gil's eyes were sad. Lily said no more about Cameron and Simon tried to cover for the awkwardness. "Did I tell you the advertising income for the paper has gone up by a third this quarter, Gil? I'll show you the figures later."

The unhappiness faded from her grandfather's face. "That's terrific. I'm guessing that some folks have taken out classifieds just to make contact with our new helper here. I even saw Mike O'Malley being nice to her the other day."

Lily chuckled. She thought the same thing about the ads and people's attitudes. It was wonderful for her battered ego.

"Eddie McPherson stops in all the time," Jenna said, mentioning a local firefighter. "I think he likes her."

Lily shifted uncomfortably. Gil looked away and so did Simon.

"What did I say?" Jenna asked.

"Lily's married, honey."

"Yeah, but she left her husband. She's living here, now." Reaching out, Lily touched Jenna's arm. "I did more than that, sweetie. I've sent him papers asking for a legal separation."

"So, good." Jenna went back to her cards. "But watch out for Eddie. They call him Fast Eddie."

"Jenna!"

"I'm not a baby, Grandpa."

Simon chuckled. "You get no argument from me about Eddie. I went to high school with him. That was his nickname then, too."

"Speaking of names, do you have them picked out for the babies, Lily?" Gil asked.

"No, not yet."

"What are you considering?"

"I'd like to keep that to myself for now. As soon as I decide, I'll let you know."

A buzzer went off in the kitchen. Simon rose. "Dinner's ready. Jenna, you can help me. Gil and Lily, why don't you go into the dining room."

When they were all seated and the food was in front of them, Simon said grace. And Lily was mesmerized by the soothing rhythm of his voice, raised in prayer. She was also struck by the notion that this must be what a real family dinner was like.

She'd never experienced one before in her life.

SIMON LOOKED OVER at Gil from his desk as he read a spreadsheet, a copy of the one Gil held in his hand. Gil said, "This is good, don't you think?"

"Yes. Though I wish we could widen the market in Gainesville."

"Let's talk about how to do that."

Simon glanced at the door, thinking of Lily and how pretty she looked in the peach linen slacks and long-sleeved shirt she was wearing tonight. Her hair was soft and shiny, too, and curled a bit from the rain. "They'll be okay?"

"We were in the way. Jenna was dying to get Lily up to her room. I heard some rumblings about makeup."

"She's a little young for war paint." And Lily certainly didn't need any.

"I hate to break it to you, Simon, but girls start with all that at about eleven."

"God forbid."

Leaning back in his chair, Simon watched the man he'd come to think of as a second father. Patrick McCarthy could never be replaced, but there was a unique spot in his heart for Gil. To ease this particular burden, he asked, "Lily hasn't said anything about what happened to Cameron?"

"Just the bare bones. I asked her to elaborate a few weeks ago, and gave her another opportunity just now, but she didn't take it. I'm guessing it was bad. I almost don't want to know how Cameron lived. Or how Lily grew up."

"Sometimes knowing isn't all it's cracked up to be." Simon was sure of that.

Gil cocked his head. "Can I ask you something?"

"Yeah, sure."

"You didn't like her at first. Why?"

"Because I was worried she was using you. I was afraid she was out to get whatever she could from you."

"That's about the last thing that's happening."

"I see that now. She seems to want to stand on her own two feet."

"She told you about Wakefield, didn't she?"

"Uh-huh. I felt bad for her. I hope he agrees to the separation."

"Mac is worried about his family. They're powerful people in New York. What changed your mind about her, Simon?"

"Seeing her interact with people on a daily basis. She's formed a bond with Jenna that can't be faked. Mr. Martini and Mrs. Billings and Miss Jameson come in just to see her." He smiled fondly at Gil. "And there's a spring in *your* step that I haven't seen in a long time."

"I'm happy, Simon."

"Good to see." He waited a beat. "Jenna was right. Eddie sniffs around her." Not that he blamed the guy.

"With good reason, don't you think?"

Simon smiled. "I'm male and healthy. Who wouldn't think that? She's very pretty."

"And she has an inner beauty."

"Does she?" He was reserving judgment on that.

"I want you to be friends." Gil waited a minute. "You know she'll never replace you or Jenna in my heart, Simon."

"Hell, I hope I'm not thinking that way."

"Probably not. I just wanted to say it out loud."

He nodded. "Let's get back to how we can increase circulation."

"All right. Just let me say thanks for accepting Lily as much as you have. It means a lot to me."

"I know."

JOHANNA WAKEFIELD stared at the legal document Derek had received earlier this week. As usual, her white hair was exquisitely styled, and her taupe pantsuit showed off her slender form. At sixty-three, she was still an attractive woman. "Well, she didn't waste a lot of time."

"No. She must really want to get away from me. With good reason."

His mother's blue eyes turned cold. "It's Liliana's style. She's not to be counted on."

"Father likes her."

"He has a soft side where people are concerned. It doesn't always serve him well."

"I gave her cause, Mother."

"A woman should not leave her husband in the dark of night. She's never been good for you. Why, we never even found out about her background. God knows where she came from."

"I wonder if she went back there."

"Where?"

"Where she came from. Wherever that—" he waved his drink at the papers "—came from."

"A law firm from upstate."

Derek slugged back his scotch and stretched out his legs. "Should I sign them?" The thought turned his stomach. He didn't want Liliana to leave him, but he was remembering things he'd done to her, and in his sober moments—few though they were—he knew she was better off away from him and his addictions. Some of which she didn't even know about.

His mother studied her drink and said casually, "We could find her through the lawyer."

"I guess." But what good would it do? He'd only hurt her again.

"Do you want her back, Derek?"

"No. For her sake."

"Then I have a better idea." She stood, went to the phone and punched in a number. "Hello, Susan, this is Johanna Wakefield. My son and I would like to see Marcus today."

"So soon?" Derek asked as she waited.

"That's what retainers are for, darling." Into the mouthpiece she said, "Yes, three would be fine. What? Oh, we're going to need divorce papers drawn up."

Derek's eyes widened and a sharp pain sliced through him. "*Divorce* papers?"

"It's for the best, Derek. We Wakefields never do anything halfway."

"No," he said getting up to fix himself another drink. "I guess we don't."

CHAPTER FOUR

"HI, LILY. NEED SOMETHING?" Evan Hill smiled up at her from his desk in the newsroom. He was a little guy with a wiry build and warm brown eyes. There were five desks in the big open space, and he was seated at one of them. Simon had his own office in the corner.

Lily nodded toward it. "I'm looking for the chief."

"He just called and said he was on his way. Go wait inside. There's a couch. Sit, put your feet up."

"Good Lord. You, too?"

"If you don't, I'll tell the Senior Brigade."

"We wouldn't want that."

In the six weeks she'd been in Fairview, the people in town had come to care about Lily, especially the older ones she'd helped with ads. She found them fascinating and loved listening to their stories. They must have sensed she was sincere because, in turn, they watched over her like hawks. Having never been nurtured before, she loved being cared for.

She wandered into Simon's office and sat on the couch. From there—with her feet up—she studied his personal space. She'd been in here before, of course, but never alone. Several pictures of Jenna, at different ages, hung on one wall. There was another of his favorite old newspapers that had been matted and framed. What was that? She rose and crossed to a small case containing trophies. For basketball. From high school. And, oh, how cute, from this year. He played in a men's league. Each day she discovered more depths to this man. And each day she found herself gravitating toward him more.

After she'd finished exploring, Lily caught sight of a typed sheet on his desk. Hmm. She'd just take a peek. His editorials were wonderful—usually on world events that small towns sometimes forgot about. He'd done one on the war in Iraq, and one on peace in the Middle East, and he'd even tackled the volatile topic of gay rights, which—because he was a proponent—had caused a stir down at the diner and over at O'Malleys' pub. She wondered what the subject of this one was and picked it up. When he walked in, she'd just finished reading.

"Hi, Lily. What are you doing here?"

She held up the paper. "I'm sorry, I peeked. Well, no," she sniffled, "I'm not sorry. Simon, this is so sad. And so poignantly written."

He leaned against the doorjamb. She noticed again how broad his shoulders were as they stretched the cotton of his shirt. The opening at the collar revealed dark chest hair and a patch of tanned skin. "It's a shame, isn't it, what goes on in those refugee camps? I wish I could do more than write about it."

"You do a lot by making people aware of the atrocious conditions. After the Iraq editorial, there was a big collection of socks and books in town. I heard from Loretta that your work spurred other action. You *are* helping."

"I guess."

She indicated the one she'd just read. "This woman, Anna. She was in a camp for sixteen years?"

He nodded his head. "Yep. Got married there, had two kids." Quietly, he added, "God knows what she endured."

Lily glanced away. He came around the desk and squatted in front of her. He tipped her chin and shook his head. "Are you crying, Lily?"

"Ignore it. I cry at everything these days."

"So did Marian." He took out his handkerchief and Lily reached for it. But instead of giving it to her, he wiped her face. She swallowed hard at the intimacy of the gesture. Up this close, she could see the green flecks in his eyes, how long lashed they were, several shades darker than his hair. She got a whiff of his cologne. Very male, very sexy.

When he finished, he stared at her for a long time. "You're something else, Lily Wakefield."

She was startled to realize how disappointed she was when he drew back. Self-consciously, she smoothed down her tan capris and long white blouse.

"Did—" he cleared his throat "—did you come back here for a reason, or just to nose around in my stuff?"

"I wanted to talk to you. I need advice and I thought you could give me some, since you're close to Gil."

He stiffened. He was so protective of her grandfather, Lily knew instantly she was doing the right thing. Though she was still wary of men, in general, she was beginning to see Simon as an ally.

"Can we sit on the couch? And close the door?"

When they were settled, Lily faced him solemnly. "Simon, last week, when Gil brought up my mother's art, I knew he was waiting for me to tell him what happened to her. He's *been* waiting."

"He mentioned it while you were turning Jenna into America's Top Model."

"And planning a world tour of all our favorite places, don't forget."

"Spare my checkbook, please." He sobered. "About Cameron?"

"If I tell Gil what happened to her, I worry that he'll be devastated. And I wonder if he really *has* to know."

His face shadowed. "As I told him, sometimes knowing the truth isn't all it's cracked up to be."

"Simon?" Intuitively, she knew he wasn't just talking about Gil. And suddenly, she wanted to know more about this man, about those secrets he said he'd been keeping. The longing was so strong, it surprised her.

"Never mind about me. Finish what you were going to say."

"All right. I thought I could tell you what happened, and you could help me decide if I should tell Gil. You're closer to him than anyone, and you'd know what was the right thing to do."

"Thanks for trusting me." He leaned back against the couch and crossed one foot over the other knee. "Go ahead."

"You know the basics. My mother never went to the home for unwed mothers. Instead, she took a bus to New York, and stayed at the YWCA. She found a job right away as a waitress."

"That must have been hard. Sixteen. Pregnant, waitressing."

Lily's hand went to her just-beginning-to-bulge abdomen. "I can't imagine. Anyway, welfare paid for my delivery and our hospital stay, and then she got a second job in a day care so I could stay there while she earned money. It was tough, but she loved me and I knew it."

"She must have been a very strong woman." He smiled. "You take after her in that respect...."

His compliment warmed her, and for a minute distracted her.

"What happened?"

"We did okay for a while. But the hard life wore on her. By the time I was in grade school, she wanted more." Lily shook her head. "She found a way to get it."

His eyes narrowed. "Not a *good* way."

"No. First she waitressed at this club. This strip club. And then she stripped. She called it dancing, but I knew what she was doing. I was mortified, but still she was a good mother."

"You told Gil she died in a bus accident."

"Another lie."

"Oh, Lily."

"She went home with one of the patrons from the club.

And never came back. They found her body on the street, near a garbage dump."

Tears flowed now. She tried to dash them away, but she was transported back to all the horror of her mother's death and the terror of being left alone.

Simon slid closer and took her hand. She latched on to it for support, but she couldn't look at him, so he pulled her close and held her.

"I'm sorry. I thought I'd dealt with this." She buried her face in his chest, as if it were the most natural thing to do. "You're the first person I've ever told this to."

"Derek doesn't know?" There was an odd note in his voice. It got that way every time he talked about her husband.

"Are you kidding? No. And he wouldn't want me to tell him. That's one reason why he won't find me here. He doesn't know about my connection to you all." Oh. "I mean to Gil."

"It must have been hard for you, Lily, living like that."

"It was, but, Simon, my poor mother... She was a good person. I think life just gave her too many knocks."

"What happened to you when she died?"

"I was sixteen, by then, and she'd left some money. She stashed it away, truly, in a mattress. With working two jobs, it was enough for me to live on."

"Didn't social services have something to say about that?"

"It's easy to get lost in New York City."

"I can't believe you were left alone." He was still holding her, and his hand smoothed down her hair. It felt comforting—and something else, too. Closing her eyes, she sank farther into him. "You were Jenna's age."

"I love Jenna's innocence. Because I never was like her. I craved it, though, and respectability."

"I can see why." He kissed the top of her head. Settled his hand at her neck.

All she wanted was to stay in Simon's arms. She'd never

felt protected by Derek. Instead, she was always taking care of him. This was such a welcome change, maybe even a needed one during her pregnancy, which had made her feel utterly vulnerable.

But it couldn't last and it wasn't reality. After a few more precious moments in his arms, she drew away, sat up and wiped her eyes. "Damn. I'm a regular fountain around you."

"This is something to cry about."

"That's why I'm torn about what to do with Gil."

"It's a hard call."

"Simon, this would hurt him so much. And what purpose would it serve, to tell him? He already feels so much guilt."

"You really care about him, don't you?"

"Of course I do!"

"I think maybe your instincts are right. As you said, what good would it serve for him to find out about Cameron?"

She released a heavy breath. "Okay, then. I feel better, knowing you agree."

Reaching out, he took her hand again. His was big and masculine and easily encompassed hers. "Let me say something. You're a wonderful person. You've survived so much. And you still worry about others."

"I ran away from Derek, Simon."

"Which was the right thing to do. You have character and strength. Remember that."

Tears welled in her eyes again.

"Uh-oh. We'd better stop this."

She looked down at her hand in his. So did he. He was right—they had to stop. Because the last thing Lily needed in her life right now was a relationship with this man. With any man. Although, in her heart, she didn't want to curtail her feelings for Simon.

This time, however, she'd listen to her head.

STILL REELING from his afternoon conversation with Lily, Simon met his sister at the Fairview Diner for dinner. The cool air inside felt good after his walk over in the warm May weather.

"Hey, Simon," Artie Conklin, the owner, said, when he came in.

"Hi, Artie. How's that son of yours doing? He just got promoted, didn't he?"

"Yep, to head of the ambulance crew. Still goes on calls, though."

"Good for him."

"How's Lily?"

"She's good." More than good. Wonderful. And beautiful. Very, very beautiful.

"Glad to hear." Artie nodded across the room. "Your sister's in the back booth."

"Thanks." He found Sara sipping a glass of wine and kissed her cheek before he said, "Hi, sis."

"Hi, Simon. That happen often?"

"What?"

"People asking you about Lily Wakefield. Right after you ask about their families?"

"Everybody asks me about her and Gil. They know her through the paper."

"I heard she was working there."

He motioned to their waitress for another glass of wine. "How are you, Sara?"

"Busy as hell." She nodded over to Mac Madison, who was at another table. "Him, too. He's with a client even now."

"Sorry you missed dinner last week. Jenna felt bad."

"Yeah. Me, too."

"You didn't really have to work, did you?"

"Of course I did."

Leaning over, he took her hand. "Let's get this out of the way so we can enjoy our meal. You didn't want to see Lily, did you?"

She shook her head. The siblings resembled each other, except her short hair was darker and her eyes greener than his. Now, there was a wariness in them. "No, I didn't."

"She's a good person, Sara. She really does have Gil's best interest at heart."

"I...found out some things about her."

"On the background check I asked you to do, right?" No answer.

"You investigated her more than that? Oh, Sara, all I wanted to know was if she was who she said she was, and from where she said she lived."

"Simon, we knew nothing about her. I wanted more on her. I found articles and pictures on the Net, society kinds of things. She's a real trophy wife."

He didn't respond.

Sara watched him. "Did you hear me? She's *married,* Simon."

"I know she's married."

"The Wakefields are influential people. I'm familiar with their law firm. Very high-powered. Rumored to be ruthless."

"So?"

"Derek Wakefield is the father of her kids. If he wants them, he's got a good chance of getting them."

"She's afraid of that." He sat back and sipped his wine. "Look, there were good reasons she left."

"What?"

"I can't tell you. They're private."

"But she told you."

He nodded.

"You're getting attached to her."

Thinking about holding her today, feeling her curves against him, loving the scent of her, he lied to his sister. "No, I like her. But I'm okay with it. Mostly, I was worried about Gil."

"I'm worried about you. And Jenna."

"Jenna *is* getting attached. She's excited about the babies."

Sara fired questions at him as if he were on the stand. "What happens to all of you when Lily leaves town?"

"Who says she's leaving?"

"Oh, Simon, she's got millions to go back to. Why would she stay here?"

For me. And Jenna and Gil. "She says she's not going back."

"She scraped her way through college. Even when she spent the required year abroad as an art major, she had to work. People who've been that poor never want to go back to a life without money."

"She says she's staying."

"Then, that brings up another problem. She'll have rights to the paper."

His initial fear, which he'd buried because he'd begun to like Lily, surfaced with Sara's warning. "I know."

"The paper that you've been planning to buy. Dreaming, all your life, to own."

He repeated, "I know. But Sara, I can't do anything about one of Gil's relatives turning up."

"You could make her less welcome. If everybody stopped being so nice to her, maybe she'd go back to where she came from and forget about the *Sentinel.*"

"I tried distancing her and it didn't work." And now, he didn't want her to leave.

"I'm just worried about my baby brother and my only niece." Sara sighed heavily. "I wish Dad was still alive. You always listened to him. He'd talk some sense into you."

He pictured his father's laughing brown eyes and kind smile. Patrick McCarthy would have seen Lily's true nature right away. God, he missed the man. "Maybe if you got to know Lily…"

"No. Somebody in this town has to stay objective about her."

Good luck. "All right. Can we change the subject now? We haven't talked in a while."

"Since Lily came to town."

"Hush. Tell me about your love life."

She snorted. "My love life is about as active as yours." When he didn't respond, she added, "Simon, you've got to start dating again. So you had a few fiascos early on. Try again. You know Ellen Priestly has been interested in you for a long time."

"I'll think about it." But instead of considering the elementary school teacher who gave off signals every time he saw her, Simon's mind settled on Lily and how she felt in his arms, how his body had responded to her. However, he kept his face blank. That was the last thing Sara needed to hear now.

THE NEXT DAY, Lily sat at a table in the drugstore visiting with Loretta Jameson. The only pharmacy in town had a soda fountain on one side, and she and the schoolteacher were having late-afternoon tea together.

"How long were you on the stage, Loretta?"

"Ten years. I gave it up because the lifestyle was too intense. I came here—I already had a teaching degree—when I decided to find a nice small town to settle in."

Lily shook her head at the story. "I love Broadway. What roles did you play?"

As she listened, she thought again of her idea for a column in the *Sentinel.* Which was one reason why she was so glad to see Simon stride into the drugstore and approach the prescription counter. He smiled at the pharmacist, Mr. Atherton, and made small talk. Lily took surreptitious glances at him. He was wearing shorts today, as she was, in deference to the warm weather. His legs were muscular, and the matching navy T-shirt outlined a chest that she already knew was sinewy. And solid. And strong.

Loretta followed her gaze. "He's an attractive man, isn't he?"

"I guess he is."

The woman watched her. Lily could see why she had been a stage star. Her face was still lovely and relatively unlined, and her auburn hair was perfectly coiffed. "I knew a man like Simon once. He wanted me to do what I ended up doing when it was too late."

"What was that?"

"Leave the stage and live a normal life."

"Loretta, if this is about me and Simon, you misunderstand the relationship."

Simon caught sight of them and a huge, delighted smile spread across his face.

Loretta arched a brow. "Do I?" She glanced at her watch. "Look at the time. I have a meeting at church. I'd better go. Take care, dear." She rose, squeezed Lily's arm and walked across the store. After speaking briefly to Simon, she left.

He headed right over to Lily and her pulse sped up as if she were a silly teenager, spotting her boyfriend.

"Hi." He nodded to the door. "Having tea with Miss Jameson?"

"Yes, but I'm glad to see you."

"And I'm glad to see you."

"Can you sit?"

"Uh-huh, I'm waiting for some medication. Jenna has a cold, and now it's turned into a sinus infection."

"I know. I hope she feels better soon."

He dropped down across from her. This close to him, she could see that he was sweaty. His hair was damp, too, making it curl even more. "Working out?"

"Running. Getting in shape for the summer basketball league."

"I saw the trophies when I was waiting in your office."

"*Snooping* in my office, you mean. You'd make a good reporter."

"You think so? Because I have an idea for the paper."

His face tightened, just a bit, which she noticed because she noticed everything about him these days. "Shoot."

"A new column called Senior Saga."

"And that would be about…?"

"The older people in town. Simon, they have so many stories. Mr. Martini was in World War II and his son served in Vietnam."

"Everybody knows that."

"But there's a whole story about the two of them being honored together in Washington."

"Hmm. That is news."

"Mrs. Billings has tales about the Depression. Her husband got laid off and she ended up going to work in a factory."

He smiled as Lily recounted other stories.

"And I think I know why the O'Malley brothers are so grumpy. There was this woman they both…"

He held up his hand. "All right, I get the picture. But I'm not sure we have the manpower to add another column to the paper."

Toying with what was left of her cookie, she shrugged a shoulder. "You've got the womanpower."

Again, he stiffened.

"Simon, what's wrong? Don't you want me to do this?"

"Nothing's wrong. It's a great idea." He played with the napkin on the table. "Does this mean you're staying in town?"

"Yes, I'm staying."

He studied her. His expression was somber.

"You don't seem very happy about that. I thought we were friends."

"We are," he said. "I'm happy you're staying."

"Then, what's the problem?"

"I'm happier than I have a right to be about that, Lily. And before I say anything more, I'm getting up and leaving."

Oh. *Oh!*

Towering over her, he no longer looked like the safe, protective man who'd held her the other day. He looked masculine and sexy, and instead of his virility threatening her, it thrilled her. "I hope you get my meaning."

"I do, yes." He walked a few steps away when she called out, "Simon?"

He pivoted around.

"I'm happy I'm staying, too. Maybe happier than I should be, but I am."

CHAPTER FIVE

DR. BETTY RABIN WINKED at Lily and then glanced at Jenna. "Ready, Jen?"

"Uh-huh. This is my favorite part."

"You should consider a career as a doctor. An ob-gyn or a pediatrician."

Jenna's eyes were wide. "I didn't know I'd like this baby stuff so much."

The doctor handed her the probe.

"I can do it?"

"Sure—it's your third time here. You know the drill."

Lily grinned at Jenna. "It's been so nice having you to share this with."

She was a full six months pregnant now, and today she was scheduled for another ultrasound. Months ago, she'd had one at her obstetrician's office in Westchester, but the babies had developed significantly since then.

"A little to the left, Jenna. There you go."

The rapid *thumpthumpthumpthump* of the first twin's heart echoed in the office. Lily never tired of hearing it, and Jenna giggled like a young girl each time.

"Now, move the probe about five inches up and three over."

And there was the second beat, just as fast and even louder. "I think that's the boy," Betty said. "Noisier already."

Jenna shook herself with joy. "I wish Dad was here."

Me, too, Lily thought. And that was beginning to be a

problem. Finally, Lily had decided to be honest with herself about her feelings for Simon. That they were sexual was something his daughter didn't need to know about, however.

"Dad?" the doctor asked. "You mean the babies' dad?"

Jenna stilled.

"No, she means Simon. Jenna wants everybody to be as excited about these little ones as she is."

"Lily told Dad he could come for the ultrasound, if he wanted to. He's over in Jefferson on a story, but he said he'd try to make it."

Lily still couldn't believe Simon would be at her prenatal appointment today, but Jenna had begged...

"Aren't you interested in all this, Daddy?" she'd asked, horrified that he might not be.

Simon had given Lily a long look before he answered. "Yeah, I'm interested."

His words had made Lily flush. She hoped Jenna didn't catch the innuendo or even register his tone of voice.

"Then come Friday. See the babies."

"If it's okay with Lily."

"Of course."

"I'll try to make it."

After Jenna had left, Simon faced Lily. "I'm sorry. She's hard to say no to. She's become obsessed with these babies."

"I appreciate the company and enthusiasm."

"Is it hard not having the babies' father to share this with?"

"The truth?"

He smiled. "Nothing but."

"Yeah. I never envisioned going through pregnancy alone."

"Do you really want me to come on Friday? I don't want to impose."

She'd answered quickly. Too quickly. "I'd love for you to come...."

"Time to transfer you to the ultrasound room," Betty told them. "Jenna, go see if your dad's here. I want to talk to Lily privately for a minute."

"Nothing's wrong, is it?" the girl asked.

"No, honey. Lily needs some time for just her and her doctor."

Jenna left and Betty shook her head, smiling. "What a doll."

"She's great. Nothing *is* wrong, is there?"

"Nope, I meant what I said. We haven't had much chance to chat about all this, with Jenna here for the tummy checks."

"I know."

"Is there anything you want to talk about? How you're feeling, emotionally or physically. A lot of changes in a woman's body this trimester."

Lily blushed. She'd been feeling changes, all right. Every time she looked at Simon in jeans or when he wore a certain shirt, or the worst, when she got a whiff of his aftershave, she reacted viscerally.

"Lily?"

"Nothing abnormal. I'm healthier than I've ever been. I hadn't realized how stressed I was in Westchester until I got away. Gil and Simon and Jenna baby me. Hell, the whole town does."

"It's sweet. Any discomfort?"

Lily groaned.

Betty laughed. "It's sex, isn't it?" When Lily nodded, Betty said, "I assume you've read about that? A woman's libido is very active during this phase."

"Like never before." She and Derek had had a good sex life for a while, but trying to conceive had killed that off. She hadn't had a sexual appetite in a long time.

"I know you're separated from your husband. Any chance of reconciling?"

"No."

"He's not interested in the babies?"

"He doesn't know about them."

The doctor's dark eyes narrowed. "Something's wrong."

"Yes, it's why I left him. He has addictions, Betty. I was afraid for the babies, and for myself. If he finds out about them, I don't know what he'd do."

"What are you afraid of?"

"That he'll seek custody. Or even just visiting rights. He's not stable, and I couldn't leave the babies with him."

"I'm sorry. No wonder you're keeping this to yourself. But he'll have to find out sometime."

"When I'm on my feet and can support them. And afford the lawyer I hired to file the separation papers."

"That explains why you don't want my bill on your insurance."

The intercom buzzed as the doctor was helping her off the table. "Dr. Rabin, the room's ready and Mr. McCarthy's here."

Nonchalantly, she said, "Simon's a great guy, Lily. My husband goes fishing with him."

"I know he is. We've become friends."

"We all wish he'd find somebody." She rolled her eyes. "Everybody in town tries to fix him up with a cousin or neighbor, but nothing's ever worked out."

Wisely, Lily chose not to respond.

Once in the ultrasound room, where it was brighter and cooler, the nurse got Lily settled and then showed in Simon and Jenna.

"Hi," Simon said softly. His expression was warm, tender. "Everything all right?"

"Just fine." Now that he was here, especially.

"We get to see them today?"

She felt her eyes moisten at the thought. "Uh-huh."

"I'm so excited." Jenna had come to Lily's side, opposite where the technician stood by the monitor. "I've never seen a sonogram of babies. Dad saw me. He said it was the best day of his life."

"It was a thrill." He'd come up close to the table, too,

and brushed back Lily's hair, almost unconsciously. He'd done those kinds of things since that day in the drugstore—a hand on her hair, on her back or shoulder. It felt natural and right. And so good. Lily had been startled to realize how much she'd come to crave his touch. "You've already had one of these, right?"

"Yes, early on. But I couldn't see much."

"You'll probably cry. I did when I saw Jenna and there she was, looking just like a baby."

"I'll probably cry. What else is new?"

"All right," Betty announced. "Here goes."

The gel was cold when the nurse applied it, as was the probe on Lily's bulging belly. A loud *whoosh, whoosh* filled the room. She turned toward the monitor. Soon, the picture began to take shape, like a Rorschach print forming as you studied it. "Okay, this is the first baby. The boy."

Jenna said, "Oh, gosh, I can see his thingy."

"His thingy?" Betty laughed out loud.

"Well, you know. His *penis.*"

Lily stared at the baby's torso, foot and head. Her vision clouded. This was her child. Her *son.*

"Now, here she is."

"Oh!" She felt a hand reach for hers and grip it. Simon.

"She's a bit more delicate. Smaller."

"Not too small, I hope?"

"No." The doctor squinted at the screen. "As a matter of fact, they're both a good size." She moved the probe around. "Maybe they're further along than we'd thought."

Simon took in a quick breath. His voice was gravelly as he said, "Lily, look at their hands."

"What, I can't…" She craned her head. When she saw what he had seen, a tear fell.

"Oh, wow," Jenna whispered. "Wait till I tell Katie."

"It's not unusual." But the doctor's voice was hoarse, too.

The babies were facing each other and had their hands up against the edge of their individual sacs. "It's like they're trying to hold hands. My babies are trying to hold hands."

For so long, she'd been on her own. And she worried about the babies having only a mother. But the picture before her made her think that they'd always have each other and would never, ever be alone as Lily had been all her life. The image on the screen was a tangible reminder. It was a sight she'd never forget.

When she looked over and saw moisture in Simon's eyes, her heart filled with a different kind of emotion—for him, as a man. She knew his response to the image of her children on the sonogram was also something that would be forever branded in her memory.

And *she* didn't feel so alone anymore.

As SIMON AND JENNA walked into the waiting area, Simon was still on an emotional high from what he'd seen. New life. Tiny babies almost holding hands. And Lily at her most beautiful.

"What are you two doing here?"

He glanced over at the row of chairs against the wall and found his sister Sara seated on one of them. She was dressed in a summer suit, so she must have just come from work.

"Hi, Sara."

"Aunt Sara!" Jenna rushed to her. "We just saw Lily's babies on the ultrasound. They were trying to touch each other."

Sara's eyes narrowed. "I see." She transferred her gaze to Simon. "How sweet."

"I'm going to the ladies' room." Jenna all but floated away.

Hoping to head off a tirade, Simon kissed Sara's cheek. "Is this a checkup or is something wrong?"

"My annual. But something is definitely wrong."

"Don't start again." He didn't want to lose the glow of

what he'd just witnessed, the feeling of closeness with Lily.

"This isn't good, Simon."

"I'm okay, Sara. She needs friends."

"Yeah, keep telling yourself that."

Luckily, Betty and Lily came out just then and Jenna rejoined them. The doctor said, "Hello, Sara."

"Hi, Sara." Lily smiled ingenuously at Simon's sister. She had no idea what Sara thought of her.

"Lily…"

The doctor turned to Lily. "Don't forget to make that appointment today."

"What appointment?" Jenna asked.

"Betty says the babies are bigger than expected. Either we're off on the due date, or she doesn't think I'll go full-term."

Simon felt his insides go cold. "I thought twins weighed less than single births, especially if they come early."

"Years ago, that was true. But with good prenatal care, twin birth weight has improved. Since Lily's been here, they've grown considerably. You can tell by her size. And any day now, she'll really pop out. It happens fast."

"What appointment does she need?" Simon asked.

"Lily needs to attend childbirth classes ASAP. There's a shortened session, three classes for twice the length, for just such situations. She should be finished by the time she's eight months along."

"Sounds like a plan," Lily said lightly.

"They're at Community Central Hospital." The medical facility served several towns and was about twenty minutes away. "Lily shouldn't drive there alone. The classes are held at night. She really shouldn't be on her own too much at all, in case she goes into labor, but especially not on dark roads."

"Maybe Gil can drive me."

"Like I said, you also need a coach. Think about it. Sara? You can come in now."

Sara was staring at Simon. Glaring, really. She didn't say anything, but he could read her mind.

Don't you dare.

"I'm ready to go back to work," Lily commented as the three of them reached Simon's car and slid inside. Gil had dropped her and Jenna off at the appointment.

Simon started the engine after Lily fastened her seat belt. She was wearing maternity clothes—a loose pink top over a matching skirt—and she had to stretch the belt. "You should rest after all this excitement."

"I could use a nap. But I want to go over the Senior Saga idea with you."

"Come back to our house." Jenna was full of ideas today. "Rest, and then you and Dad can talk afterward. I'll cook dinner." She grinned hugely. "We can call Grandpa. Maybe he's done with his doctor's appointment in Lewisville."

Doc Jacobs insisted that Gil be seen by a heart specialist once every few months. Simon had gone with him a time or two.

Lily looked to Simon. He said, "Fine by me."

"Okay, then."

"We'll have some sparkling grape juice to toast the babies, who were almost holding hands." He glanced in the rearview mirror. "That was *the bomb*. Right, Jenna?"

She rolled her eyes. "Right, Dad."

The minute Lily hit the couch in Simon's family room, she fell asleep. While Jenna was upstairs doing homework, Simon watched Lily for a while. Lying on her side, she had her hand cradling her belly. The lashes against her cheek were dark and thick. He shouldn't offer to be her chauffeur for the prenatal classes. He definitely shouldn't volunteer to be her coach. Though he'd argued his sister down, in most ways Sara was right. This was happening too fast. Jenna could get hurt.

So could he, he finally admitted, if Lily left.

Frustrated, he forced himself to get up and go into the

den to work. He called up her e-mail about the Senior Saga column.

After reading it again, he sat back in his chair. Her idea would be a good addition to the paper, and if she expanded it to neighboring towns, the column would increase distribution. He had to let her do it, even if she'd become more involved in the business—which still scared the hell out of him. That day at the drugstore when she'd suggested the idea and admitted she planned to stay in Fairview, he'd had conflicting feelings. He feared her claim to the paper, but he'd also wanted to drag her out of her chair and kiss her soundly.

Pushing the thought away, he called up the paper's Web site, which was run by an independent company, and was making notes on some changes he had in mind when he heard Lily yell in the family room. Bolting up, he hurried out there. She was thrashing on the couch. "No. Somebody... Can't somebody help me?"

He raced over and knelt beside her, grasping her arms. "Lily, wake up. You're dreaming."

"They're going to die." She started to cry. "Please, don't let them die."

"Lily, wake up."

"Dad, what's wrong?" Jenna, from the doorway.

"Lily's having a nightmare." He shook her gently. "Lily, wake up."

She returned to consciousness slowly. Her eyes were wet with unshed tears. "What? Oh, Simon, the babies... They died."

"No, no, Lily, they didn't. You were dreaming."

Sinking back into the pillows, she rubbed her hands over her face. "I was in labor, and the babies were coming out and there was no one there to get them. They were going to die."

He brushed back her hair and let his fingers graze her cheek. "Someone will be there. The doctors, if no one else."

"I know. It was just so real." Her defenses down, she admitted, "I guess I'm more worried about all this than I thought."

Damn it, she shouldn't be alone during all this. "Maybe your fears were brought to the surface because of what Betty said. You need childbirth classes and a coach."

"You think?"

"I do. After Marian went through the sessions for Jenna, she felt more confident about the delivery."

"Good."

"Dad, I could be her coach."

A sixteen-year-old? "No, honey, you're too young for this kind of thing."

"Maybe Grandpa Gil?"

"No," Lily said. "I'd be embarrassed."

"Dad can do it, Lily. He did it with me."

"Oh, Jen, that's a terrible position to place him in. Simon, don't even answer that. I won't put you on the spot."

Simon didn't say more, because the doorbell rang just then.

Jenna got up to get it. Lily took his hand. Linked their fingers in a gesture that connected them even more. "I mean it, Simon. I can do this on my own."

"You could. But it would be better if someone was with you."

"Dad, this guy is here looking for Lily. Evan told him you called in and that she was at our house."

Over his shoulder, Simon saw the little man with glasses and an ill-fitting suit who'd followed Jenna inside. To Lily, he said, "Are you Lily Wakefield?"

Simon stood and towered over the guy. "Who are you?"

"Excuse me, sir. Are you?" he asked Lily again.

Sitting up, Lily managed to get off the couch and stand. "I'm Lily Wakefield."

He handed her an envelope. "Consider yourself legally served." With that, he turned and walked out.

Lily stared at the papers. "What could this be?"

Simon touched her arm. "Maybe they're the separation papers from Derek." Her hand began to tremble. "Want me to open them?"

"I'll do it." She ripped the envelope.

"Is that what they are?"

"No, they're divorce papers." She looked up. "Derek wants a divorce."

LILY'S HEAD WAS SPINNING, as she and Simon pulled up to Gil's house. He stopped the car and turned off the engine. "Stay for a minute."

"Okay. It's dark inside. I guess Gil isn't back." Earlier, her grandfather had called her cell phone to say the heart specialist had given him a clean bill of health, and he and Doc Jacobs were having dinner in Lewisville at a restaurant they favored.

Simon buzzed down the windows to enjoy the warm June air. Then, he turned to her. "How are you feeling?"

"Rested, after the nap."

"That's not what I meant."

"I know." She laid her head back on the leather seat. "It's a lot to take in. The babies coming early. The sonogram, the classes, now this." She nodded to the floor, where she'd put her purse. The divorce papers stuck out of it at an angle.

"Are you disappointed?"

"What do you mean?"

He shrugged a shoulder against the door frame. "I don't know. Maybe you thought Derek would come after you, when you sent him separation papers. You'd be easy to find now."

"No, Simon, I didn't think that. And I certainly wasn't hoping for it." She sensed his doubt. "There was a piece of that last night that I didn't tell you about."

In the moonlight, she could see his features harden. "What?"

"Derek hit me."

"What?"

"When I went to tell him about the babies and found him snorting coke, he became enraged and he hit me. I was afraid for myself and for them. That's why I left so fast."

"That bastard. I could strangle him with my bare hands." After a moment, he asked, "Why didn't you tell me that part?"

"It's so awful to have someone you care about treat you so badly. Turn on you like that. I didn't want anybody to know. I didn't even tell Gil."

"That settles it. You're never going back to him."

"I never planned to."

He ran his palm over the steering wheel. "I've been afraid of your going back."

"Because of Jenna and Gil?"

"No. Yes." He shook his head. "For them, yeah. But for me, too."

Lily's heart began a slow gallop in her chest. "Why, Simon?"

"Before I say this, I want to know something. Are you still in love with him?"

She waited before she answered. "I'll always love Derek. But I'm not *in* love with him anymore. He pretty much killed that. I'm sad about this." Again she pointed to the papers. "But it has to happen. For me and for the babies. I could never trust them with him now."

Simon gripped the gearshift. For a few moments, the noise of crickets was the only sound in the night.

"Why did you ask?"

He let out a huge breath. "Maybe I shouldn't say this, shouldn't throw it at you now after everything that's happened today, but…" He faced her fully. "I care about you, Lily. I have feelings for you."

"Feelings?"

"Yeah, feelings." He stared at her. "And they're not platonic."

Oh, thank God. "They're not?"

Resting his arm on the seat behind her, he grasped a strand of hair and rubbed it between his fingers. "No, Lily, they're not. They're the man, woman, *thingy* kind of feelings."

She laughed. She couldn't help it, she was so glad he'd made this confession. Raising her hand, she grasped his wrist. "What a coincidence. I've been having those same kinds of feelings."

He held her gaze. "Midpregnancy sex drive?"

"Maybe, but I don't think it's just that."

"No?"

"Nope, these are very specific feelings. Very directed. And after getting these papers, I can tell you how I really feel."

"The truth?"

"Oh, this is true. I care about you, too, Simon. I have strong feelings for you. The…" She lifted a shoulder. "The *thingy* kind, too." Inching closer, she whispered, "I have for a long time."

When he leaned in, she inhaled that wonderful scent that was Simon.

"Well, then. I guess I can kiss you."

"Please, God, do that." Her gaze dropped to his lips. "I've been daydreaming about your mouth on mine."

"It's amazing we've gotten any work done. I can't stop fantasizing about touching you."

"How?"

With a sexy smile, he slid his hand around her neck and settled it there. "Like this." He tugged her as close as the gearshift would allow. Lifting his other hand, he grasped one of her shoulders, rubbed up and down from there to her elbow and back. "And this." He tipped her chin. "And, ah yes, this." He lowered his mouth to hers.

The kiss came gently like summer rain and cool breezes. He brushed his lips over hers. Once, twice, three times. Coaxing open her mouth, he slid his tongue inside.

She matched his actions, and sighed. He moaned as she grasped his neck and anchored him there.

Summer rain turned into torrents and those cool breezes escalated to gale force winds. He deepened the pressure of his mouth. Held on to her tight. Her nails dug into his back. Moans and groans—his, hers—melded.

"God, Lily…"

"Ah, yes, Simon."

They were breathing hard, when she felt a series of kicks that startled her. "Oh, Lord." Her hand went to her abdomen. "Sorry, they've never kicked so hard before."

Instead of frustration at the interruption, Simon chuckled. Without asking permission, he placed his hand on her tummy. The babies jabbed and pushed and prodded. "I love that. I love touching you so I can feel this." His eyes were sparkling as they held Lily's gaze. "So, what do you think, Lily? Are they celebrating or are they angry?"

She kissed his jaw—it felt scratchy—and then moved on to the other side. "Oh, they're definitely celebrating." She whispered against his lips, "So am I."

CHAPTER SIX

LILY FINISHED her Senior Saga piece on Mrs. Billings and then sat back in front of the office computer. In the two weeks since the column had first run, it had become such a big hit that they'd expanded to people from surrounding areas. Lily was having a great time interviewing the older set.

She glanced at her watch. Simon would be at an appointment for a while longer, so she decided to take advantage of her time alone and check out an Internet site before he came back. She clicked onto Primer on Collecting Old and Historic Newspapers. His fortieth birthday was coming up in a month, and she wanted to get him something special.

As she searched the entries, though, her spirits plummeted. "Damn." Way, way out of her price range. Unless... She glanced at her purse. She'd borrowed Gil's car today and had brought along her engagement ring. She was planning to drive to Clearhaven after work and sell it there, so no one would know what she'd done. She'd need money soon to pay for the hospital bills, as well. Would she have some left over to afford a gift for Simon?

For a minute, she felt bad about hocking the ring and about the divorce. She'd loved Derek for a long time and she mourned the loss of that relationship. At first, she'd thought about him every day, but those moments had dwindled. Sometimes, she still dreamed about him, but not in a sexual way. Only in a sad *goodbye* kind of way.

Nothing like how she thought and dreamed of Simon

these days. He'd been so solicitous and affectionate, and
she'd basked in his attention. They'd shared more kisses
and caresses but had agreed not to make love until her
divorce was final and the babies had arrived.

Sometimes she wondered about his past relationships
with other women. As long as she'd been here, he hadn't
dated anyone, and especially not lately, not since the kiss
and their declarations in the car. But Ellen Priestly, the
pretty schoolteacher, still stopped by the *Sentinel* on occasion, in order to flirt with him. And Lily didn't like that
one bit.

Her stomach growled and the babies kicked. She needed
food, so she printed off the pages and exited the site. She
didn't want Simon to happen upon it, if he used this
computer.

The bell over the door tinkled just as she was heading
to lock it for the lunch break. In walked Simon's sister.

"Hello, Sara."

"Lily. Is my brother here?"

"No, he's out on assignment."

"I can't seem to catch him these days." Generally, Sara
looked like Simon—except now, when she scowled
fiercely. "He's busy with you most nights."

"You're welcome to join us anytime. As a matter of
fact, I'm cooking dinner tomorrow at Gil's for all of us.
Would you like to come?"

"No, thanks." Now, she glared at Lily. "I can't watch this
happen."

"Watch what happen?"

"You two falling in love." Sara's scowl darkened as she
looked to the side of the office. "What are those things?"

"Presents for the babies."

"From whom?"

"People in town. Sort of an informal shower, I guess."

Sara studied the gifts. "They're pretty expensive."

They were. Two beautiful bassinets, one from Mr.
Martini and one from Loretta Jameson. A vaporizer and a

swing. One by one, the townspeople had dropped in with their precious cargo. Lily was overjoyed and deeply moved by their thoughtfulness.

Still frowning, Sara picked up two tiny sweaters with matching hats, one in pink and one in blue.

Lily said, "Mrs. Billings made those. I'm going to bring the babies home from the hospital in them."

"Seems you have everybody on your side."

"Sara, there aren't any sides. Please, can we talk about this?"

When Simon's sister looked up, her expression was even darker. "There's nothing you can say to change my mind."

"I'm here to stay."

"I hope so, Lily. But I don't trust you. This town is nothing like the place you came from. You're going to get tired of the absence of five-star restaurants and living in a small house." She swallowed hard. "Do you have any idea what Simon and Jenna have been through?"

"Some, I think."

"They were devastated after Marian died. For years, until Jenna got better. Please, be careful about what you're doing. I don't know what will happen to them if you leave."

"I don't plan to leave."

"The best-laid plans," Sara quoted. And then she walked out.

Saddened, Lily felt tears well. Just moments ago, she'd been happy. Then, jealous. And now, she felt bad about Sara. She'd been on this emotional roller coaster for weeks. After staring at the door for a long time, she gathered herself together and went back to the kitchen.

She'd have some soup and crackers. When she opened the cupboard, she saw that both had been shifted to the top shelf, completely out of her reach. After glancing briefly at the step stool and rejecting the idea of climbing it, she crossed to the closet and got out a broom. Back to the cupboard.

Gently knocking the crackers with the end did no good. Hmm, this was harder than it looked. Poke, poke. Slide, slide. The box tumbled down and hit her on the temple. "Ouch."

Her stomach growled. Damn it, she was going to have lunch! She stepped to the side, to get out of the way, and managed to move a soup can right to the edge. It came crashing down onto the floor.

She yelped, then heard behind her, "What are you doing?" Simon's voice, harsh and angry.

He was in the doorway, standing there with fury written on his face.

"I was…"

"Going to get hurt. That soup can could have hit you in the head." He stalked over to her and tilted her chin. "What's this? Hell, Lily, you're bleeding."

"I am?" She touched her temple and felt the wetness. "The edge of the box caught me as it fell."

"What's wrong with you? You've got to be more careful. You have babies to consider."

And just like that, Lily burst into tears. Huge, racking sobs that came as quickly as her smiles did at other times.

"Aw, hell." Simon drew her to him. She went willingly, cuddling against his chest, holding on to his white dress shirt. "Shh. I'm sorry I yelled at you."

"I—I— First the price, and then the ring, then Sara, and then I couldn't reach the food."

"I don't know what all that means, but I'm sorry for my part in making you cry."

She stayed in his arms until she was calm. When she eased back, she wiped her face and looked up at him. "No, I'm sorry. I don't know where that outburst came from."

"My idiocy. Your hormones."

"Not idiocy. But I *was* trying to be careful."

He cradled her chin. "I'm sorry. I overreact about the safety of the people I care for. Just the thought of something happening to you—" he touched her abdomen "—or them, makes me crazy."

"I understand." Sara had just reminded her, too.

"As I said, I overreacted."

Stepping closer, she managed a superficial smile to lighten the mood. "At least I got to cuddle with you during the day."

He slipped his hands around her hips. "You like this?"

"I sure do."

He took out a handkerchief and blotted the cut on her forehead, then put it away. "There. Now you can eat. After this."

Dragging her close again, he held her as if she belonged to him. When his mouth closed over hers she forgot about soup, hocking the ring, the divorce and everything else.

THE CHILDBIRTH EDUCATION nurse stood in the front of the small room at Community Central Hospital and addressed the class members. "All right, partners, ease Mom down to the floor. That's it. Mats comfortable, ladies?"

Lily said "Yes," as did the others. The ten participants had introduced themselves the first week. There were three married couples and a two-female couple, plus Simon and Lily. She'd introduced him as her friend.

Like hell, Simon thought. He was more than her friend and he intended to keep it that way. In some ways, he thought, as the instructor outlined the three stages of labor, it was the best and worst of times. He was enthralled with Lily and the babies. He loved being with her. But he wanted more. Not just sexually, though waiting to make love until the babies were born might possibly kill him. He also wanted an emotional commitment.

Lily's divorce wasn't final yet, and Simon was old-fashioned enough to want to wait to declare his love until she was free. Both deprivations were torture sometimes, but he'd just have to content himself with being near her.

The petite instructor continued. "Now, in that final stage

of labor, you're going to be in a certain amount of pain."
She flashed some information on the screen. "Here are the
choices you have."

Everyone studied the options.

"Why don't you talk among yourselves about whether
you think you'll choose an epidural, other medication, or
go without."

"I don't want an epidural or any drugs," Lily said firmly.

"There's nothing wrong with having a little help."
Simon brushed back her hair. "Labor hurts, sweetheart."

"I don't care."

She was so brave and she'd done so much on her own.
A fierce wave of protectiveness came over him. That was
all past now. He was here with her, to help her with decisions such as this one. "I think we should do some more
reading about the effect of a spinal block on the babies."

When the class ended, they headed to the nearest ice-
cream store, just as they had the previous time. Lily ordered
a hot fudge sundae with extra nuts, and they sat outside in
the warm July air.

"I'm getting so fat." She shook her head in disgust.

Her doctor had been right—one day Lily's stomach had
just popped out. Now, at just over seven months, she looked
really pregnant. But still beautiful. Her dark hair was natu-
rally wavy, Simon had learned, and she no longer straightened it with a blow-dryer. She hadn't cut it since she'd
arrived, either, so it swirled around her shoulders.

"I gained five pounds this week."

"You should be gaining weight at this point in your
pregnancy." He took her hand. "Besides, you look better
with some meat on your bones."

She toyed with the straw in her water. "I've spent my
entire adult life trying to stay thin. It was chic, you know."

"No more. I like my women rounder. Like in a Rubens
painting."

"I've seen several of those in the Louvre. Maybe not that

round." She lifted her gaze to his. "But I do want to be attractive to you, Simon."

"If you were any more attractive to me, I'd be in constant misery."

Instead of laughing at his joke, she frowned. "Are you sure this is all right? That you want to be there during the delivery?"

She'd asked this before. "Of course."

"It's messy—and intimate. Won't it gross you out? I mean we haven't even…"

"No, Lily, it won't gross me out. And I know we haven't even… Believe me, my body reminds me every night."

"I'm sorry, it must be hard."

"Choose your words more carefully, babe."

She laughed. "You always do this. Joke around and put me at ease."

He glanced down. "This is no laughing matter."

"Simon? After the babies are born—after six weeks. I promise." She picked up his hand and kissed his knuckles. "I'll make it up to you."

He moaned. "Please, don't flirt with me."

Her look was saucy. "Oh, I'm going to do more than flirt afterward. A lot more."

"Change the damn subject," he said shifting in his seat.

"Seriously, if it's bad, we could…"

"No, we couldn't. We're waiting till the divorce is final, and you're back to your old self again."

Quietly, she said, "I'll never be my old self again."

"Babies change you."

"No, I mean that I'll never be the woman I was before. And I'm glad."

"Me, too, love."

GIL SAT NEXT TO LILY on the bleachers for a game of the men's basketball league. He nodded to Simon on the court. "Things have changed between you two, haven't they?"

Looking up from her sketch pad, Lily met her grandfather's gaze directly. He deserved to know the truth, though he'd obviously already guessed it. "Yes, Gil, things have changed."

"Does my heart good."

She scowled. "How *is* your heart?"

"Fine. I wish people would stop worrying about me."

"Angina attacks are serious, Gil."

"This wasn't a full-blown attack. It was just a few pains. And it only lasted seconds."

"It's been too much for you, taking care of me."

"Nonsense. The specialist in Lewisville said I'm fine."

"I just found you..." Her voice was raw. "I don't want to lose you."

"I'm not going anywhere." Sliding his arm around her, he kissed her cheek. The affection had come easier in the past couple of months. "Except to go over and talk to Doc about our bowling banquet." He bounded down the bleachers as fast as Jenna climbed them. They passed each other with high fives. Seemed as if everybody was happy these days—even the babies, who were constantly kicking up a storm.

Jenna dropped down beside her. "What are you doing?"

"Sketching your dad." Lily glanced down at the court. "I think he looks cute in his shorts."

"He's not bad for an old guy." Jenna stared at the men warming up. "Don't put those stupid pinnies in the drawing, though."

Lily sneezed, and cursed the cold she'd gotten. She fished a tissue out of her maternity jeans.

"You okay?" Jenna asked.

"A stupid cold is all."

"I hope you feel better soon." Picking up the baby name book, Jenna began to leaf through it. "How about Nathaniel? I'm reading *The Scarlet Letter* for Advanced English next year."

"Nate's cute." Lily hid a smile. She already had chosen

the names but she wasn't telling anybody. Besides, Jenna was having fun with this.

"Cecilia. We could call her Cessy for short."

"That's interesting. Wait a minute. The kid in *Dark Water* was Cessy." She shivered at the thought of the DVD she had recently watched with Jenna when Gil and Simon had been at a town meeting. "No, thanks."

"Or Joan. It means God's gracious gift."

"They are that."

Jenna smiled. "Dad said I was, too. A gift from God. He wanted to name me Joan, but Mom chose Jenna after her mother."

"You were a gift from God, honey, no matter what your name is. Your dad loves you very much."

Easily, as if she was talking about the weather, Jenna replied, "He loves you, too."

The pencil skidded across the paper. Lily didn't respond.

"I know you guys are taking this slow. Dad told me. I think it's stupid, but it's totally obvious that he loves you."

Crazily, Lily looked to the court for Simon's help. He was down there gliding in for a layup, which he sank with ease.

"Uh-oh." Jenna's gaze had shifted behind Lily. "Man, how do they keep finding you?"

Lily raised her eyes to see a frowning Matthew O'Malley come into the gym, look around, then head right for them.

"How do you know he's here for me?"

"Duh! He didn't come to see Dad play. And he's carrying something. Everybody knows about this league. Mr. O'Malley probably brought you another present. Though it's not his style." A light came on in her eyes. "See, *they* expect you to be here watching Dad."

Lily smiled as the older man did indeed stop at the empty bleachers in front of them. "Harrumph. Should you be sitting up there, Mrs. Wakefield?"

"We're up here so I can lean against the wall, Mr. O'Malley." Her back had been hurting a lot these days, and Simon hadn't even wanted her to come tonight.

"Young lady," the man barked to Jenna. "Come and get this." He held up a big paper bag. "It's Irish stew. Word has it Mrs. Wakefield's got a cold."

She chuckled. "I do." And because of the babies she couldn't take anything for the symptoms, so she was feeling rotten. "Stew will be delightful."

"Michael made it. He wanted you to have it tonight, but he was too lazy to walk it over himself." He glanced at the game, which had just started. "Young pups. Anyway, there's enough for the three of you, and your grandpa, too, if he wants some."

After Mr. O'Malley left, Lily watched Simon again. He was so graceful, yet so quick. He'd played Division Three at Ithaca College. He didn't talk much about college or his life with Marian. He'd said he was keeping secrets, and lately Lily had begun to want to know all of them. Staring down at the picture in her lap, she studied it. She'd drawn him facing forward, the ball under his arm, listening to the coach. His brow a bit furrowed, his stance loose limbed. God, he looked good. He was so handsome and sexy, she wanted to jump his bones.

Nice thought to be having next to his daughter.

Lily focused on the drawing, trying hard not to think of what that daughter had said to her earlier. That her father was in love with Lily.

But she couldn't ignore the fragile hope budding inside her that Jenna was right; that a really wonderful man like Simon cared for her, would be there for her. And wouldn't turn on her. She'd always lived with the knowledge that she was on her own, just her against the world. Despite what she'd learned about life in those years, Simon McCarthy had brought her to a whole other way of thinking about the future.

"Oh, Betty, you don't mean that. I'll go crazy." In Fairview, doctors made house calls, and right now Lily's stood at the side of the bed in Cameron Gardner's old room. For Betty Rabin's demure five-foot height, she could be a tyrant.

"I do mean it. The cold you had drained you. And the babies are big. They're pressing on your cervix. The longer we can keep them inside you, the better off they'll be."

"But bed rest? I'm not even eight months along."

"You can get up to use the bathroom and shower. I'd prefer you didn't go downstairs to eat."

"That'll be such an inconvenience."

The doctor packed her things in her bag as she talked. "Gil will have help."

"What do you mean?"

"Once the town finds out you've been sentenced to bed rest, they'll inundate you with all the food and company you want. The latter's okay, but don't tire yourself out."

"All right." Lily rested her palms on her huge belly. "I'll do anything for the babies, but, hell, I hate inactivity."

"You'll have all the activity you can handle in a few short weeks." At Lily's pout, Betty said, "I know this is hard. But you just have to do it. Do you have a cell phone?"

She'd left hers in Westchester and couldn't afford a new one. "No, why?"

"Because I want you to be able to call Gil or Simon if something happens."

"They have cell phones." She pointed to the nightstand. "I can call them on this extension."

"Good. We'll need to tell them to keep theirs on at all times."

"Do you think I'll deliver soon?" Lily asked. Now she was getting scared. She'd chosen annoyance over fear, but Betty's caveats were sinking in. Lily wished Simon was here with her.

"I hope not, but you never know." The doctor smiled. "Everybody's invested in these babies, Lily. Just enjoy the pampering you'll get."

"This is so different from where I used to live."

"Do you miss it?"

She saw Derek's face, high on drugs. Felt the slap across her cheek. And pictured Johanna Wakefield's disdain. "No. I've signed the divorce papers and sent them back."

"I heard."

"I can't believe nothing's private here."

"Get used to it. So, do we have names yet?"

"Uh-huh. But I'm not telling." She rolled her eyes. "I gotta keep *something* from the whole town."

The doctor laughed. "I'll go get Gil. Then, I'll stop by the paper and talk to Simon, too." She made the visit to him sound like the most natural thing to do.

"He was worried when I didn't come in today."

"You got a good guy there." Her face sobered. "He deserves happiness. So do you."

She didn't bother with a denial. Once again, the whole town probably knew what was going on between them. "Thanks."

Gil visited. Lily ate a light supper, and then she fell asleep. She woke to find the room dim and cool. Someone was sitting in the shadows. She knew, without really seeing him, that it was Simon. "Hi."

"Hey, there." He came over to the bed and sat down next to her. "How are you feeling?"

"Okay. But Betty's worried about the babies." She gripped his hand, terrified at the thought. "Simon, what if they come early?"

"Betty said they'd survive just fine, even if they were born now. They're big for twins. Still, the longer you can give them, the better."

"I hope I can do this."

"You can. And I'll be there to help."

"Promise?"

"I promise."

She relaxed a bit. When he told her things like that, she believed him. Dragging a second pillow close to her own, she tugged on his hand. "Lie down with me, Simon. Hold me for a while."

Without question, he kicked off his shoes and climbed onto the bed beside her. He pulled her flush against him and engulfed her and the babies in a huge embrace. With him there, she wasn't afraid anymore.

CHAPTER SEVEN

WITH EVERY BONE in his body aching, Simon sat on his porch, sipped his coffee and stared out at the backyard. The early-August morning air crept in through the open screens. He was exhausted, but he hadn't been able to sleep when he got home. He still couldn't believe the miracle that had just happened.

It's okay, love. I'm here, we're going to the hospital right now. Luckily, he'd been with Lily the day before when she'd come out of the bathroom and into Cameron's old room to tell him her water had broken. She'd made it through two weeks of bed rest.

Grabbing on to his arm tightly, she'd said, *I'm scared, Simon.*

That's all right, I'll take care of everything.

Stretching, he grinned foolishly. The babies had come a mere two hours after they got into a birthing room.

That's it, Lily. Breathe.

Come on, Lily. Push.

Oh, sweetheart. I can see one of their heads. Dark hair, just like yours.

She'd been sweating and swearing and crying, all at the same time. And soon, there they were. Two beautiful babies, six pounds, four ounces for the boy, and six pounds even for the girl. They were big for twins. Lily was announcing their names today. But with or without names, they already were as special to him as Jenna had been.

"Hey, Dad." His daughter materialized in the doorway

wearing shorts, a T-shirt and a huge smile. "You just get home?"

"A while ago. I stayed the night with Lily in the hospital. I left when Gil came back this morning."

Both Jenna and Gil had paced the waiting area while Lily was in labor, and after she delivered Gil had driven a sleepy Jenna home.

"I thought we'd go back right away. I wanna *see* them again."

"As soon as I shower."

With a dreamy expression on her face, Jenna poured herself cereal and sat down. "They're so beautiful, Dad. They're not even mine, and I love them already."

I know the feeling. Which scared him some, now that the babies were here. But he truly believed that nothing bad was going to happen. He wouldn't think that way, especially today.

"And they're all coming to stay here. I'm so psyched."

Doc Jacobs, who'd been at the hospital when Lily went in, had found Simon after the birth….

Simon, Gil can't handle two babies and a new mother at his house. It's too much for his heart.

He okay?

He's an old man, with a weak ticker. Even the stress of waiting during the labor and delivery wore him out.

Lily can stay with Jenna and me.

The doc had put his hand on Simon's shoulder. *You sure about that, son? It's quite a commitment.*

Not any more of a commitment than his heart had already made. Actually, he was thrilled at the thought of Lily and the babies being under his roof, and Jenna had gone wild with excitement. They'd yet to tell Lily, but at least Gil had reluctantly agreed to the plan.

"Dad, stop daydreaming and go shower. I wanna be at the hospital."

Gulping down his coffee, he stood. "Okay." But he continued to stare at his daughter.

"What?"

"The twins' birth has made me remember when you were born."

"Oh, Daddy. Were you this happy then?"

"Yes, I was. I've always loved you as much as Lily loves them, Princess."

They left the house after Simon cleaned up and were in Lily's room forty-five minutes later. She was asleep, with the babies in their Isolette a few feet away. They didn't even need an incubator, because Lily had brought them close enough to term. Gil was stretched out in a chair, his eyes closed, too. Simon and Jenna tiptoed inside and quietly went over to the babies.

"Oh," Jenna whispered as they stood over the tiny bed. "Their heads are touching."

The smells of new baby—powder and milk—made Simon smile. "I read that twins gravitate toward each other in the crib, just as they did in the womb."

"They're so beautiful."

"Yes, they are," Gil said from behind them.

"This is so awesome, Grandpa." Jenna took out her cell phone. "Can I take a picture?"

"I think so." Gil looked weary as he rose and came around the bed to have another look at the babies. "I feel bad about them going to your house. I could hire a nurse. They could still stay with me."

"Gil, we may have to do that anyway. Two babies are a lot to deal with. Jenna and I might not even be able to handle them."

"Think Lily will be okay about going home with you?" Gil asked.

"I'm sure she will be."

She'd said as much.

They'd been alone in the birthing room, each holding a baby.

I wish...

You wish what, sweetheart?

That you could be there. When I go home. I'd feel better,
more confident. I guess because you got me through the
labor and delivery.

I'll come every day.

It won't be the same.

No, it won't.

"Hello, there."

Everyone turned to find Lily awake, sitting up in bed.
And looking absolutely beautiful, even with messy hair and
a rumpled hospital gown. Her face was aglow and her eyes
were bright.

"Hey, there's my girl," Gil said. "How are you feeling?"

"Remarkably well. I can't believe it."

"I wish your mother could be here to see this." Gil
flushed. "I'm sorry. That was the wrong thing to say."

"No, no, it wasn't. You must be thinking of her giving
birth to me."

"Alone."

"She had a friend with her, Gil."

"She did?"

"Yeah, a girlfriend."

"Oh, that's good."

"Speaking of my mother…" She nodded to Jenna.
"Could you bring me my daughter, honey?"

Carefully, Jenna picked up the baby the way the nurse
had shown her and brought her to Lily.

"Come closer, Gil." When he was nearer the bed, she
smiled up at him. "I want you to meet Cameron. We'll call
her Cami."

Gil just stared at Lily. Then he looked away. After a
moment, he cleared his throat. "I…I don't know what to
say."

"Just say hello to Cami."

Jenna was so excited she was practically hopping up and
down. "What's *his* name?"

"Simon, could you get my son?"

Simon scooped up the other twin, and once again his

chest got that tight feeling in it. There was nothing quite as wonderful as holding an infant. He carried the babe over to the bed, but Lily didn't take her son from him. "You keep him while I introduce you. Simon, Jenna... I want you to meet Patrick Simon."

Simon's jaw dropped. Then moisture welled in *his* eyes.

Jenna teared up, too. "That was Grandpa's name, Lily. Dad's father."

"I know, honey. Your dad talks about him a lot. I think he'll be a fine namesake."

Simon couldn't speak.

Jenna's gaze narrowed on Lily. "You had this planned all along, didn't you?"

"For a while."

Gil touched little Cami. "Thank you, Lily."

Simon still couldn't speak.

"Simon?"

"Dad?"

"I can't..." He looked around. "Could I have a minute alone with Lily?"

"Sure thing." Gil grabbed Jenna's hand. "Come on, kiddo. Let's go get a doughnut."

When they left, Simon placed Patrick in the Isolette and nestled Cami alongside her brother. Then, he returned to the bed and sat down. Taking her hand, he said simply, "I love you, Lily."

"I love you, too, Simon."

Three weeks later

"YOU'RE EXHAUSTED. Go to bed now, or I'll drag you there." Lily tapped her foot to accompany her order. Dressed in loose pink shorts and top, she was feeling stronger today than Simon was. He'd been up all night with Patrick. "You're done coddling me, Simon McCarthy. Everyone is."

"Yes, ma'am." His easy acquiescence told Lily that she

was on target. Simon had run himself ragged working at
the paper and taking care of the babies. Though they'd had
help. Her friends in town had organized a schedule of all
able-bodied women to come over, deal with the babies,
cook meals and even clean. The first week, a couple of the
more experienced mothers had stayed during the night, as
well. With two babies waking up at all hours, the women
had been a godsend.

"*Now,* Simon."

"I'm going." He crossed to her. "Want to come with me?
Believe it or not, we're alone in the house—except for the
screaming meemies."

They *did* have powerful lungs, especially when they
got each other going. Usually, Patrick began the routine
and Cami followed soon after.

Simon placed a hand over her heart. "What do you
think?"

"I'd love to, but I haven't seen Betty yet. My appointment isn't for another three weeks. I'm afraid we have to
wait until then."

His sappy grin turned into a frown. "You haven't gotten
the official divorce notification, either. We said we'd wait
for that."

"I'm tired of waiting." She wrapped her arms around his
waist.

He kissed her soundly. "There've been too few of these
in the past month," he murmured against her jaw.

"I know. Can you believe the babies are so much work?"

"More than double what Jenna was."

Arms linked, they walked to Simon's bedroom. He was
so tired that he stripped off his shorts and T-shirt while she
was standing there. Though he'd been in the delivery room
and seen her in all her natural glory, she'd never gotten even
a glimpse of him naked.

She gawked. He was gorgeous. Tight glutes. Muscular
thighs. When he turned toward the bed and went to climb
in, he caught her staring. "What are you…" He followed

the direction of her gaze and looked down. "I'm sorry. I'm so tired, I wasn't thinking."

She gawked some more. Then she raised amused eyes to his. "Not so tired."

Swearing at his erection, he slid under the covers. She crossed to the bed and dropped down beside him. "Simon, I could…" She whisked her hand across the sheet to where it covered him.

He stayed her motion. "No, we're waiting until it can be us both."

"Well, it could be for us both. Just not intercourse."

"Call me old-fashioned but I want to wait until you're divorced." As he burrowed his head into the pillow, he mumbled, "I hate that you're still his," and then fell asleep.

Gently, she kissed him on the cheek. "I'm not his, Simon. I'm all yours."

Still, she was bothered by his reaction, so she went downstairs and, praying the babies would stay asleep, dialed her lawyer's number. When she hung up, she had a sick feeling in her stomach. Derek's attorney had not returned the final divorce papers. Mac Madison said he'd call about them today.

The chill, the bad feeling, stayed with her until Patrick woke up and then promptly woke Cami, and Lily had her hands full, trying to breast-feed them both.

Three weeks later

SIX WEEKS AFTER THE BABIES were born, Simon had forgotten completely that it wasn't his name on the birth certificates. In the parking lot of the *Sentinel,* as he buckled the second baby into a car seat, he thought of them as his own children and not those of some other faceless man. Closing the door, he turned to find his sister beside him. Late September had her wearing a light jacket, like his. "Hey, Sara. I haven't seen much of you lately."

"You've been busy." She nodded to the car. "You have them both? Alone?"

"Uh-huh. Lily brought them in to see the staff, then left to go shopping with Jenna. I'm taking them home."

"I'm impressed."

"Want to take a look?"

Sara hesitated. "I don't know."

"Honey, please, be part of this. Share them with me. I'm so happy I could burst." Not seeing his sister was the only thing that marred that glow.

"So, it's working out?"

"Of course it is."

"Why not?" Sara opened the door and poked her head inside. "Oh, God, they're gorgeous. All that black hair. And Lily's blue eyes." When she pulled out, she whispered, "She named the boy after Dad."

"I know." He even sounded like a proud papa, which was fine by him.

"Dad would have loved that."

He wished so much that his parents were alive to share his joy. "It's times like these when I miss them even more." He grasped her arm. "And you, too, Sara."

She just watched him.

"Want to come home with me? You could visit with them." He slid his arm around her shoulder. "And me. I hate this estrangement between us."

"Maybe. I miss you, too. And these two are like the Second Coming in town."

Sara followed him to his house, and when she pulled up behind him in the driveway she helped him get the babies out of his car, which was practically impossible to do alone. They each carried one inside.

Two frisky kittens scurried to meet them at the door and trailed them into the family room. "You have cats, too?"

"One's Jenna's and one is Lily's."

Sara sat down and unzipped Cami's jacket. "They're shopping, you said?"

"Yeah, Jenna has a holiday school dance in a month and they're looking at dresses." He didn't, of course, tell Sara that Lily had first gone for her six-week checkup today, which meant…a lot of things.

Cami yawned and Sara placed her in the bassinet, but then Patrick started to cry. "Want to get the little bruiser out of his coat and hold him while I make a bottle? He's hungry all the time."

Sara took Patrick and eased him out of his jacket. Both twins wore one-piece rompers. His had Winnie-the-Pooh on the front. "Lily isn't nursing anymore?"

"Yeah, but she's not here right now."

"So I see."

"Now, how can you see her, if she's not here?"

"Shut up and get their food."

As Simon fixed a bottle, Sara held the baby and walked him back and forth in the kitchen. "So, she's living here?"

"Uh-huh. She has her own room, if that's what you're asking."

"No, it's not. Are you going to make this arrangement permanent?"

"As soon as she gets the final divorce papers, I'm asking her to marry me." He handed Sara the bottle. "Here, you do it."

"Me? Why?"

"Because in about sixty seconds, Cami'll wake up."

"How do you know?"

"They have a sixth sense about each other."

She glanced down at Patrick. "It'll be fun to feed Dad's namesake."

Sure enough, loud cries rent the air. Sara laughed, and Simon joined in. "I'm so glad you're here, Sara. Now everything is perfect."

They crossed into the family room. "I guess this might work out."

"It will." He picked up Cami and nuzzled her. "Here I am, honey. Let's eat."

He and Sara chatted like old times until the babies finished their bottles and Simon put them down and wheeled their bassinets into the den. These days, they slept better when they were isolated from others.

"How about some wine?" he asked his sister when he came back to the family room.

"Love some."

The doorbell rang. "I'll get that. You get the wine." She kissed his cheek. "I'm glad I came, Simon."

He was whistling when Sara returned. But when he saw her face, he stopped abruptly. "What's wrong?"

Completely pale, she nodded over her shoulder. A man stood behind her.

He looked as if he'd stepped off the pages of *GQ*. Tall, handsome, with thick black hair and startling blue eyes. He wore an expensive-looking leather jacket, and even at first glance Simon could tell his clothes were designer. They were like Lily's clothes.

Simon clutched the stems of the wineglasses. "Who are you?"

"Derek Wakefield. I've come to get my wife and children."

LILY AND JENNA were laughing with Gil as they entered the house from the garage. "Think he's frazzled?" Gil asked.

"Nah. He's had the two of them alone before and he did pretty good." This from Jenna.

Lily called out to him. "Simon, we're home. Look who we brought with us."

Coming farther into the kitchen, she could see Simon on the couch and Sara next to him. How sweet that his sister had come over. He'd said more than once how he'd missed her, and Lily suspected he felt even worse than he admitted.

She noticed the two of them were staring at something out of her range of vision. She couldn't tell what it was until she reached the entrance of the family room.

"Oh, my God!" She dropped the cheesecake they'd picked up for dessert. It registered, when the box split and the cake splattered out onto the floor.

"Hello, darling." Derek stood and approached Lily. He grasped her by the arms and kissed her on the mouth. "It's so good to see you."

She yanked back. "W-what…when…did you…" She stepped even farther away, realizing how close he was. "What are you doing here?"

"I've come to bring you and the babies back home."

Her heartbeat escalated. "You…you know about the babies?"

"Yes. And I couldn't be more delighted. We're going to be a family now, Liliana."

Panicking, Lily looked at Simon. The color had drained from his face and his shoulders were tense. Sara had linked her arm with his. From the corner of her eye she saw Jenna lean into an equally stricken Gil.

And in that moment, Lily realized that the life she'd only just built in Fairview could very well fall apart.

CHAPTER EIGHT

DEREK ASSESSED the dynamics in the room. Among the many things that Alcoholics Anonymous had taught him, he knew he had to be attuned to others and not be self-absorbed. "I'm sorry to cause such a stir. It's clear you've all embraced Liliana. For that I'm grateful." He stared at his wife, who looked sensational in a red pantsuit. She was no longer so thin, and her complexion had a healthy sheen to it. "I'd like to see the babies, honey, and then go somewhere and talk."

The guy, Simon, who'd said little and just stared at Derek before Liliana arrived, broke away from his sister, strode over to Derek's wife and tugged her close. The old Derek felt his blood pressure rise and his fists curled tight. But the man he'd become—or so he hoped—quelled the angry reaction. This Simon person addressed him. "Things have changed, Wakefield."

Smiling at his wife he said softly, "For me, too."

"Lily's built a life here."

"In five months?"

The older man came forward. "Simon, it might be a good idea for Derek to see the babies and let him and Lily talk."

Liliana finally spoke. "In a minute. If you'll excuse us."

Derek frowned as she took Simon's hand and pulled him down a corridor and out of sight into another room. Confused, he faced those who were left. "Might I ask who you people are? What connection do you have to Liliana?"

"I'm Lily's grandfather, Gil Gardner."

"I didn't know she had any living relatives."

"There's a lot you don't know." This from the girl, who did what all teenagers seemed to do—she became surly.

"And you are?"

"Jenna McCarthy. Lily's been staying here at our house."

"Really? Why not his?" He nodded to Gil.

"We've been helping with the babies."

At the mention of his children, Derek smiled. "Twins. I can't believe it." Joy filled the holes and all the dark places inside him. "I really want to see them."

"I can take you into the den," Gil offered.

"No, thanks." He glanced down the corridor and frowned. "I'd like my wife to introduce me to my babies."

PALE AND SHAKING, Lily leaned against the washer and wrapped her arms around her waist. Simon hated seeing her like this, hated anyone hurting her—especially a man who'd already made her life so miserable. Even before today, Simon had harbored considerable ill will toward Derek Wakefield. "Are you all right, sweetheart?"

"The truth?"

He smiled, albeit weakly. "Of course."

"No, I'm shocked and upset. You?"

He shook his head. "I can't believe Derek just showed up here."

"Oh, I can. It's so him."

"Do you think he really wants you back?"

"Yes. He likes new toys."

"What?"

"We'd be new toys. This is Derek's m.o. He'd amuse himself with us, and then he'd lose interest in a little while. I've seen it happen before."

Simon took Lily in his arms. For a moment, he just held her close. He said a brief prayer to himself that they'd get through this and that he could do the right thing for her.

Then he drew back, knowing he needed to see her face for a moment. "I have to ask. You're not... You wouldn't... You wouldn't go back with him, would you?"

She seemed offended. *Thank you, Lord.* "No, of course not!" She clutched his shirt with her hands. "I am worried about the babies, though. He has a legal claim to them, Simon."

"We'll deal with that together. I promise." He kissed the tip of her nose. "What do you need right now, Lily? What can I do?"

"Tell me you love me."

That surprised him. "I love you. More than I can express." And certainly far more than Derek Wakefield had ever loved her.

"I won't leave with Derek," she said again, knowing intuitively that he needed to hear it a second time. Then, she kissed him sweetly and kept her arms looped around his neck. Having her close, breathing in her scent calmed Simon.

"Damn, you know what today is?" she asked.

He laughed and bumped his middle with hers. "How could I forget?" Though right now he had more important things on his mind than sex. Still, he was grateful that she'd lightened the moment. "I guess we'll get around to that *thingy* thing someday." He sobered. "Want me to stay with you while you deal with him."

"No. Liliana would have let you, but I've gotten stronger, because of you and Jenna and Gil. I can talk to Derek alone."

He started to object, to say he had a bad feeling about that, then thought better of it. "Fine. I'll be here, in the house, anywhere you want, just in case."

"I can't tell you how much that means to me."

But when they left the laundry room and Simon watched Lily go to Derek and lead him into the den, the bad feeling grew into a deep primal fear. And because the situation reminded him of Marian and his past, he couldn't quell his reaction, no matter what promise Lily had made him.

THE DEN WAS DIM and the babies were still asleep, so Lily switched on a small light in the corner. Despite her assurances to Simon, she was rattled by Derek's appearance in Fairview. It had only been six weeks since the babies were born and her hormones were still out of whack. She wished she'd gotten over the postpartum ups and downs before she'd had to face this man, who was still, after all, her husband.

Derek walked over to the bassinets. She'd forgotten what an imposing figure he was—he looked so big and masculine, standing there, staring down. She saw him swallow hard, reach in and touch one of the twins, then the other.

When he looked up, his face was streaked with tears. "I can't believe it."

Lily had seen him cry before—when he'd gotten drunk and missed a dinner she'd cooked, after a fight he'd instigated—but this was different. She'd never seen him weep for joy. She had to steel herself against this side of him.

He cleared his throat. "I take it they're one of each, by the colors?"

She nodded.

"Do they have names?" He ran a hand through his black hair, mussing the stylish cut. "Of course they do. What are they?"

"Cameron, for the girl. Cami for short."

"That was your mother's name." She'd told him that, but never the whole story of her background, fearful he'd think less of her.

"Yes, it was."

"And the boy?"

"Patrick."

"For a reason?"

"Yes."

He waited.

She didn't tell him about Simon's father. Instead, she said, "Derek, surely you didn't mean what you said out there. I've been gone five months. I would have thought you'd moved on without me." The old Derek's style.

"Like you have." He nodded to the other room. "Something's going on with that guy, isn't it?"

"The McCarthys have been wonderful to me. Especially Simon. And to answer your question, yes. I'm in love with him." She expected a tirade. They came whenever he was crossed.

But there was pain in his voice, when he simply said, "So quickly?"

"I—"

He held up his hand, his palm toward her. "No, I shouldn't have said that. You had cause to put me out of your life."

The fear came back then, as she recalled their last confrontation. "I did."

Tears in his eyes again. "I finally remembered, or let myself remember, what happened before you left."

She touched her cheek, which had been red for a full day after he'd hit her.

He approached her and rested his knuckles against her cheek. Gently, he caressed her skin. "I'm so, so sorry. I want to make amends."

The phrasing was odd. Not at all like Derek. Once again, she stepped back from him. "What's happened to you?"

"I've turned my life around, Liliana. I promise you, I'm not the man you left."

"What do you mean?"

"When I got notice of the babies' birth, I cleaned up my act."

"You've done that before, but it's never lasted." She frowned. "And how did you find out about the babies?"

"Through our insurance."

"They weren't supposed to use my card. I arranged to pay in cash."

"An error in bookkeeping that saved my life, I guess."

She didn't respond. This wasn't the old Derek, and she didn't know how to handle him.

"I'm sober and I'm staying that way. I've been going to Alcoholics Anonymous. I have help from my home group and from a Higher Power now. In time, I'm going to be a man worthy of you." He nodded to the bassinets. "And them. I'm asking for another chance, Liliana."

GIL WATCHED LILY come into the family room and his heart ached for her. His granddaughter's shoulders were slumped and her walk was slow. Since he was closest, he stood and hugged her. "Was it bad?"

"Yes." She looked around. "Where are Sara and Jenna?"

"Jenna went to bed," Simon answered. "I assured her everything was all right. But she was upset."

"Should I go up?"

"No, she's asleep. Gil checked on her."

"Sara left?"

Simon just nodded.

"She must be angry at me now, more than ever."

"I'll leave you two alone," Gil said, "but first I'd like to know what happened in there."

"All right." Lily sat on the couch next to Simon. Who looked as if he'd been hit by a train. Who looked just the way he had when Marian died and Jenna had been hurt.

"Are you all right?" she asked him.

"I told you I was. I'm mostly worried about you."

She picked up his hand and squeezed it. "Me, too. About you."

Gil sat across from them. "He's gone?"

"For now. He went to his hotel in Clearhaven."

"Why is he staying in Clearhaven?" Simon asked.

"You won't believe this. There are Alcoholics Anonymous meetings in a church there. He's joined the organization and has been sober since he found out about the twins."

"That's good, isn't it?" Gil asked.

Gil saw Simon's hand tighten in Lily's.

"If he stays sober. He's a complicated man, Gil. He means well, but… I guess he's weak. Time will tell if he's really changed. Meanwhile, he's spouting the AA mantra about taking one day at a time. He's got almost six weeks of sobriety in, and he felt he could come here now."

"And take you back," Simon said, disgusted. "Damn him."

"I told you that won't happen. But Simon, he has a right to see the babies."

"He does," Gil put in. "It's a horrible thing to lose your child. To never see her grow up." Even though Lily had forgiven him, Gil would never forgive himself for letting Cami go. "I wouldn't wish that on my worst enemy."

"Well, right now Derek Wakefield's feeling like mine." Simon faced Lily. "You were worried he wasn't responsible enough to see them. Be alone with them."

"I still am. That won't happen for a long time."

"What *is* going to happen now?" Gil asked.

"Derek's coming back after his morning AA meeting tomorrow. We're going to talk more."

"Do you want me with you?" Poor Simon, he sounded so worried.

"No, he has a right to private time with me. And Cami and Patrick."

"That's all he has a right to, Lily."

"I know." She kissed him on his cheek. "Don't worry."

Gil stood and put on his coat. "I'm going. Walk me out, honey?"

"All right, Grandpa."

The two men grew still. In the midst of all this turmoil, Gil felt a surge of happiness so great it silenced him.

"What?" Lily asked, distracted.

"You never called me Grandpa before."

"No? I guess in my mind I have. It must have slipped out."

"I'm touched."

"It's about time, don't you think?"

"I do." Sliding his arm around her shoulders, Gil hugged Lily close as they walked to the foyer and when they reached it he turned to face her. "I don't want to make this harder for you, Lily. And I love Simon like a son, so I don't want him hurt, either. But I feel sorry for Derek. Don't deprive him of his kids."

"I won't. Legally, I couldn't, even if I wanted to. But he'll have to prove he's stable and sober for good before I'd ever leave them with him." Her eyes hardened. "And he can forget about me as part of the package."

"I understand. Now say it again and I'll leave."

She smiled. "Good night, Grandpa."

"Good night, Lily."

DEREK TOOK THE BOTTLE from Liliana and frowned at it. "Are you sure this is all right? I mean, you said you're still breast-feeding."

She held up the second bottle. "This is fine. We try to give them one of these every day so they get used to it. Then when I go out, or when I go back to work, they'll be accustomed to having it."

"You shouldn't be working." He hated the idea of his wife having a job. Especially now, when she had his children to take care of. "You should be able to stay home with them."

"Go ahead, feed Patrick."

Picking up the baby from the bassinet, Derek held him close for a minute. "Hey there, son. How are you today? Do you know who I am? I'm your daddy." Even if he didn't deserve them. But did he deserve what he'd found when he got here—that another man had usurped his roles as a father and a husband? Like hell.

He caught Liliana watching him. She'd done a lot of that

in the three days he'd been here. Stare at him, as if she was dissecting him, trying to figure out if he was who he said he was. "I think he knows my voice."

"I'm glad for you, Derek. We need to talk today." He nodded. "Let's wait till Cami wakes up."

"Will she?"

"Uh-huh. Simon gives her about a minute, then she lets loose."

Simon. Liliana mentioned him a lot, and Derek hated the way the man touched her. He wondered if they'd slept together. At the thought, Derek felt the darkness well inside him again, begin to surface.

He pushed it back by silently repeating the Serenity Prayer, as Cami did, indeed, wake up, and Liliana began to feed her. She never breast-fed the babies in front of him, and it made him feel bad.

Confront your demons, Wakefield. "All right, let's talk. You go first."

"Surely you know I can't go back to Westchester with you."

"No, Liliana, I don't know that. I've changed, I promise you. I'm sober, by the grace of God, and I'm going to work the steps so I can stay that way. I've stopped using drugs and I've also got the gambling under control."

"Gambling?" The bottle slipped out of her daughter's mouth and Cami began to cry. Liliana slid the nipple back in. "I didn't know about this."

"I know you didn't. And I could have let you come back without telling you. The old Derek would have, but not me. I'm a different man."

"I'm glad for you, Derek, really I am." She drew in a breath. "How much debt do you have?"

"I've kept it at bay. We're fine financially. You can come back and not worry about anything."

"I've built a new life here."

"Honey, you've only been gone a few months. We were together more than ten years. We're husband and wife."

"I signed the divorce papers."

"I didn't."

"I wondered."

"I don't think you wanted me to. I think, in your heart, you wanted me to come after you."

She shook back her hair, which was longer now, and wavy. He liked it. "No, Derek, I just wanted to get away from you."

"I don't blame you for that. But I've changed, and I'll do anything you want me to, if you'll stay with me. I'd even move here, so you can be near Gil."

"Oh, God, no. That would be the last thing I'd do."

"Whatever you want, Liliana." He waited. "I know you've had trouble with Mother and Father. I'll stand up to them, I promise, if that's holding you back."

"Derek, making all these promises… It's not what I need."

"What *do* you need?" He wondered if he'd ever asked her that before and felt bad that he probably hadn't.

"I need to stay here." ·

"With McCarthy."

"Yes." She added, quickly, he noticed, "And Gil and Jenna."

"Why does he deserve this from you, Liliana? You've only known him a short time. You and I have a history. Can you throw it away because of someone you just met and think you love?"

Her eyebrows raised.

"I'm not stupid, darling. I can see what you think you feel for him. But answer this. Have you stopped loving me, a man you committed yourself to legally, the first man you ever loved?"

Tears came to her eyes.

And they encouraged him, so he pushed. "I know I don't deserve you. If you tell me you don't love me anymore, I'll rethink staying here."

"No, Derek, I never stopped loving you. I just can't live

with you anymore. I'm still angry with you for your drug
use, and how you reacted when I found out. Now I hear
about the gambling. These things can't be fixed just
because you want them to be."

The fist around his heart had loosened. For the first time
in a long while Derek felt hopeful. "You're wrong. They
are fixable. And if you can admit that you still love me, then
we do have a chance." He hoped that all the love he felt in
his heart showed on his face. "I promise, Liliana, this time
I have changed."

IN THE TWINS' ROOM at his house, Simon rocked Cami back
and forth, one hand on her soft, wispy hair, the other
cradling her bottom. His heart swelled in his chest with the
thought of how much he loved her. And Patrick—who
slept, finally. What would Simon do if he lost them now?
No, he wouldn't think that way, wouldn't let that happen,
despite the upheaval they were experiencing. It didn't
matter that Derek Wakefield had burst back into Lily's life
a week ago, claiming legal rights to the twins. Simon
would always consider them his babies and himself their
father in the true sense of the word. The guy had him
spooked, was all. Had him questioning the future. Okay,
Lily was acting strangely, too, but what could you expect
with the appearance of Wakefield and her still-unstable
emotions?

He heard her come out of the bathroom down the hall.
Jenna was staying overnight with Katie Welsh, so it had to
be her. He rocked Cami a few minutes more, then put her
down and headed toward Lily's room.

She was sitting up in bed wearing a blue nightgown,
looking almost ethereal resting against the pillow. He was
struck by the thought that he loved her so much that sometimes it frightened him. Mostly this had occurred to him
since Derek had turned up. "Tired?" he asked.

She looked up at him. Her gaze was warm, but there was

something in it that increased his unease. "I am, but I haven't been able to fall asleep right away lately."

Leaving the door ajar so they could hear the twins if they woke, he crossed to her bed. When he sat, she placed the book she'd been reading on her lap. "I know a surefire way to make you fall asleep." He kissed her nose, inhaled the wonderful scent of her bath. "After."

She flushed. From desire or something else? "Do you think that's a good idea?"

He didn't laugh. They'd always joked about their deliberate celibacy, and under ordinary circumstances he would have made a bawdy comment. But tonight, he didn't want humor. He wanted her. He wanted to possess her. Make her his, irrevocably. He wanted—needed—to have the physical connection that would bind her to him. Gently, though his hand was a bit unsteady, he placed it on her gown and traced the neckline with a finger. "It's time, sweetheart."

"It's a bad time." She shifted uncomfortably. "Things are in such a state of flux."

He drew his hand back abruptly. "I know. But not between us."

"Still, I'm not sure…" She moved restlessly again, causing the book to slide off her lap and onto the floor.

Simon picked it up and got a glimpse of the cover. *Living with the Alcoholic Husband. One Woman's Story.* His fist curled around the binding. "Tell me you didn't buy this book."

"I didn't." Twin slashes of red on her cheeks betrayed her discomfort. "Derek's AA sponsor sent it to him, to give to me."

"I don't believe this. Lily, talk to me. Tell me what's going on."

"I already did!" In contrast to his gentle tone, her voice had risen a notch. She was angry? At him for wanting to make love? "Don't harp on this."

"Harp?"

Guiltily, she glanced away for a moment. "I'm sorry, I

didn't mean to snap at you. I feel so out of control of my emotions these days."

He waited a beat before he spoke again. "Lily, let's not fight. We need connection. We need to be together, emotionally and physically." At least *he* needed that. At the moment, her needs were unclear to him.

"Please, Simon, I'm tired. I want to sleep now."

Panic swamped him. He couldn't believe she had turned him down after weeks of yearning to make love. And for the first time, he seriously considered the possibility that she might go back to Derek. Though it broke his heart, he also saw that she was so weary, tiny blue veins were standing out on her pale face. He couldn't go off on her now. So he stood. "I see. I don't want to keep you awake."

He left, to the sound of her calling him back.

Had she been more forceful, seemed to mean it more, he might have turned around.

HOW COULD SHE HAVE BECOME so confused in just ten days? Lily couldn't believe it. But Derek had breezed into town and turned her world upside down.

No, that wasn't fair. He hadn't breezed in. He'd crawled in, groveled his way in, and he was obviously hurting. He was truly trying to make amends.

"Hi." Simon came to the doorway of the glassed-in porch. It was early, and Lily had gotten up with the babies so he could sleep. His stubbled jaw and bloodshot eyes were evidence that he wasn't getting much rest. What had happened the other night in her bedroom had remained between them like some invisible force field, keeping them apart.

"Hi. There's coffee."

"I thought you weren't drinking it while you're still breast-feeding."

"I'm not. I made it for you."

He poured some into a mug, came to the table and kissed

her head. "Thanks." He looked down. "You're dressed already?"

She'd put on a sweat suit, no longer comfortable around the house in her pajamas. "Um, yeah."

Taking a chair, he stared out the window. The end of September had begun turning the leaves red and yellow. Simon had told Lily he loved this time of year, but lately nothing seemed to please him. The strain between them eclipsed everything else.

"So," he finally said. "Are we ever going to talk about why Wakefield hasn't gone home yet?"

She wished there was rancor in his voice—his wariness and pain were worse. Especially since her own emotions were still bouncing all over the place like Ping-Pong balls.

"He has a right to stay and see the babies, Simon. He is their father."

Simon's mug stopped halfway to his mouth and his expression was clearly stunned. Lily hated hurting him— actually she felt the pain, too. But they both had to acknowledge the truth. "I was beginning to think I was their father, in every way that counted."

"I'm sorry. This is hard for me."

"He's staying till he wears you down, Lily. You just can't see it."

"That's not going to happen. I promise you." In reality, she had no idea what Derek was doing or how she was standing up to his subtle coercion. Things were fuzzy, like a photograph that was out of focus, and she couldn't get anything into perspective.

"Isn't it?" Simon's voice was achingly tender. "Then, why haven't we made love? The six weeks have turned into almost eight."

"You wanted to wait until the divorce was final."

His face flushed and his beautiful eyes clouded with misery. "I made it clear the other night that I'd changed my mind."

She just stared at him. All right, she *had* put him off,

but she was too confused to do anything else. Why couldn't he see that?

"I feel like I'm losing you, Lily."

"You're not. I'm just mixed-up about all this."

"That doesn't make me feel better."

She didn't comment.

"Derek came to see me at the paper. You were right, he's charming and charismatic."

"What did he want?"

"He asked me to step aside. Told me he loved you more than anything in the world. He wants me to give him another chance with his family. He made me feel like the other man."

"In a way, you are."

Simon stared at her, horrified.

"What did you say to him?"

"That I wouldn't even consider it." He studied her. "But you are, aren't you?"

"Simon, I…" Lily felt her stomach roil. "I don't know what I'm thinking these days. My hormones are crazy. It's still all this postpartum stuff. I need some time."

There was a gasp from the doorway. Jenna. "You're going back to Derek?"

Slapping the mug down on the table, Simon stood up and crossed to his daughter. "Honey, you weren't meant to hear any of this."

She stared at Lily wide-eyed. "Tell me, Lily."

"Jenna, this is complicated. No, I'm not really considering going back to Westchester, but the whole situation isn't as simple as it seems. Derek's changed and he's got a right to the babies."

"But they're ours."

Lily waited a beat. Some things had to be said here. Now that Derek knew about the twins, and wanted them, he would be their father no matter what happened. He'd be part of all their lives, and she couldn't let Jenna or Simon think otherwise—no matter how much it hurt them, or her.

With a heavy heart, she said simply, "No, honey, they're not yours."

Simon pivoted. His look mirrored Jenna's. Lily couldn't believe that those words had come out of her mouth.

"I NEED SOMEONE TO TALK TO. I know you're not the best person, that you love her, too, but I had to come." Simon stared at Gil. This visit was so selfish. Some days he felt he was acting more like Derek Wakefield than the guy himself was.

"It's all right. You're like a son to me, Simon."

"Thanks for saying that." He got some coffee and joined Gil at his kitchen table.

"Where is she today?" Gil asked.

"At the zoo." Could this hurt any more? The notion of Lily and Wakefield together with the twins on a family outing sickened him.

"A little cold for that."

"Wakefield wants to do 'daddy' things, I guess."

"Ah. How long is staying?"

"As long as it takes to get her back." Simon ran a weary hand over his face. "It's working, Gil."

The older man didn't say anything. Simon knew what silence meant these days.

"It's excruciating, watching her slip back into his clutches."

"He's her husband, Simon. The father of her children."

"Oh, my God." This just kept getting worse. "You think she should go back to him."

"I—I've spent some time with him. He seems reformed."

"Until he falls into his old ways. My God, Gil, he hit her."

"He came to see me, Simon. He confessed everything. He cried when he talked about how he treated her."

Wakefield had been making the rounds. "He's good with the crocodile tears."

"I'm going to say something, son, and you won't like it. I never got over letting Alice send Cami away. I've lived my whole life tortured by that mistake. It's hard to want that for someone else." He cleared his throat. "In my heart, I wish I'd had the kind of courage Derek Wakefield's shown, and that I'd fought for my child."

"Gil, she can't go back to him. I'm worried about Jenna. She's become sullen. Withdrawn. She won't pick up the babies. She's afraid. Hell, so am I."

Gil didn't respond. But the look on his face spoke for him.

"Did you tell Lily all this? How you feel about Derek coming back?"

"I thought it was best."

And the awful truth crystallized. Gil was on Derek's side. Simon had come to him for reassurance and he'd gotten the exact opposite. From the man who was a second father to him. But he needed to hear the words. "We have reason to be scared, Jenna and I, don't we?"

"Yes, Simon, I think so."

Two WEEKS AFTER Derek turned up in Fairview, Simon arranged to spend some time with Lily alone. They had dinner at his house, where conversation was strained, as they had little to talk about these days except their problems. Now, they were in the family room. Simon was hurt when he learned that Derek was with the babies at Gil's tonight. Everything that happened these days hurt him, and it was nearly killing Lily. At least Jenna was staying at Sara's. Lily stared at the picture on the wall that she'd drawn of the girl. It seemed like a lifetime ago.

"You know we have to talk about this, love."

"I know."

"I wish you didn't look as if you were going to the guillotine. I'm me, Simon."

"I know." She was repeating herself, stupidly. So she cut to the quick. "You're sick of waiting."

"Yes. You've got to make a decision, Lily. It's too hard on all of us. You, Jenna, me. Even Gil's heart. We can't all be waiting for the other shoe to fall."

"I need more time. I can't help it, Simon—nothing's clear to me."

The love on his face, the absolute, deep love in his eyes shamed her. She hoped hers were filled with the same emotion.

"It's clear to me. You have to make a choice."

"Please, Simon, I'm not ready."

He ran a hand through his hair. "This is bringing back something difficult for me, Lily. Something you don't know about."

"What?"

"It concerns Marian and me."

She hadn't expected that. "Tell me."

"People thought we were the perfect couple, but we weren't. She got pregnant in college and we had to get married. And Marian was never happy after that."

"Oh, Simon, I'm sorry."

"I lived with her for years, knowing she was unhappy. Hell, I was, too, but I told myself we had to make it work for Jenna. I focused all my attention on her, and unknowingly I made things worse. Marian tried, we both did, and some years were good, but some weren't. Then, she met another man.

"The night she told me about him, I ordered her out of the house. I didn't care if she left. But she had to leave Jenna with me. She accused me of loving Jenna more than her. Then she took her, in the night, while I was sleeping."

"And crashed the car."

"Yes."

"Simon, I'm not Mar—"

He held up his hand. "No, let me finish. Jenna's injuries devastated us all. Our lives revolved around them for years."

She saw the pain on his face. Why was he telling her

this? To fight for her, or—oh, no, it couldn't be—to hurt her as she was hurting him?

"I'm telling you all this because I've already lived in limbo once. I won't do it again. You've got to get us out of this situation."

Lily just stared at him.

"And there's more to the meaning of this story. Staying together for the kids, giving marriage a shot for the wrong reasons, it doesn't work. Unless you really love each other."

A long, excruciating silence stretched between them.

"I'm waiting for you to tell me you don't love Derek anymore."

"I can't tell you that," she blurted out. "I said it before, I never stopped loving him. But that doesn't change how I feel about you."

"Funny, Marian said the same thing about her new guy."

"Derek isn't new, Simon. He's the first man I ever loved."

"He's back for a couple of weeks and already I'm second fiddle."

"I didn't mean it that way."

"Don't do this, Lily. Don't choose him. Choose me."

"Simon…"

"Think about all we have together. About the family we've built."

The guilt that had been edging into Lily's consciousness surfaced. In some ways, she'd been so wrong. "Behind Derek's back. I did it all behind his back."

Simon's eyes widened. "He's brainwashed you."

"No, he hasn't. But I have a responsibility to him."

"What about me? I know that sounds selfish. But I have to say this. Don't you have a responsibility to me?"

"Of course I do. But I have children to consider."

"And what about *my* child?" His voice rose. Finally, he was angry. "You've let her love you like a mother."

"Simon, nobody's going to win here."

"Oh, I don't know. It looks to me as if Wakefield's going

to snag the brass ring. He gets you and the twins. Even Gil feels something for him."

Lily didn't know what to say.

"I'm done with this waffling. You have to choose, Lily."

Damn it. Damn him for pressuring her. "Don't say that, Simon. I'm not ready."

"Well, I am. If you can't choose me and Jenna now, tonight, if you're not certain enough of us after all we've been through, you and I are finished."

"Simon."

"And know this, before you answer. I won't take you back. When he turns into the real Derek Wakefield, there'll be no place in our lives for you."

"I can't make a decision now, Simon."

He stared at her for a long time. "You just did." He rose to his feet. "I want you out of here tonight."

Just like Marian. The thought made her cringe. "You don't mean that."

"I'll go to Sara's. I'll stay there with her. Take what you can carry—we'll give the gifts from the town to the Salvation Army. Derek will probably want to buy you all-new things. Be gone by nine." He took a step away. "And take the cat. He reminds me of you and I don't want him around." He walked toward his front door.

"Simon, wait."

"No, I'm done waiting," he said over his shoulder. "Goodbye, *Liliana*."

The front door slammed shut. Lily just sat there dazed. And scared to death about losing Simon. And indescribably hurt. She shook her head at the irony. In the past, all she'd ever wanted was Derek's undying love. But now that she'd gotten it—chosen it?—the searing pain of losing Simon and Jenna made it impossible to be happy.

JENNA WAS FROZEN TO THE SPOT out of sight in a corner of the living room. She'd snuck out of Aunt Sara's house because she knew her dad and Lily were having a big talk and she wanted to know what was going on. She wished she hadn't. She couldn't move. Lily was *leaving*. Lily had chosen her other family, her *real* family over Jenna and her dad.

But it was more than that. Her father had never told her the truth about her mother. Her father, whom she trusted more than anyone in the world. He'd lied. Lily had lied. Her own mother had lied. Sinking to the floor, Jenna couldn't believe this was what life was really like.

What was the term? Pollyanna. She'd been a Pollyanna all this time. Well, no more. She wouldn't be a Pollyanna anymore.

With that, she got up and crept out of the house and into the night.

CHAPTER NINE

Five months later

THOUGH LILY WASN'T a praying woman anymore, she stood in the foyer entrance to St. Peter's Church with Cami and Patrick, who were sound asleep in their double stroller and said, to whatever deity might exist, *Please just let them sleep through the service.* As the reality of where she was and why she was here began to sink in, she tried to smother her emotional response. No room for grief now. That would have to wait. Last month, she'd buried a husband, and today she would bury her beloved grandfather. Lily couldn't afford to let go of her equilibrium because she was afraid, if she did, she'd never get it back. And she had major battles to fight.

The cruel February wind swirled around her legs when the heavy front door opened. Two people entered the church—Mrs. Billings and Mr. Martini. Briefly, Lily forgot about what had happened in this town, and her spirits lightened at the sight of them. But Mr. Martini's blue eyes were somber and his face tight as he tipped his fedora hat to her, said nothing and averted his gaze. Mrs. Billings turned her face away. Their actions weren't anything Lily hadn't expected, but the slights hurt just the same.

Checking her watch, Lily saw it was almost ten. Mac Madison, who was still her lawyer, had called to tell her of the service. At least the horrible news of Gil's death hadn't come by phone. Doc Jacobs and Loretta Jameson had driven down to Westchester to tell Lily in person, and for that she would always be grateful. Both had been kind when they'd informed her that Gil had died quietly in his sleep of a heart attack. Her own heart, already bruised and battered by her circumstances, hadn't stopped aching since.

Then, Mac had called about today. *The service will be at ten. The burial will have to wait because the ground is frozen.* So Lily only had to endure this funeral, then she could go back to Gil's house and wait until tomorrow when the will would be read.

I don't want anything from Gil's estate, she'd told Mac. *Since you're in town, it would be more convenient for my office if you were there.*

Lily figured she owed it to him for how he'd tried to help her over the past month.

The strains of "Amazing Grace" began and Lily pulled herself together. If she could just stay in the back of the church and go unnoticed, maybe she'd be able to handle this final goodbye. Slowly, she pushed the stroller through the big double doors of the sanctuary and off to the side behind the pews. The completely filled pews. Everyone in town had loved and admired Gil Gardner, including his prodigal granddaughter. At least she'd seen him once a week since she'd left here, either meeting him halfway between Fairview and her house, or on occasion in Westchester, if Gil drove down.

The scent of candle wax and incense permeated the church. Just as the priest offered words of welcome, Patrick let out a howl. The sound echoed like a gunshot, so loudly in the solemn atmosphere that the priest stopped midsentence and heads craned. Lily panicked and picked up her son, held him close and began to walk him. Murmurs rumbled though the crowd. She kept her face close to the baby's and whispered soothing words to him.

Finally, he quieted, the priest began again, and heads swiveled back to the altar. "We're gathered here to say goodbye to a good man."

Then Cami started up a minute later. *Oh, no.* Lily would have to leave the service now. She didn't even deserve to say goodbye to Gil. She tried to get Patrick back into the stroller, but he started to kick, stiffened his legs and screamed again. He was teething.

Lily felt a hand on her shoulder.

"Let us help you." Loretta Jameson had come up to her. The expression on her face was kind. "We'll take them down to the fellowship hall, so you can mourn Gil properly."

Behind Loretta, Mac Madison and his wife reached the end of the aisle. Hannah Madison said, "You stay and say goodbye to Gil."

Before Lily could object, Loretta eased Patrick away from her and Hannah wheeled Cami though the sanctuary door.

Mac took her arm. "Come on, Lily, let's get you seated."

She shivered, even though she was wrapped up in a black wool coat. "I'm all right back here."

"Gil would want you up front, dear."

Oh, God, was this her penance? As she let Mac escort her down the aisle, she felt like Hester Prynne on the day she was released from prison, being paraded in front of the community. Only Lily's letter brand was a scarlet *D*, for deserter.

Let's name him Nathaniel. I'm reading The Scarlet Letter.

Nate might be cute.

Lily forced away the memory of her exchange with Jenna that day on the bleachers when they were watching Simon play basketball. They'd all been so happy, then. And Gil had been alive and well. She couldn't think about Jenna any more than she could think about Simon. The notion that she'd had them both and had foolishly abandoned them for Derek would level her if she thought about it too much.

And then she saw him. Mac led her into the pew behind

Simon and Sara, then mercifully sat next to her. Where was Jenna? And who was that thin girl, dressed in odd black clothes, with the short hair? She turned and looked at Lily. Jenna? Oh, dear Lord, no! She remembered her sweet-faced and innocent, with a broad smile. This prematurely old teenager wore black lipstick, heavy mascara, painted black fingernails and a scowl the size of the Pacific. One lone remnant of the old Jenna surfaced when she turned back and leaned against her father.

Simon. He didn't look back, so Lily couldn't see his face. But his shoulders—were they wider now?—filled out a navy suit that she'd never seen before, as one strong arm encircled his daughter.

When Lily remembered how his arms had comforted her, she thought she might be sick. She'd missed him, his presence, his touch, every single day she'd been gone.

Don't, she ordered herself. *Just don't.*

The priest finished speaking. As the verses from the Bible were read, one by Sara and one by Doc Jacobs, grief filled Lily and began to seep out. She pictured her grandfather's face, saw him smiling at the twins....

Every time I come, they're bigger. Say hi to Grandpa, Cami.

She saw his gaze, direct and full of understanding.

It's not going so well with Derek, is it?

And on his last visit…

Come back with me, Lily. Derek's dead. There's nothing here for you but a constant battle with the Wakefields.

She'd wanted desperately to flee to the safe harbor of Fairview. But she didn't go with Gil because of Simon and Jenna. She owed it to them not to return, not to remind them of what she'd done to them. As it was, she was planning to leave town tomorrow, right after her appointment with Mac, in order to avoid any further contact with them.

And go where? She had no idea.

She heard the priest say, "Now a few words from Simon

McCarthy, who knew Gil probably better than any of us did."

Briefly, Lily closed her eyes and stifled a moan. She hadn't anticipated this, or if she had it was just another thing she'd hidden from herself in the past five months, during which time she'd become very good at denial. Telling herself to be strong, she watched the man she still loved with all her heart rise from the pew, kiss his daughter's cheek and walk stiffly to the lectern.

WHEN SIMON LOOKED OUT at the people who had come to pay their respects to Gil, he vowed not to single out Lily. He'd heard the murmurs when one of the babies had cried, caught Jenna's reaction when she turned around and sensed Lily's presence behind him. But he blocked her out now, as he had in the past five months, by forcing himself to remember the kind of person she really was and what she'd chosen for her life.

He glanced at his notes and then looked out at the congregation. "Gil Gardner was an honorable man. Kind, loving, giving. There wasn't a person in town who didn't love him."

Some coughing, some muffled sobs. Sniffles.

"For me…" He cleared his throat. "Gil became a second father when my dad died, and for Jenna he was a grandfather. For you, he was a friend, confidant and a significant contributor to our community, not only in running the *Sentinel* for decades, but in every way that mattered."

Simon drew verbal pictures of Gil. His ordering the same fish fry every Friday night at the diner. His bowling exploits. Early in his career, facing down a big-city lawyer who didn't like an editorial Gil had written about the man's client. Chuckles, which Gil would have liked, resounded throughout Simon's talk.

He clenched his fists at his sides, dug his nails into his palms so he could finish these remarks without breaking down. "None of us know what this world, this town, will be like without Gil Gardner in it. His death has left a hole inside of me that probably can't ever be filled. But you know what? Gil would want me to try to fill it."

He saw Jenna crying. Sara hugging her. Doc Jacobs and countless others wiping their eyes.

"He'd want us all to go on and live happy lives, remembering his goodness and his joie de vivre, his sense of humor and his vitality, and most of all his welcoming, loving nature, which influenced an entire town."

Just as he finished and looked up from his notes, his gaze collided with Lily's. Her eyes were dry. So were her cheeks. But on her thin, ashen face was an expression of acute suffering. Simon turned his head and stifled his sympathy.

After all, anything she was feeling now she'd brought on herself.

As soon as she entered the church hall, Jenna saw the babies across the room. Miss Jameson and Mrs. Madison must have brought them down here when they'd started to cry in the sanctuary. So what? Let them scream or do whatever. Jenna had cut them out of her freakin' life, just as she'd cut out Lily. And tried to cut out her dad, although he wouldn't let her. She'd hung on to some of her rebellion, but he'd pretty much worn her down. And the counseling she'd gotten had helped to change things.

"There you are." Her dad approached her and slid an arm around her shoulders. "You okay?"

"Yeah. I can't believe it, Daddy. Grandpa Gil's really gone."

"I know, Princess." Her father's eyes were bloodshot and there were deep lines around his mouth. "I can't, either."

For some stupid reason, Jenna's gaze strayed to the babies. Lily was with them now, holding Cami. Mrs. Madison held Patrick. "They're so big, aren't they?" she whispered.

Her dad pivoted away to avoid seeing the twins. "Are they?" He sipped some punch. "I'd prefer not to see them."

"Think she'll go right back to New York?"

"I hope so."

"Uh-oh, Dad…" Lily had handed Patrick to Miss Jameson and was heading toward them. "She's coming over."

Her father's jaw tightened. Though he'd tried to keep his suffering over Lily's leaving them hidden from Jenna, it came out in telltale signs like this one. And at night, when she heard him up at all hours. During the holidays, which had sucked out loud, they'd both tried to put up a good front, but it hadn't worked. Instead, her dad's pain had mixed with her own, and it was what had driven Jenna to Hank and the clothes and the other things her father didn't even know about.

He said, "We can handle this, honey."

Lily reached them. "Hello, Jenna." Then, more hesitantly, "Simon, your eulogy was wonderful."

Jenna stared at the woman she'd once thought might someday be her mother. Her face was pale, her blue eyes dull and she'd lost weight. "You look like hell, Lily."

Her hands went to her cheeks. "I do, I guess."

Jenna's father squeezed her arm. Then he faced Lily. "Hello, Liliana."

Lily recoiled as if she'd been slapped, and it took Jenna a minute to realize why. The name her father used was what the Wakefields called her.

"I wanted to say how sorry I am." Lily sounded sincere, but she was good at that. "I know you must be devastated."

Her dad kept his cool. "As you must be."

"I want you to know I would have left the church right after the service, but the twins were down here."

He nodded.

Jenna bit her lip, so she wouldn't ask about them.

"There's something else. Mac insists I be here for the reading of the will tomorrow. But then I'll leave town."

"Whatever," her father said.

"Do you think it would be all right if I stayed at the house? Gil's house?"

"Why ask us?" Jenna made her tone as nasty as she could. "You don't care about our feelings." Even though Lily had written that e-mail right after she left, saying she did love Jenna, she was sorry for the hurt she caused and maybe eventually Jenna could forgive her.

That'd be the day.

"Jen, Gil wouldn't want you to talk to Lily this way." He said to Lily, "Do what you have to. Just stay away from us."

He grabbed Jenna's arm to leave, when a baby's scream filled the air. And before anyone could react, Miss Jameson was there with Patrick.

Jenna wanted to puke, but she couldn't tear her gaze away from the baby. He was so beautiful. His eyes had stayed blue and he still had dark hair just like Lily's. When Lily took him from Miss Jameson, he stopped crying and stared over at Jenna and her dad.

Jenna couldn't help herself. She said, "Hi, Patrick."

The baby's eyes widened, as if he recognized her voice.

"Dad?" She looked at her father, but he'd turned his back to all of them.

"Come on, honey, we need to do some things." He walked away.

Jenna glared at Lily. "This is mean." She followed her father out, vowing she'd forget the look on Lily's face and how her lips trembled. She'd forget about how scared and almost sick she'd seemed.

This time, Jenna wasn't being taken in by Liliana Wakefield.

FROM BEHIND HIS DESK, Mac Madison stared over at Lily and Simon, who sat across from him. Simon had moved his chair as far away from Lily as possible, but he could still feel her presence, smell her subtle perfume, even sense her breathing. Jenna had been right, she looked like hell. Today, she'd dressed in a black skirt and a red sweater, and the color washed her out. But even that didn't ease his visceral reaction to her nearness. Cursing himself, he shifted in his seat. "Can we get this over with?"

Mac nodded. His expression was strained. This wasn't easy for anyone. "The two of you are here for a reason. You and your children are the beneficiaries named in Gil's will."

"Mac," Lily said, "I told Gil repeatedly, I didn't want anything from him."

That had always been true. Simon remembered it from when she'd first come to Fairview. Maybe Gil had just left her Cameron's things. Maybe the house, too. Simon didn't care, just so he still had his options to buy the *Sentinel* without interference.

"I know you did, Lily. But Gil was worried about your circumstances."

She shot a wide-eyed glance at Simon, then back to the lawyer. "I'm fine, Mac. Leave it alone."

"What circumstances?" Simon asked because she didn't seem to want him to know.

"Gil left Simon a letter, explaining why he did what he did in his will, Lily. Simon's going to find out, anyway."

Lily flushed and looked down at her hands. Fingers linked, she curled them tight around each other. "Go ahead, then."

"Simon, Lily's financial circumstances are dire."

He snorted. "The Wakefields have millions. New York has community property laws."

"There's nothing left of Derek Wakefield's estate. After he died last month, it was discovered that not only had he gambled away their savings, but he'd sold off his stocks and Lily's jewelry, and had taken out a third mortgage on their house. Lily has her clothes and a bit of cash in her own name. That's all."

This was news. Gil had told him Derek had died, but

he'd said nothing more than that. Simon looked at her then. "How did this happen?"

She was practically squirming, but she lifted her chin. "Derek's recovery was short-lived."

Simon remembered something.

We'd be like new toys to him. As soon as the novelty wore off, he'd return to his old ways.

Yet she'd gone back to him. Sometimes, in the dark of night, he still couldn't believe it.

"Look, Lily, I'm sorry Derek died. He didn't seem like a bad person. And I'm sorry if you don't have any money. But your kids will be okay. Derek's parents' assets will go to support them. In any case, it's none of my business." Simon faced the lawyer. "Just read the damn will, Mac."

"But it is your business, Simon. And for the record, Lily's in-laws have disowned her and the kids."

"Why?"

"Mac, please, do we have to drag all this out? I'm mortified."

"It's in the letter."

Simon sighed. "Tell me now, then."

"The Wakefields are suing for custody of the twins."

"What?" If nothing else, Lily was a good mother.

"They're putting financial pressure on her, knowing she can't stand up to it. Derek's bills, supporting the twins, the bankruptcy…"

"Just like everything else," Lily said, her tone defeated. "They think they can buy anything. Even my babies."

"Why would they do this to you?" Simon's shock overcame his resolve to shut her out.

"They hate me. They blame me for Derek's relapse and overdose."

It must have been a nightmare.

"Knowing all this will make Gil's bequests more understandable, I think." But Mac shifted uncomfortably in his seat.

Fear took shape in Simon's stomach. "What are the terms of the will?"

"In brief, Gil left you ten percent of the stock in the *Sentinel,* Simon, and the option to buy the rest."

"I only want the option. I don't want ten percent free and clear."

"This is how it reads. He also left money in trust for Jenna. A good chunk. She won't want for anything." He smiled. "And he left her his new car."

Mac directed his gaze to Lily. "Lily, Gil left you the remaining sixty percent of the stock."

"What?" Her jaw had dropped.

"But you aren't allowed to sell it to pay your bills or anything else for six months. And Simon has the sole legal right to buy the shares within that time period. Until then, the stocks must remain unsold. He was sure you'd be approached by the Heard Corporation again, so he specified that point."

Simon felt his throat constrict. "I can't afford to buy them in six months. I don't have that kind of money or income. Unless... Did he want me to use Jenna's inheritance?" Which seemed convoluted and stupid. Why leave it to her, then?

"No, you can't touch her money. Neither can she until she goes to college."

Lily shook her head. "I don't want the stock."

Steepling his hands in front of him, Mac sighed. "Don't be too quick to say that. Gil meant this as a way for you to fight your in-laws. He was honestly afraid they would, could, take the children away from you. That a judge would see that you can't support them. Now, with this kind of stock and the income it represents, you won't be such a sitting duck."

"There's got to be another way to keep the Wakefields at bay."

"You and I have tried and failed to find one in the past month."

"You two have been in contact?" Simon asked.

"Yes, Lily called me after Derek's death to consult about the financial aspects of her life."

"I get it." He faced her. "You talked Mac into convincing Gil to leave you the paper."

"I did not!" She slapped her hand on the arm of the chair and her eyes sparked with anger. "This is a shock to me."

"And I should believe that why?"

Mac stiffened. "I'll let that insult to my integrity go, Simon, because I know you're stunned by this news and grieving for Gil. But he was the one who made this decision. As I said, it's all in the letter."

Ashamed of his outburst, Simon took in a deep breath. "I'm sorry, Mac." He stood. "I need to get out of here. Is there anything else?"

"Yes. Lily, Gil left the rest of his money to the twins on the same terms as Jenna's bequest. And he left you the house."

"The house?"

"So you could have a place to live."

"No! No!" Simon couldn't believe this. "You can't stay in Fairview."

Lily stared at him openmouthed.

"Jenna couldn't handle that." *And neither could I.* "Lord, Lily, please don't do it. Please don't stay in town."

Mac said, "I'm sorry, Simon. I'm not sure she has anywhere else to go."

CHAPTER TEN

HER CAT, BLACKIE, curled at her feet, Lily sat at the desk in Gil's den while the babies were in the living room, supposedly taking their afternoon nap in their portable cribs. Simon and Gil hadn't given her things away after all, but stored them in her mother's bedroom, as if Gil knew she'd come back someday.

Lily could hear the twins cooing and babbling, though not crying. Cami would go to sleep first, and Patrick might or might not doze off. Mostly, he was a good baby and amused himself, except for outbursts when his gums hurt or he was hungry. Lily didn't know what she'd do if they were cranky and colicky.

She was glad they were occupied because she was meeting with Mac at four and she wanted to get a handle on her finances before he arrived. Picking up the checkbook that lay in front of her, she stared at it blankly. No matter how she figured and refigured things, she couldn't go much longer than another week without any income. She'd spent the money she'd saved on a doctor's visit and medicine for Patrick because he had an ear infection, on food and on some clothes for the twins because they were outgrowing everything. Medical insurance was the big thing, though. She'd only recently been informed that her coverage had expired soon after Derek's death. Either she'd have to buy a policy or she'd need to get a job that included health care in her benefits. She'd never known until now just how terrifying it could be to have no plan for covering medical bills.

Glancing at the *Sentinel,* she let out a heavy breath. There was no job for her in Fairview, and if she went anywhere else she wouldn't have a place to live or access to good child care. She'd trust babysitters here for her children, but in a new town...? No way.

Restless, she rose from the desk and walked around the den, touching all the things that had been Gil's, biting back the emotion that flooded her whenever she wasn't busy. She fingered one of several bowling trophies that filled a shelf of the bookcases. A picture of her mother sat on the sideboard. She picked it up. "What would you do, Mama? Run again, like you did before?"

Lily was sick of running. She didn't feel well herself from the emotional drain and grief of losing Derek and then Gil, and from the physical demands of caring for twins. If she could sleep better... But she woke with nightmares that she couldn't handle the babies, or sometimes she dreamed about Simon's anger, and she rarely went back to sleep.

A sketch she'd done of the twins with their great-grandpa was sitting on a table. Lily had spent a lot of time drawing after she'd gone back to Westchester. She'd done this one from a picture she'd taken when Gil had come to visit. Then she'd drawn it and framed it and had given it to him the next time they'd met.

"Thank God we saw each other every week, Grandpa," she whispered, tracing his strong jaw, his wide shoulders, where his hands clasped each baby. "Who knew?"

Derek had objected to her seeing Gil. At first, he'd welcomed her grandfather. But as the weeks wore on and things had started to disintegrate, he'd balked.

Why does he come so much? He's dragging you down, Liliana. He's making you remember that place. That guy. Toward the end, Derek had become completely irrational about Fairview and Gil and especially Simon. And the tantrums had begun. Just the thought of them made her cringe.

There was a knock at the front door. She went to answer

it, glad that Mac had remembered not to use the bell. But instead of the lawyer, she found Loretta Jameson on the porch. She was dusted lightly with snow and her face was rosy from the cold February afternoon. "Loretta, hi."

"Hello, Lily. Is this a bad time?"

"No, I'm waiting for Mac. He said he'd be here around four."

"I won't stay long." She held up a covered dish that smelled spicy. "I brought you some supper."

Lily's throat hurt. In the aftermath of the funeral, the townspeople had cooked meals, but all the food had gone to Simon's house. Rightfully so. "Thanks. Can you stay for some tea?"

"I'd like to." She removed a stunning forest-green cape, revealing matching slacks and a light green sweater.

"You look beautiful, as always." Lily led her friend to the kitchen.

As she fixed tea, Loretta took a seat at the table. "How are you holding up?"

"I'm sad."

"And exhausted."

"Hmm."

Once the task was done, Lily sat with Loretta over steaming mugs of Earl Grey.

"You need some help."

"I'm fine, Loretta."

"I can see that's not true."

Lily glanced down at her sweatshirt and jeans, then tugged at her unkempt hair, which was pulled back in a ponytail. "I'm a mess today. I didn't sleep well."

"One of my former aides has two school-age children. She's a loving mother and a good person. She's available to come over mornings after her kids leave for school and take care of the babies. Maybe you could get some rest then."

Embarrassed again by her circumstances, Lily flushed. Loretta covered her hand. "I'll pay her, dear."

"Everybody knows, right?"

"Most of it. Small towns. Things leak out."

"Well, I suppose it doesn't matter. They hate me anyway."

"When you left, they felt abandoned, just as Simon and Jenna did. You'd become one of theirs, and they felt your loss acutely."

Lily shook her head.

"And they don't hate you." Loretta shrugged. "Give them a bit of time—they'll come around."

"I doubt that. But I appreciate your loyalty."

"I understand what you did, Lily. Even if it didn't work out."

That was an understatement. In the cold light of day, it was tough to face the biggest mistake of your life. "Maybe you can help me with something, though. I need a job. One that has medical insurance."

"Oh, Lily, I didn't know.… Your circumstances are that dire?"

The bald statement of her situation caused her to panic. But she worked to push it down. "Yes."

Loretta's brow furrowed. "That's going to be tough here in Fairview. There's waitressing jobs and the like. I can check to see if anything's open at school, but you'd need full-day child care if you got something like that."

The thought of leaving the babies for eight hours made her stomach roil. "I don't know what to do."

The older woman waited a significantly long time before speaking. "You own a newspaper, Lily."

"I can't cash in the stocks, even if I wanted to. Which I don't. The *Sentinel* belongs to Simon in every way that matters."

"You could work there. Get yourself on their group insurance. You could even bring the babies to nap in a back room in the afternoon."

"I can't do that to Simon."

Another knock on the door. Loretta finished her tea and stood. "Think about it. I'll walk out with you."

A few minutes later, Mac sat in the den with Lily. His kind face was lined with concern, as well as grief over his friend's death. "I hate to be the bearer of bad news, but I received notice from the Wakefields' attorneys. They've filed suit for custody of the children."

Lily shook herself to get control of the fear that always hovered in the back of her mind. "I can't believe this."

"You have to start believing it. You've got the resources for future income, but I'm worried about the present. I heard you paid cash for Patrick's doctor's appointment and medicine. Having no insurance looks bad. My biggest concern is that the Wakefields could prove unfitness right now and get the twins on a temporary injunction."

Lily gripped the edge of the desk. "I won't survive that, Mac. I can handle everything else, but I won't survive losing the babies, even temporarily."

"I know. And you're their mother, so of course that will work in your favor. But if you could show some means of support, the Wakefields wouldn't be able to do this to you. And the health care has to be addressed ASAP."

"I can sell my car to cover it."

"The Wakefields are taking your car. It's in their name."

For some reason, that single fact caused the reality of her life to come crashing in, and this time she couldn't control her terror. All the security she'd carefully built up was slipping away piece by piece. That it reminded her painfully of how tenuous her childhood had been, never feeling safe or secure, made the fear more intense. Black despair filled Lily. "C-can they do that?"

"Yes. Derek didn't have the money for it. They bought it and it's in their names."

Now anger replaced the fear. Damn Derek. She remembered when he brought the vehicle home, a month after she'd gone back to Westchester. She didn't want a new

BMW, but he'd been adamant about giving her presents.
"No. I won't let this happen."

"You have one option." He suggested it.

"Loretta said the same thing."

"It's a good solution. Maybe you and the McCarthys can
smooth things over, too."

"My being at the paper would hurt Simon."

"I'd lend you money, Lily, but the Wakefields might find
out and it won't help in the long run."

"I'd never take-your money."

"Then go back to the paper. It seems the only way."

SIMON LIFTED THE BARBELL over his head for the tenth repe-
tition. He was sweating and his muscles screamed, but he
was determined to complete four sets today. He'd just
returned the weights to their holder when he saw his sister
approach him. "Done?" he asked her.

"Yes. And so are you."

As Simon sat up, he felt a twinge in his back. "I thought
I'd hit the treadmill."

Sara got that big sister look on her face. "You're doing
it again."

"What?"

"Obsessing with exercise. Just like when she left."

"This has nothing to do with her."

Sara touched his arm, which was slick with sweat. "Hey,
this is me you're talking to. I was there when she went back
to her real life."

When Simon hit bottom. He nodded. There were no
secrets between him and his sister now. "Point taken."

Looping a thin towel around her neck, Sara asked, "Are
things bad?"

He shook his head and wiped his face with the hem of
his shirt. "I miss Gil so much, I can hardly stand it. Add
Lily staying in town… Sometimes I think I'll go crazy."

"Jenna's still in counseling, right?"

"Yeah. She's hanging on okay."

"Maybe *you* need to talk to someone."

"I *need* for Lily to get out of my life."

Sara looked away.

"What?"

"I heard something. The legal world is small, anyway, but it's minute in Fairview."

"Is it about her?"

His sister nodded. "The Wakefields are trying to get her kids."

"I know that."

"She has no money, Simon."

"She owns the freakin' paper. Gil left it to her to keep her in-laws at bay."

"But right now she has no cash. If she sells the house, she won't have a place to live. She can't sell the stocks. They're even taking her car."

"You're kidding. She has to have a car in case of an emergency with the twins."

"The in-laws must think if they put enough financial pressure on her, she'll either give up the babies, at least temporarily, or they can prove her unfit and unable to support her children." She watched him for a moment. "There's legal precedent for grandparents obtaining custody of their grandchildren."

He eased off the bench. "Yeah, the Wakefields did such a good job raising their own son."

They headed to the locker rooms. "Do you still hate her?"

"I never hated her. I loved her, which was the problem. I might even be able to forgive what she did to me, but not to Jenna. Never to Jenna."

He thought of the letter Gil had left him, explaining his bequests. It had made sense and Simon was glad for Gil's concern about all of them. But the end of the note disturbed him.

I know I have no right to ask this of you, son, but I'm
afraid for Lily. I know things are over between you
two, but if you can ease her circumstances in any
way, I want you to do it. Take care of Jenna and
yourself, but please watch out for Lily and the babies.

When he and Sara reached the locker rooms, Sara said
softly, "I don't know what to say to you, Simon."

"Just letting me vent helps." He checked his watch. "I
have an appointment in an hour." He hugged her.

"I love you, Sara. I don't know what I would have done
without you all these months. Thanks."

The glow of Sara's support waned as he switched to
reporter mode and covered the opening of a new store on
the edge of town. Trying not to think of Lily and her des-
perate circumstances or Gil's letter, he drove the icy roads
back to the paper feeling conflicted. God, he didn't want
Lily around. But, hell, what was going to happen to her?
And to the babies? He couldn't bear to think about them
in the hands of the Wakefields.

Evan and Sammy were out on a story in Gainesville
when Simon got to his office at the *Sentinel.* He stopped
short at the door. Lily was on his couch, sleeping like a
dark-haired Goldilocks. He hadn't seen her since the
reading of the will. She looked even worse today, in jeans
and a sweatshirt that was stained. Her hair was limp and
smudges made dark circles under her eyes. He leaned
against the wall wondering how on earth to handle her.

She stirred and came awake. "Oh. Oh! I'm sorry, I must
have dozed off."

"You're exhausted."

"No, I'm fine."

"Yeah, sure." He tried to gentle his tone as he took off
his leather coat and threw it on the couch. She was still
wearing hers. "Why are you here?" The expression on her
face was so conflicted, he added, "I'm not going to scream
at you or anything. Just tell me."

"You may scream at me."

"Why?"

"The truth?"

He didn't smile at their old joke. It made him bristle inside.

Lily must have realized that the familiarity was hard on him and she just said, "Simon, I'm in trouble."

He could make her go through the whole thing, but he remembered Gil's letter and tried to be civil. He dropped down on a chair opposite her. "I know. I heard."

Those eyes closed briefly again. "Everybody in town knows."

"You remember what it was like here. The good and the bad of small-town living."

She expelled a heavy breath. "Well, my humiliation is complete. So be it. I hate to do this to you, Simon, but I'm coming back to work at the paper."

"What?"

"I'm coming back. I'll do anything, clean after hours, answer phones, whatever, but I have to have a job, a salary and health insurance. Mac says there's a company policy I can hook into."

"Wait a minute. Wait a minute. You want to work here, every day? I'd have to see you every day?"

"I could try to stay out of your way. Or work nights?"

God, why hadn't he expected this? Why hadn't Sara seen the possibility? Because the thought was unbearable. "No, you can't do that."

She bit her lip. "Simon, I'm not asking permission. I...I don't have to."

His pulse beating double-time, he stared hard at her. "So, you'll ruin my professional life as well as my personal one?"

She flinched. "I have no intention of ruining your professional life. The stocks are yours, no matter how long it takes you to buy them. I'm only interested in supporting myself in the immediate future to stop any legal action from the Wakefields. I promise, Simon."

I won't leave with Derek. I promise.

"We both know how much your promises are worth, Lily."

She took the jab stoically. And he remembered something else she'd said a long time ago, when she told him that Derek had hit her. *It's so awful to have someone you care about turn on you, treat you so badly.*

Bending forward, he linked his hands between his knees. "I don't mean to hurt you. And I see your plight. But some things happened after you left... There are reasons you can't become a part of the paper—or our lives—ever again."

"Jenna."

His eyes narrowed. "Who told you?"

"Nobody. Gil didn't talk to me about you or Jenna, at your request."

"You made the same request on your end. I never knew it got so bad with Derek." He cocked his head. "Then, who? Mac? Miss Jameson?"

"I figured it out myself. From seeing her."

"Huh. She's a lot better now."

Lily's eyes widened.

"Oh, yeah, it was worse. She overheard that last conversation of ours before you left Fairview."

Her brow furrowed as she tried to remember. When she did, her eyes moistened. She didn't shed a tear at the funeral or after, but now a few slipped out. She dashed them away. "Jenna never knew about you and Marian?"

Simon shook his head. "No, and she couldn't handle it. On top of you and the babies leaving, she just turned into another person."

He could still see her, in the bathroom, with scissors in her hand, chopping off all that beautiful golden hair. It had broken his heart.

What are you doing?

Growing up.

Then, there was the guy.

You can't see him. He's not good for you.
Yeah, like Mom wasn't good for you, Dad?

Thinking Lily might change her mind, he told her all of it. "She started sneaking around, and then the Goth phase came. She dyed her spiked hair black, which finally grew out, thank God, bought black clothes. It was a nightmare."

"I'm so, so sorry."

"We're better now, but not completely. She's in counseling. I've been afraid Gil's death will set her off again." He gave her a meaningful stare. "And I worry that your coming back might make things worse."

Lily ran her hands through her hair, making a mess of it. He'd never seen it so unkempt. "I'm sorry, Simon. But I don't know what else to do. If there was another way..."

"Please, Lily. Find one."

The bell in the outer area sounded.

He stood. "Someone's here. Why don't you leave now. We'll talk again, when I've had time to think about this and you've tried to figure something else out."

She followed him out of the newsroom, and he was thinking of how his life couldn't possibly get any worse when he found a woman in the reception area. Tall, slender, wearing a beautiful suede coat that set off her white hair and fair coloring, she nodded to him.

As pleasantly as he could, he said, "Can I help you?"

"Yes, I'm looking for Liliana Wakefield."

Behind him, he heard a gasp. And then Lily stepped to the side. Her hands clenched so tightly that her knuckles turned white. "Hello, Johanna."

The woman's gaze raked Lily as if she were a cockroach. "I want to talk to you."

LILY COULDN'T DO THIS. She just couldn't. Gil's death. Simon's story about Jenna. The fatigue that went deep into her bones. And now Derek's mother. "I have nothing to say to you."

"I have much to say to you." Her haughty gaze rested on Simon. "You must be Simon."

"I am. Simon McCarthy."

"So she came running right back to you."

"She came back for her grandfather's funeral."

The shell cracked a bit and Johanna's hard expression softened. "Yes, I'm sorry about that, Liliana. I know you cared for him." She adjusted the strap of her purse. "We must talk, though. When you didn't return to Westchester, I decided to come here to reason with you." To Simon, she said, "I'm sorry for your loss, too. I know what it's like to lose someone you love. But if you'll excuse me, Mr. McCarthy, you're the reason things could never work out with my son and Liliana."

"What do you mean?"

"All right. I'll talk to you," Lily said hurriedly. "Simon, can we use your office?"

"Uh, yeah, I guess."

Lily led Johanna back to Simon's office. When they were seated on the couch, her mother-in-law faced her. "I'm asking you to let the babies go without a fight."

"You have to be kidding. They're my children."

Johanna took in Lily's appearance. "Look at you, you're a wreck. You're incapable of taking care of yourself, let alone them."

Sometimes, that felt true. She'd been so conflicted, she left home in a state she'd never have allowed herself to be seen in before. But to Johanna she said, "You're wrong."

"We had to hire a nurse to help when you came back."

"I didn't want the nurse. Derek insisted."

"It didn't make a difference. You still didn't give Derek enough attention."

Liliana, you're always with them. What about me?

"Babies take a lot of time, Johanna. Especially two at once."

"You should have made more time for my son, and then

perhaps he wouldn't have slid back into his old ways. He was doing well before you returned."

Lily was so tired of this argument. In the month after Derek died, her mother-in-law had battered her with accusations. Bruce Wakefield had tried to intervene, but nothing worked. "Johanna, Derek stopped going to AA meetings. He went back to drugs and to gambling. That wasn't my fault."

"I don't see it that way." She nodded out the door. "He knew your feelings for that Simon person. He told me."

Derek had told her, too.

You're still in love with him. I know it.

Derek, please, I'm doing the best I can here.

I don't hear a denial.

She couldn't give him one, no matter how much he badgered her. And that had lead to another chain of events that she hoped like hell he hadn't told his mother about.

Johanna stared at her. In her eyes, Lily saw a hurting woman, grasping for purchase. "They're all we have left of Derek. Please, Liliana, I'll beg. Let us have them."

"Johanna, no. I'm sorry you're in pain. But I can't give you my babies to ease it."

Her chin came up and the traces of vulnerability fled. She'd seen the transformation happen in Derek, too. From friend to foe in sixty seconds flat. "Then, I'll forge ahead with legal action. I don't want to, but I will."

"You won't get them."

"You have no job. No medical insurance, for God's sake. No way to take care of them. And I've arranged to have the car brought back with me." When Lily started to speak, Johanna held up her hand. "Yes, yes, I'm aware that you inherited stocks. But I talked to a judge we know, and he said that any adjudicator worth his salt will see that in the interim, you're incapable of taking care of our grandchildren. And once we get them, well, possession is nine-tenths of the law."

"They aren't a commodity, for God's sake."

"I'll win, Liliana. I always do."

"No, not this time, Mrs. Wakefield." Simon had come to the doorway.

Oh, God, he'd eavesdropped. Now her mortification was complete. Simon had witnessed how utterly vulnerable she was, had seen her at her worst.

"You won't win," he continued, "and you're misinformed. Lily's here today to make plans to work at the *Sentinel* again. She'll have a good salary and benefits. The babies can come to the office in the afternoons, so she won't be away from them all day long." He smiled at Lily, but she could see it didn't reach his eyes. "Right, Lily? We have it all figured out."

Johanna stood. "If this is a ruse, I'll discover it. If not, there are other ways to get what I want. I'm not giving up."

Lily rose, too. Now that Simon was here, she felt stronger. "Neither am I."

Without saying more, Johanna swept out of the office.

Stunned, Lily frowned at Simon. "Why did you do that?"

He motioned after Johanna. "Like you said, there didn't seem to be any other way."

"I don't know what to say."

"Say you'll handle Jenna with kid gloves."

"I promise. I'll do anything you want me to."

"And stay away from me as much as possible. I mean it."

"All right."

He turned and walked out of the office. She called after him, "Thank you, Simon." But he didn't look back.

CHAPTER ELEVEN

THE STACK OF FOLDERS on the cabinet made it clear where Lily could start filing on her first day back at the *Sentinel*. Technically, she was the receptionist again, but she was determined to do more to earn her salary. And to keep busy and forget she'd left her children with a babysitter this morning. It was the first time she'd gone to work since they were born and she missed them so much she hurt inside. She wondered if all working mothers felt this way. The twins had been smiling and babbling when she'd left them with Marta, whom she'd liked right away and trusted fully after she'd spent some time with her over the past week.

Her back to the door, she straightened her shoulders, but the ache wouldn't go away. The babies were teething and Cami had woken up first during the night. She'd wanted to be held and rocked. Then Patrick had taken his turn. They'd finally fallen asleep when she'd put one of them under each of her arms on the bed and snuggled them close.

The bell over the door sounded and Lily turned to see Mrs. Billings coming inside. Wearing a heavy navy-blue coat and boots, she unwrapped a crocheted scarf from around her head. The woman's face was as blank as it had been at Gil's funeral, and she regarded Lily coldly. "Is Simon here?"

"He's out on a story with Sammy." She gave her a tentative smile. "How are you, Mrs. Billings?"

"What about Evan—or even the temporary receptionist?"

"Evan's working at home today. Simon isn't using a temp agency anymore. I took over that position."

The woman's gray brows rose. Clearly she didn't know about Lily's return to the paper. "I have an ad to place." She frowned, and for a minute Lily missed her old smiling approval so much that she wanted to cry. "Guess I'll have to do it with you."

Lily drew in a breath. "Yes." At the desk, she asked, "Is it ready or do you need help with the wording?"

She produced a paper. "Please read it before I leave, to see if it's suitable."

Taking the sheet, Lily blinked hard to clear her vision. She remembered her first months in Fairview and Mrs. Billings bringing her tea or sitting with her while she tried a new cookie recipe. Now, the woman didn't even want to deal with her over an ad. Lily forced herself to read the handwritten text. "It's clear." She looked up. "I didn't know it was Mr. Martini's birthday on St. Patrick's Day."

"You miss a lot when you leave town."

"How will this be a surprise?"

"His cronies have gone to great lengths to make sure he doesn't see the paper until that night."

"That's so sweet."

"Friends are priceless, Lily."

She nodded.

"They shouldn't be treated lightly."

Her throat painfully tight, Lily looked down. "I'll make sure Evan sees this. I think he's handling the ads."

"He was supposed to continue the Senior Saga, but it didn't work out."

"I know. I saw last week's paper."

Mrs. Billings sniffed, wrapped the scarf around her head again and reached the door before she spoke. "How are they? The babies?"

"Wonderful. They're so big. They'll be spending afternoons here, if you'd like to see them."

Her back to Lily, she nodded. "I would. Children shouldn't pay for the sins of their mothers."

After Mrs. Billings left, Lily stared at the door. She hadn't expected anything different. But she didn't know how much the aftereffects of her abandonment would hurt.

Be glad for what you have. A way to support the twins, a roof over your head and a job.

Now, if she could just find a car. True to her word, Johanna had had the BMW taken away the day she'd come to town last week. It was impossible to have two babies and not own a car. As it was, after Marta dropped off the twins today, she was going to have to wheel them home from the paper in their stroller. At least the car seats fitted right into the carriage mechanism. She hoped it wasn't too cold at six o'clock, and that she could protect them from the March wind.

Dismissing these thoughts from her mind, she finished filing, then went to the desk, wiped off its surface, straightened drawers and dusted the entire reception area. The whole office needed a good cleaning. A notice in the previous week's *Sentinel* mentioned the service that was taking care of the office had left town for lack of business.

Lily took calls, and soon it was noon. She settled on the couch with some soup, and was checking the want ads for a cheap car that she could buy on credit, when there was a knock at the door.

It was déjà vu. Jenna stood outside the locked door. Lily went to let her in and noticed a truck in the driveway, along with Gil's Saturn, which Jenna had been driving since the funeral.

"Hi, Jenna. Come on in."

The girl stepped inside. Today, she was wearing black corduroy jeans, black cowboy boots and a black fringed vest. Her hair was soft and curling around her ears.

A sudden motherly instinct hit Lily with sledgehammer force. She tried to quell it, but what she felt for Jenna had never gone away. "Can I do something for you, Jenna?"

"You're kidding, right?"

"Excuse me?"

Stiffly, Jenna reached out and put something on the table in the entrance.

"What's that?"

"Car keys."

"Whose?"

"Yours now. They're for Grandpa Gil's car." Her voice was hoarse, the way grief had made it. And suddenly she seemed younger, more sensitive, like the old Jenna.

"I don't understand."

The teenage mask fell back into place. "You gotta have wheels, Lily. Don't be stupid."

"I'm not stupid. I'm looking for a used car now."

"You need a reliable one. Besides, I don't have to have a car. Hank takes me pretty much every place."

Lily glanced out the window. "Is that Hank?"

"Yeah." Lily couldn't fathom the sneer on her face. "A dad's worst nightmare."

"Jenna…"

"Stop it!" Her voice rose a notch and her eyes flared with anger. "I don't want anything from you. I can't. Why did you have to…?" She stopped and shook her head furiously. "Just take the damn car." Jenna turned to the door. "I'm outta here."

For a long time, Lily just stared at the keys.

"WANNA GO BACK TO SCHOOL?" Hank asked from the driver's side of his red Ford truck. His head was freshly shaved, making the diamond stud in his ear stand out more.

"What do you think?"

"Thomason said one more skip and you were in deep shit."

Jenna sighed. She was so tired these days, since Lily had come back. "I'm already in deep shit. What's the difference?"

He started the engine. Jenna watched him. He wasn't as bad as she'd told Lily, as bad as the town thought he was, which was probably why she could stand to be with him. Down deep, she wasn't really a badass, either.

"Where do you wanna go?"

"I want some pot."

"You stopped doing that since you been seein' that shrink."

And she'd thought·she was on her way to feeling better. Until Grandpa died and Lily came back. "So much for progress."

"We'll have to go back to my place."

"What are you waiting for?"

Tenderly, Hank took her hand. "Everybody'll know you're there, Jen."

Her dad would be upset, but she tried not to think of him now. She had to get the picture of how Lily looked at her—like a concerned mother—out of her mind. "So?"

"Damn, I can't believe I'm gonna say this, but you were doin' better. You weren't actin' out so much."

Jenna stared out the window. When Hank got like this, all soft and tender, she couldn't keep the feelings inside. "I hate that they're back. I hate that bitch."

"Why'd you give her the car, then? Daddy tell you to?"

"He doesn't know what I did."

"How come, then?"

"For the babies. Kids shouldn't suffer just 'cuz their parents are assholes."

"You know, underneath that makeup, you're still a nice kid."

She didn't want to be nice. She wanted to be mean and surly, and hurt Lily the way she'd been hurt. "I'm not a kid." She sidled in close. "And if you take me back to your place and get me high, I'll show you."

"You're on, dollface." He kissed her hard and tore out of the parking lot.

In the rearview mirror, Jenna watched the *Sentinel* building disappear. She only wished the woman inside would disappear as easily.

SIMON HAD STAYED AWAY from the office as long as he could. He'd called in several times to see if he was needed, but Lily told him everything was fine. It stung, at first, to hear her answer the phone. Damn! Was nothing about this going to be easy? He turned down a street to go into the paper by the side entrance, hoping the babies were in front with her. Maybe, if he was lucky, he could avoid seeing them today.

Who are you kidding? That one glimpse of Patrick at the funeral stole your heart.

Well, he'd have to steel himself against them, he thought, as he quietly let himself inside. He'd reached his office, when Lily poked her head in the back. "Simon, is that you?"

"Yes."

"Oh, okay. I just wanted to make sure."

"All's well. Go back to work." He kept his back to her, so he wouldn't see what she wore, or how her hair looked, or if she was rested today.

He worked in his office until four, and then his cell phone rang. "Simon McCarthy."

"Simon, this is Loretta Jameson from school."

"Hello, Miss Jameson."

"Jenna missed English class after lunch. And I checked with her last period teacher. She missed Creative Writing, too. We're giving her a break around here because we know how close she was to Gil, but truthfully, I'm worried."

Please don't let this be starting again. The absences from school. Those long stretches where I didn't know where she was or who she was with. "Do you have any idea where she went?"

"One of the students said she was going to the *Sentinel* for lunch. But she never came back."

"I'll check it out. Thanks for calling."

Hell, he'd have to see them sometime. Bracing himself, he left his office and opened the door from the newsroom to the front. Lily sat at the computer, engrossed in some kind of drawing program on screen. She wore a plain white blouse with a black V-neck sweater and black pants. She didn't see him, and his willpower waned. He looked off to the side.

And there they were. Both babies in the same playpen. The small details overpowered him.

They could sit now, propped by colorful half-moon pillows. And they were cooing, babbling. He'd never heard the sweet sound before—both had been too young when they'd left to do much more than cry.

Patrick's dark hair was spiky, as Simon had seen at the funeral, and his hands batted at a toy in front of him. Entranced, Simon watched as the infant grabbed for the plush blue dog.

Cami was smaller, her hair lighter, wispier. And she seemed quieter. She was on her back, staring up at something. He raised his eyes and saw the whirling ceiling fan. She kicked her legs and grabbed her feet, tugging off a sock.

Oh, my God. She rolled over and scrunched herself up into a sitting position. He remembered when Jenna had passed that particular milestone.

Jenna. He had no business staring at the babies when his own child was in trouble. Again. "Lily?"

A hand slapped against her chest. "You startled me."

"You were into whatever you were doing."

She didn't volunteer what it was.

"Everything okay?"

Nervously, she glanced at the babies. "Yes, great."

When they babbled even louder, he gave a grudging smile. "Do they always amuse themselves like this?"

"A lot of the time during the day. I'm very lucky."

He didn't contradict the absurd statement. Her circumstances were dreadful. Two of the people she loved most had died recently. He wouldn't think about her loving Derek, though. Wouldn't think about what she'd been doing with her husband these past few months while Simon had torn the covers of his own bed, wondering about it.

"I need to talk to you."

"Of course. What is it?"

"Did Jenna come by today?"

She nodded. "I was going to ask you about it, but you stayed back there and I figured you didn't want to see us."

"Why did she come here?"

Lily reached into her drawer and drew out something that jangled when she held it up. "She brought me these."

"What are they?"

"Keys to Gil's car."

"Why on earth would she bring them to you?"

A long hesitation. "I thought maybe you told her to do it."

"I didn't tell her to do anything."

Her wide blue eyes softened. "That makes the gesture even more special."

"What are you talking about?"

"She wants me to have Gil's car. She says I need it for the babies."

Thank you, God. *That* was the real Jenna.

"I can't accept it, of course."

"You have to."

Her eyebrows rose beneath her hair, which was parted off to one side. It was longer now than when she'd left and shiny in the overhead light that kissed the silky strands.

"It shows she's coming out of herself. Thinking of others. And maybe forgiving."

"No, she made it clear this wasn't for me, it was only for the twins."

"Still, if she wants to do this, let her."

"Simon, there's only so much I can accept from you two."

"You said you'd do anything for her."

"I would."

"Then take the damn car."

At that moment, one of the babies let out giggles. They were lying down, turned to the side, facing each other and trying to touch hands. When they succeeded, the giggles began.

It was such a beautiful sound, and for a minute Simon lost himself in it. But then he remembered that the worst thing he could do was let Lily and her children into his heart again.

So, snapping more than he meant to, he said, "Keep the keys. And go home now. I don't want any of you here."

She sucked in a breath. "All right." Before he left, she asked, "Simon, is something wrong? About Jenna? Is that why you came out here asking after her?"

"Nothing I can't deal with."

Later that night, as Simon sat in his den and listened to the clock chime ten times, he wondered if his earlier assurance to Lily was true. He'd gotten home—through truly foul weather—to find a message on the machine. When Jenna didn't want to talk to him, she'd call the house and not his cell, knowing he wouldn't be there to answer the phone.

I'm fine. I'm with Hank. I'll be home by ten—my curfew. Then a hesitation, *I promise, Daddy.*

She was trying. He knew that. But how long could a father be patient when he was worried sick about his child? He heard the front door open and close. Some rustling in the foyer, and then she appeared at the door to the den. "Hi, Dad."

"Hi." She just stood there. "You okay?"

"I guess."

He nodded out the window. "It's rough out there."

"Hank's a good driver."

"Come and sit."

Her boots clicked on the hardwood floor. At least these were more feminine then the black combat pair she'd worn for a while. She dropped down in a chair.

He waited.

"I skipped my afternoon classes."

"Yeah, your favorite ones. Why?"

She shrugged a too-thin shoulder.

"I know you went to the paper. Not to see me."

She stared out the window behind him, looking much older than her age. "It was the right thing to do. Grandpa…" She sniffled. "He would have wanted Lily to have the car if he knew she needed one."

"Maybe."

"She can't *not* have one, with babies."

"I know. But she might have managed otherwise."

"That's what she said." His daughter focused on him now. "Do you mind?"

"No."

She bit her lip. "I didn't see them."

"I did."

"How are they?"

"They can do a lot of things." He waited. "Do you want to know?"

"Uh-uh. It all sucks."

For me, too. "Okay. What about school?"

"I couldn't go back. I was bummed."

"Where'd you go?"

"That's TMI for you." Too much information. Her signal that he wouldn't want to know.

Give her space to work this out, the counselor had told him. *Don't pressure her to tell you everything.*

God, it was hard to follow that advice.

"All right. But you'll have detention for a few days at school."

She nodded.

"And you're grounded through the weekend."

Her meek acceptance of the punishment cut him to the quick. He didn't recant, though. He'd learned how to be firm with her. The counselor had also said that was important. Having never had to mete out discipline before this year, it was a new and unpleasant experience.

"I'm gonna crash," she said and stood up.

"Fine. Do I get a hug?" He wasn't supposed to force affection, either.

She came around the desk, surprising him. As he held his daughter tightly, he prayed that they could both get through Lily's return to Fairview with a minimum of damage.

But when Jenna went to bed and Simon felt the emptiness inside him grow and expand, he didn't think his prayer had been heard.

THE ATMOSPHERE at the *Sentinel* was so tense—from Simon and the other employees who were all in today—that Lily decided to take her lunch hour to go out and do a few errands. She arranged for Marta to bring the babies to the paper a little later than usual. First, Lily stopped at the drugstore to pick up a prescription cream for diaper rash. Waiting in line, she looked around, remembering the previous spring when she'd been here with Loretta and Simon had come in. It was the first time he'd hinted at his feelings for her.

Which were now obviously dead, as he could barely speak to her since the incident with Jenna. The loss continued to hurt her heart, and it hadn't gotten any easier to face.

When she reached the counter, Mr. Atherton scowled at her. "What can I do for you?" he asked, as if she were a stranger who'd come in from the cold.

For a few seconds, she couldn't answer. Hell, she should be used to the rudeness by now. To people ostracizing her. But she'd been isolated in Westchester, when she'd gone back there, and busy with the babies. Besides, she had no real friends in that town. In the two weeks since she'd come back to Fairview, no one but Loretta and Mac had spoken to her unless they'd been forced to, like now.

"I need this prescription filled, Mr. Atherton."

A crack in his demeanor. "Heard they're good." He frowned at the prescription. "Diaper rash?"

"Patrick."

He cleared his throat. "The wife's asked about them."

"Tell her they're fine. She can stop by the paper and see them anytime." Which some townsfolk had been doing, although they acted as if Lily were invisible.

While she waited for her medicine Lily was browsing in the baby aisle, when she sensed someone staring at her. She looked over to see Sara, Simon's sister, standing down the way with a full cart. She wore a tailored navy suit under a leather coat. She was probably on her lunch break, too. "Hello, Sara."

"Lily."

"Got a full load there."

"I'm going on vacation for two weeks. Though I hate to leave Simon now. Because of you."

What could Lily say?

Sara wheeled closer. Her face was tight and her eyes cold. "How could you come back here? *Stay* here?"

Lily started to turn away, but Sara grabbed her arm and forced her around. They were even in height, but Simon's sister was in better shape, and once again Lily felt overpowered by her circumstances. "Answer me. How could you come back to town? And work at the paper? That's sadistic."

"If I'd had any other choice, I would have done things differently. But I have to provide for my children, Sara. And I've had to make hard decisions in order to do it."

"You don't know what happened to him after you left. The only thing that seemed to help was working out, so I joined a gym with him."

"That's why he's...bigger."

"The holidays were a nightmare for all of us. They... Oh, never mind."

Gil hadn't told her that, when he'd come to spend Christmas Day with her. Jenna had loved Christmas so much…. God, Lily couldn't stand what she'd done to both of them. "I know I hurt him."

"And Jenna. I hold you completely responsible for what happened to her."

Lily felt her eyes moisten. "I can't tell you how bad I feel about her. She's doing better, though, according to Simon."

"She was. What do you think is going to happen to her now that you're back?"

"I'll try to minimize my contact with her."

"A lot of good it will do. You bulldoze your way into their lives, and there'll be collateral damage."

"I don't know what you want me to say, Sara. I'm doing the best I can."

"For you and your kids. But not for Simon and his daughter."

"If you know anything I can do to make this easier for them, tell me and I'll do it."

Grabbing her purse out of the cart, Sara slung the strap over her shoulder. "There's nothing you can say or do to make your return to Fairview in any way palatable. You should just go away again."

Devastated, Lily watched Simon's sister leave the loaded cart midaisle and storm out of the store.

Though she didn't feel like eating after this confrontation, Lily needed to keep up her strength. So following a stop at the post office, she went to O'Malleys' Pub. Hopefully, any new animosity for her that Mike and Matt had built up over the past six months would be disguised by their natural grumpiness.

Mike was behind the bar. His wizened face didn't change when he saw her. He stared at her for a moment, then scratched his white beard and returned to his task of washing glasses.

Taking the nearest booth, Lily picked up the menu and decided on a corned beef sandwich. Good protein and the scent of cooking meat made her stomach growl. To busy herself until a waitress came over, she took out her to-do list and began adding to it.

Buy Cami a new jacket.

Check Patrick's spring clothes.

Get groceries—don't forget Cheerios.

She caught a glimpse of her watch. Ten minutes had passed. She looked around the pub. Other patrons were watching her. Matt had replaced his brother behind the bar and Mike was now waiting on some businessmen next to her. When he finished, Lily called out, "Mr. O'Malley, I'd like to order."

Again, nothing. He simply walked past her.

Lily sucked in a breath. And the word *lonely* took on a whole new meaning.

SIMON AND HIS STAFF were sharing Lucy's Lunch Basket meals in the newsroom when he heard Lily come through the front door. Evan was in the middle of a story about a bicycle race in Clearhaven, Sammy was laughing at his descriptions and even Tom Barker had been able to join them today. Since Lily had left, the staff had gotten closer. And since she'd returned, they were all uncomfortable and had needed this downtime together.

Unfortunately, Lily came into the kitchen, silencing them and dousing their good humor. "Oh. Sorry, I was just looking for some soup."

"You said you were going out to lunch." Sammy's stare and her tone were harsh. She'd cared about Lily a lot, and just like the others, she'd felt abandoned when Lily had left.

Lily's eyes widened as she took in their meals, the kind she'd once shared, when Simon treated one Friday a month. "Um, I... Never mind." Turning, she hurried out and the door closed behind her.

"What was that all about?" Tom asked.

"Who knows?" Simon made the comment, but in his heart *he* knew what was wrong. He'd intentionally excluded her from their lunch and had hurt her, a lot, if the expression on her face was any indication. Damn it, why did he feel bad about that?

"She looks like hell," Evan said. He'd been a big fan of hers, too. "She's already too thin. She should get the soup."

"She said she was going out to lunch." Simon picked up his burger and took a bite.

They were quiet for a while.

Tom nodded to the door. "Can't fathom what it's like for her to be back here. I don't know what I'd do in a small town if nobody talked to me."

"Maybe she'll leave," Sammy put in.

Simon sighed. "She doesn't have anywhere to go. She's here to stay, and we need to find a way to deal with her."

Putting down her half-finished sandwich, Sammy stood. "I've got a class at the college. I'll see you tomorrow."

The party broke up and Simon shook his head, thinking about how lunch had been ruined. Like a lot of things since Lily Wakefield had come back.

When they'd cleaned up, he couldn't stop thinking about her, and the fact that she did look thin. Her green skirt and sweater were too loose. And she'd come in for soup. Hell. He went out and found her at her desk. By her hand were a Coke and some crackers.

"I thought you ate when you went to do your errands."

"Um, I ran out of time."

He came closer to her desk. "Oh, that's a good substitute."

"It's fine."

"We're done. Go back there and get the soup."

She wouldn't look at him, and that was okay. The sight of those blue eyes filled with wariness and fear most of the time did something to his insides. When she didn't answer, he said, "Did you hear me, Lily?"

"Uh-huh. Don't worry about me."

"I'm not worrying about you," he snapped—because, of course, he was. "I just don't want you to get sick and force us all to help you."

"I won't get sick, I promise."

As promises went, it was a stupid one. But he guessed no more stupid than all the others she'd made to him.

THE WIND HOWLED OUTSIDE, and Lily pulled her sweater tighter around her. March had come in like the proverbial lion, and even the trees were protesting by batting the branches closest to Gil's house against the siding. Cami and Patrick had been disturbed by Mother Nature's furor. Even the white-noise maker in their room hadn't helped to calm them. They'd fussed themselves into exhaustion, though, and had finally conked out around ten.

Lily was at the dining room table with pictures and Internet downloads in front of her. When she'd been back in Westchester, her art had been the only thing to keep her sane.

Drawing makes me happy, Lily. I'm going to teach you, so it helps you through the rough spots, too.

Her mother had been right about that. So tonight, with the isolation of the town wrapping around her like a black blanket, Lily turned to her pad and pencils and charcoal. She'd poured herself a glass of wine and sipped as she sketched. She lost herself in the task until a branch swatted the window behind her, making her jump. Then, her mind began to wander.

To sketching Jenna.

Oh, Lily, this is so mag.

To sketching Simon at the basketball game.

He's in love with you.

Sometimes the enormity of her loss was nearly suffocating.

Lily kept drawing, though.

Until glass shattered and she screamed. Loud howling wind came from the kitchen, its sound eerie and frightening. She raced out to find that a window had shattered. Glass had splintered onto the floor, and the curtains billowed, allowing in the frigid air. For a moment, Lily just stood there. What should she do? Who should she call?

An ugly laugh escaped her. No one. There was no one to call. She'd have to take care of this herself. But how?

Turning on an outside light, she saw the little wooden shed out back. Okay, maybe there'd be things in there to board up the window. Finding her heavy jacket and stuffing her feet into boots, Lily stepped outside. The wind whipped her face and stung her eyes. It tried to force her back as she made her way to the shed. Her legs were freezing because of the skirt she had on.

Thank God, Gil had put a light in the shed. She found some plywood inside, and on a shelf, a hammer and nails. She glanced back at the window. Luckily, she could reach the opening from the ground. First, she dragged one piece of plywood across the hard bumpy lawn and then she went back to get another.

On her return, the wind slapped a branch in her face. She swore at it.

She dragged another board over and made a final trek to the shed. Fortunately for her, one summer in college, Lily had helped out on the building of a Habitat for Humanity house, so she knew the basics of wood and hammers and nails.

Still, with the wind as her worst enemy now, and the darkness and the absolute freezing cold, she barely managed to get the first piece of plywood in place and hammer it to the frame. Through her thin Italian leather gloves, her fingers were getting close to numb. The second board took even longer. Somehow, she completed the task.

Taking the hammer and nails with her, she practically crawled inside the house and collapsed against the door to the mudroom, sliding down to the floor. She sat there in her heavy coat and boots until she warmed up. Finally, she stood and took off her outdoor wear.

Back in the kitchen, she saw the glass-covered floor and

sighed. She went back to the mudroom, put her boots on again and got out the broom and dustpan.

She'd just finished sweeping when she spotted a last piece of glass under the table. She reached past the chair to pick it up. "Ouch!" It was jagged, and bigger than she thought. "Son of a bitch. Damn it."

Blood oozed from the pad of her palm, dripped down onto her sweater. And Lily said aloud, "Great. Now I can't even draw tonight."

Stuffing the fear that she wouldn't be able to make it on her own, Lily crossed to the sink and began to wash the glass out of her hand. Five minutes later, the cut was still bleeding. What to do? She couldn't go to the hospital. There was no one to call to watch the twins. Loretta was out of town, and it was midnight.

She glanced at the refrigerator. On it was a magnet that listed emergency numbers. One was the volunteer ambulance. Would they come to her home and help? Only one way to find out. After wrapping her hand in a towel, she picked up the phone.

CHAPTER TWELVE

ON ST. PATRICK'S DAY, during a break from work, Lily was sitting on the couch giving the babies their afternoon bottles. Her habit was to hold and feed one, while the other sat in a low carrier next to her and fed himself. She'd switch the twin she held halfway through. Thank God they could hold their bottles now, making mealtimes much easier.

The front door to the *Sentinel* opened and Mr. Martini hobbled inside. In the four weeks she'd been back, the seniors and other townspeople had come in one by one. Some ignored her, some managed to be civil, but they'd all fawned over the babies, who were often out front in a playpen or Jolly Jumper, or on a blanket on the floor. It warmed Lily to see the older set making a fuss over the twins. After the fiasco with the broken window and the realization she had no one to call for help but strangers, Lily was resigned to their apathy toward *her*. It was especially hard today when she was feeling lousy—Cami and Patrick had had colds, and she'd gotten one from them. She'd taken medicine so she'd feel well enough to work.

Mr. Martini tipped his fedora and glanced at Patrick. Of all of the townsfolk, he'd been friendliest. "He can hold that thing already? Bright boy."

"Yes, he is. Would you like to sit with us?"

"Maybe." He shuffled over to a chair and scanned the office, taking in the shamrocks, the posters and green crepe paper. "Jenna decorate?"

"She and Simon. They're Irish, after all."

And tonight there was going to be a party for the holiday to coincide with this man's birthday surprise. Lily swallowed hard, knowing all the people in town that she cared about would be there. And, of course, she wouldn't be with them.

He picked up a magazine from the table and leafed through it. "I'm surprised the paper's not out yet this week. Can't recollect that ever happening before. Hope young McCarthy isn't losing his stride."

"I've caused a stir, Mr. Martini. Things got delayed because of me." Then, she added, "There have been a lot of complaints."

The old man met her gaze directly. "You *have* caused a stir, girl." His brow furrowed. "Heard about your window. You called the glass people over in Clearhaven to fix it."

"Yes, I did."

"Why?"

"I wasn't sure anyone in Fairview would come out to do the job."

He gestured to her hand, which had a bandage on it. "That the reason you called the ambulance?" She nodded. "Artie Conklin's son said you should've gone to the hospital."

Lily had known news of her recent plight would get out, but when the EMT who treated her turned out to be Tom Conklin, she realized word of her accident would spread like wildfire. He'd been nice to her, though.

"No worries. My hand's good. And the window's taken care of."

Thank God. She'd wondered if the draft coming in through cracks between the boards had caused the babies' colds. She sneezed.

His face softened. "You sick, Lily?"

She touched her cheek with her free hand, and it did seem warm. "The babies have a cold. I've caught it."

"Gotta take care of yourself. So you can take care of them."

"I will, Mr. Martini." She switched the twins, so she could hold Patrick.

When Cami grinned as she took her own bottle, Mr. Martini chuckled. "Good idea." He raised his gaze to her. "You're a fine mother, Lily."

Again, the door opened and Lily turned her head to see who came in. A stranger. He was dressed in a suit and carried a leather briefcase. His expression was serious when his gaze landed on her. "Lily Wakefield?"

"Yes."

"I'm Mark Kramer. I'm from the Department of Social Services."

Lily gripped the bottle tightly. "What can I do for you?"

"I'd like to talk to you. I went to your grandfather's house, but you weren't there."

"I'm working here, at the *Sentinel.*"

"So I heard."

Mr. Martini leveled a stern stare on him. "And for the record, it's Lily's house now, not Gil's. I always wanted to buy it myself, but I guess Gil was saving it for his grand-daughter."

"And you are?"

"Her friend." Mr. Martini looked innocent. "Lily has a lot of us in town."

A bald-faced lie at this juncture.

"May I sit?"

Lily nodded.

Kramer took a chair and cocked his head at Mr. Martini. "I'd like to speak with Mrs. Wakefield alone, please."

Unbuttoning the coat he had yet to take off, Mr. Martini shrugged out of it. "Don't mind me, I'll just read my magazine."

His reaction gave Lily strength. "Where are you from, Mr. Kramer?"

"Westchester County. I've been sent at the request of the Wakefields. As part of their custody suit, they're conducting a formal investigation into your fitness as a mother."

Mr. Martini snorted.

"I'm legally informing you that you have a right for your own county's social worker to make a report, and that person can be contacted at this address."

Willing her hand not to shake, Lily took the card he offered. It was from the social service office that covered Fairview and the surrounding small towns.

The man removed a slim notebook computer from his briefcase and set it on his lap. "May I ask you a few questions?"

Mr. Martini said, "Lily, maybe Mac should be here."

"Mac?" Kramer asked.

"My lawyer."

"You think you need a lawyer?"

Lily raised her chin. "Look, Mr. Kramer, let's get this out in the open. I know the Wakefields will do anything to get my babies. I'd have the devil himself here, if I thought that would help. But I have nothing to hide. Ask away."

"First, I'd like to know your daily schedule—your work hours, who watches the children, and so forth."

When she gave him the information, he frowned. "You bring the children here? To the office?"

"Yes, and it's going fine."

"More than fine," Mr. Martini added. "We all stop in to keep them company."

The questions came fast and furious. "Where do they sleep here? What if they cry when you're busy?"

Lily answered his queries honestly.

"What happens if you get sick, Mrs. Wakefield? Pardon my candor, but you don't look well today."

"The twins have colds, Mr. Kramer. If you have any children of your own, you know parents often get sick when their babies do. I'll be fine."

Mr. Martini leaned forward. "Lily has a babysitter who can come if she needs to."

"What about at night?"

Again, Mr. Martini spoke up. "There's people willing

to help out, just like when the babies were born. Experienced mothers, teenagers. A whole townful."

"Sounds like one big, happy family." Kramer's tone was edged with sarcasm. "I'll need a list of those people to interview. Fax it to this number." He handed her another card and prepared to leave. "I hope all this is true, or you are in danger of losing your children."

"You calling us liars, Kramer?" Mr. Martini's tone was offended.

"No, of course not. I'll be back in touch."

Kramer left and Lily faced Mr. Martini, her heart thrumming in her chest. He *had* lied. Panic triumphed over calm. "It's not true. Nobody's going to help me in town. I don't have anybody. What am I going to do?"

Mr. Martini grasped her arm. "Whoa there, Lily, don't be upset. You'll have people to help." He slipped back into his coat and buttoned the front. "As soon as I send out the word."

"Why would you do that, any of you? You've made it obvious you hate me and don't want me back here."

He took a bead on her. "You were one of us, girl, before you left. And now you're back, we'll take you into the fold again—especially since you're in trouble." His smile was reassuring. "We take care of our own here in Fairview."

SIMON PUT THE FINISHING touches on an editorial about a kidnapping attempt over in Gainesville, printed a copy to edit in the morning and shut down the computer. He only had a half hour to get to the party in order to surprise Mr. Martini. From inside the small room where the babies slept, he heard one of them cry. On his way out, he stopped in the doorway. They were sleeping, but all the same Patrick stirred and Cami fussed. They were sick. Colds. He remembered when Jenna was little and caught colds. She wanted to be held all the time. How would Lily manage two at once?

Not your problem.

He headed to the front to tell her he was leaving. Outside, the wind whipped and the windows in the front rattled. Just like last week. News had gotten around that a window had broken at Gil's place—Lily had boarded it up herself and arranged for it to be replaced by someone from another town. She'd also gotten hurt and called no one but the paramedics. He'd brushed it off as none of his business until he'd seen the bandage on her hand. Damn, that had bothered him.

Lily looked up at him. Her eyes were bloodshot and her nose was red. She'd put on a heavy sweater over the lighter one she'd worn to work. "Leaving?"

"Um, yeah. I gotta be somewhere."

"I know. Have fun at the party."

To avoid looking at her, he checked the clock. "Aren't you going home? It's six."

She nodded to the back. "As soon as they wake up."

How would she get them into the car in this weather?

Not your problem.

"Have a good time, Simon."

He watched her. "You okay? You look peaked."

"Got their cold." As if to confirm it, she sneezed. "I'm all right. I took medicine but it's starting to wear off."

"Well, take some more."

Feeling like a deserter, he left the building and drove to the Fairview Diner, where the party was being held. He tried to think of how surprised Mr. Martini would be, but the roads were icy and again he worried about Lily driving. Did Gil's car have good tires? Was she accustomed to maneuvering in winter conditions?

Not your problem.

When he arrived at the diner, he found almost everybody there, including Jenna. Delighted to see her wearing green tonight, instead of black, he crossed over to her.

"Hi, Dad. This is crunk, isn't it?"

"I take it crunk means good."

"Uh-huh. You okay?"

"Yes." He removed his heavy snow-dusted jacket. I'm distracted by the weather, I guess."

He scanned the room. About seventy-five people had shown up. Too bad Sara couldn't attend, but she was out of town on a well-deserved vacation. He caught sight of Ellen Priestly, dressed all in green, which went well with her auburn hair. She waved when she saw him.

Jenna was checking out the room, too. "Something's wrong."

"About the party?"

"Yeah, people are…I don't know, quiet."

"Probably getting ready for the surprise."

"Maybe."

Promptly at six-thirty, the guests migrated to the right side of the room or to the back, so Mr. Martini wouldn't see them when Doc Jacobs brought him in for dinner. The old man entered first. "It's too nasty out to be having dinner, Jake," he said as he entered. "Don't know why I let you talk me into this."

"Because it's your birthday."

"The hell with my—"

"Surprise!"

The greeting echoed around the diner, and Mr. Martini looked shocked. It was fun to watch the pleasure spread across the old codger's face.

People milled around before dinner, and Ellen came over to Simon and Jenna. Simon hadn't asked Ellen for a date since Lily had come back to town, but they'd gone out several times in the months before her return.

"Hello, Simon. Jenna."

"Ms. Priestly. How are the kids?" There had been a time when Jenna had volunteered in her fifth-grade classroom, but she hadn't helped out in ages.

"They're fine. They miss you." She squeezed Jenna's arm. "Come back."

"Maybe."

Ellen turned pretty dark eyes on him. "How are you, Simon? I haven't heard from you in a while."

"I've been swamped at the paper."

They made uncomfortable small talk for five minutes. Then Simon saw that Mr. Martini was alone, at last. "If you'll excuse us, Ellen? We need to say hello to the guest of honor."

Ellen pursed her lips. "Of course."

As he and Jenna headed over to Mr. Martini, Jenna said, "She's into you, you know. And pissed."

"Jenna, the language."

"When was the last time you called her?"

"Um, a few weeks ago." Fortunately, they reached Mr. Martini before Jenna could grill him further.

"Happy birthday," they both told him.

"Too old to be celebrating." He smiled at Jenna. "Looking good, child."

She smiled, but toyed self-consciously with the hem of her green blouse.

Simon motioned to the room. "A good turnout on such a wicked night."

Mr. Martini studied the guests. "Lily couldn't make it, I guess, because of the twins?"

Loretta came up behind him. "Lily wasn't invited," she said coolly.

The older man frowned. "You don't mean that."

Simon shook his head. "All your friends and acquaintances were invited, Mr. Martini."

"How?"

"Word of mouth. Then a reminder in this week's paper, which by the way, came out on time."

The old man's eyes twinkled. "I'll be damned. I was just asking Lily about that a few hours ago." Again the dark look. "Poor girl."

"Katie's here, Dad. I'm gonna go talk to her. Don't forget, I'm staying overnight there."

When Jenna left—to escape talk of Lily, he guessed—Simon asked casually, "You saw Lily today?"

"I was at the paper when some highbrow social worker came looking for her." He related the story.

"So, they're going through with it." Simon sighed. "Even though she has a job and insurance?"

"They're gonna dig into her life until they find something. The man asked about her getting sick, and who would help with the babies if she did."

Next to Simon, Loretta straightened. "I would. Who was this person? I'll call him."

Mr. Martini told them how he'd already lied about everybody being willing to help her.

"Oh, sure," Loretta said. "Like they helped with the window."

"She never called anybody in Fairview, Miss Jameson." Simon sounded defensive because...he felt that way. And in truth, it was eating at him that Lily was being treated like a pariah.

"People will do this, Loretta, even if nobody invited her here." Mr. Martini shook his head. "It ain't right."

Simon tried not to think about Lily the rest of the night. He made a point of spending time with Ellen, and they made plans to have dinner on the weekend.

But it was damn near impossible to forget about her when the presents were opened and among the pile there was a gift from her. After he ripped off the pretty paper Mr. Martini couldn't speak, he just stared for a long time at what looked like a drawing of some sort. Simon sat stoically by as Mr. Martini turned it around so everyone could see.

Next to him, Jenna said, "Oh, shit, this is awful."

Lily's gift was a collagelike sketch, with a young Mr. Martini in the center of it, wearing his World War II uniform. Behind him and to the side were a battle scene, medals, an American flag, his children and his wife.

Somebody asked, "Who brought this to the party?"

"I did." Miss Jameson's look was scathing. "Shame on all of you."

"OH, SURE." Lily stood over the playpen. "Now you sleep. Just because I wanna go home, you're dead to the world."

It was nine o'clock, and she headed into the last room she had yet to clean in the office. Though no one expected this of her, she was feeling a little like Cinderella, who'd been left out of the ball and sentenced to spend the night scrubbing. Since it had gotten worse outside and she hated driving in foul weather, not to mention that the twins were asleep, she began the task of sprucing up the place. She had to do something, or she'd go crazy thinking of the party no one wanted her to attend. Cleaning wasn't the best idea, though, she thought as she entered the bathroom. She'd just finish this room and then she'd lie down. Maybe the weather would get better soon and she could go home.

First, she sprayed the sink with cleanser. Its strong scent set off a bout of coughing.

As she dropped to her knees to clean the toilet bowl, she let out a sardonic laugh. "You didn't come very far, did you, Lily?"

When she was young and needed money, she'd worked as a maid at a hotel. She used to plan her future, as she swished bowl cleaner, just as she was doing now. She'd wished for a good job. Then, a wonderful husband. A nice place to live. And finally, babies.

Funny, how you could get everything you thought you wanted and still be miserable.

"Stop feeling sorry for yourself."

Next, she mopped the floor, and finished at last, she whipped off the plastic gloves, carefully washed her hands and applied a new bandage. In the mirror over the sink, she caught a glimpse of herself. Kerchief on her head. Wet spots on the sweat suit she'd had in the car and put on when she decided to clean. Her cheeks were flaming red. Must be she just wasn't used to hard labor.

As she came out of the small room, she stopped short and clapped a hand over her chest. "Oh!"

"What the *hell* are you doing?" Simon's harsh voice matched his stern expression.

She sneezed. "I'm sorry. What?"

"What are you *doing?*"

"Cleaning. The place needed it and the babies..." She grasped on to the sink. "Oh."

"What's wrong?"

Her hands went to her face. "I'm not feeling well. I'm a little dizzy."

"Smart thing to be doing then, cleaning the office. All those fumes are really good for you."

Damn him. What right did he have to be mad at her for helping out while he partied with his friends? "I felt better after I took more medicine, but then it wore off." Furious at having to defend her actions to him, she said haughtily, "Besides, I had the time tonight."

"Why didn't you take the babies home, like any sane person?"

Exhaustion, feeling ill, being treated like an outcast, all made her temper snap. "Don't talk to me that way. The twins are sleeping. I didn't want to wake them up. And I thought I might wait out the storm."

"You could have rested on the couch."

"Simon, what's this all about?"

"Nothing, damn it."

She shook her head, growing dizzier. And crankier. "Then leave me alone." She tried to brush past him, but he moved in front of her. When she pivoted to get around him, her head spun again.

And the world dimmed.

Dazed, she suddenly felt herself being picked up and carried. "I'm okay," she murmured, nosing her face against his chest. He still smelled the same—the unique scent that was Simon. For the first time in more than six months, she felt comforted.

"You almost fainted, for God's sake."

"I just got dizzy and swayed a little."

Out front, he laid her on the couch, and when her vision cleared, she saw that he'd sat down next to her. His eyes were harder than before. What had she done now? Damn it, she was getting *fed up* with this. "What's the matter now?"

"You almost fainted. Like women do when they're pregnant." His temper seem to build. "Are you? With Wakefield's child again?"

The hell with this. "No, Simon, I'm not."

"How do you know that?"

"I just do."

"How?"

"Because I can't possibly be pregnant."

"What do you mean?"

"Damn it, Simon. I can't be pregnant because I never made love with Derek after I went back to Westchester."

WHEN SIMON CAME to Lily's bedroom door, he saw that she'd done as he'd ordered. She'd showered, changed into pajamas—a pretty deep blue that made her eyes look like jewels—and had gotten into bed. Her face was still flushed, though. Beside her was the cat, Blackie, whom he hadn't seen in months. It was bigger, like the twins.

He softened his tone intentionally. "Did you take more medicine?"

"Yes. It's just a damn cold, Simon."

She'd tried to pick a fight on the way home, but he wouldn't be part of it. He'd felt like a heel all night at the party because the town had excluded her, and because he was worried about her driving home in the bad weather. He'd gone by the paper and saw her car there, and he'd gotten angry again. His pique had increased when he found her cleaning, for God's sake, and he'd behaved badly—

until the revelation about Derek. That little tidbit had doused his temper and preoccupied his mind as the babies had awakened and as they'd fed them at the office. He'd gotten them into their car seats and had insisted Lily wait inside where it was warm. She'd been sputtering ever since he left his car at the paper and drove hers to her house, but he ignored her complaints.

"You don't feel well," he told her now. Even he could hear the tenderness in his voice. "You needed help."

Which was why he was here. Well, partially why. He wanted some answers. Still in the doorway, he stalled. "How come you're sleeping in here?"

"What do you mean?"

"Gil's room is bigger."

Her shoulders sagged and the fight went out of her eyes. "It's hard to even go in there, let alone sleep in his bed."

"I guess it would be."

She tossed back her hair, which was damp and curling around her shoulders. "You can leave now. The babies are asleep, and I'm in bed."

"I'll go when I've had my say."

"What's gotten into you? When did you turn into such a tyrant?"

"I want some answers, Lily."

Looking down, she petted Blackie. "Go away. I'm tired. As you said, I don't feel well. And I'm sick of being pushed around. By everybody."

Instead of leaving, he entered the room and dropped down into a chair near the bed. "I heard about the social worker."

"Of course you did! Everybody knows my whole sordid situation. I'm sure they're rejoicing."

Like hell. The party had been somber, especially after Mr. Mancini had opened her gift. In the month she'd been back, there'd been a lot of thawing toward her on everybody's part. "The drawing was spectacular."

Her eyes lit up. "Did he like it?"

"Yes. How did you do it?"

"I downloaded pictures from the Internet, mostly, and found some that were archived at the paper. Then, I drew them. I've been drawing a lot since I left Fairview."

"It was the most unique present he received." And she hadn't been there to see the emotion on the old man's face when he'd opened her gift. "I'm sorry. You should have been there, Lily."

"Fine. Now will you go, Simon?"

"Why, Lily?"

"Because I wanted to do something special for him."

"That's not what I mean and you know it."

Stubborn silence.

"Why didn't you make love with Derek when you went back to him?"

"That's none of your business."

Like hell. "I want to know."

"Please, Simon, don't make me go through this."

"I'm not leaving until you tell me. I need to know why."

She sank back into the pillows, her face tight, as well as pale. Old protective feelings rushed to the surface and Simon had to quell them to get the answers he wanted.

"When I left Fairview and got back to his house, I couldn't let him touch me. Just the thought of it made me ill. It didn't seem to matter, because he didn't try. Finally, he brought it up. Said the alcohol and drug withdrawal had killed his sexual appetite."

"So, eventually you wanted to, but he couldn't?"

"No, I didn't want to. Stop putting words in my mouth."

"How long did this last?"

"Close to two months. Then he was repulsed that I was still breast-feeding. He said he wanted sex, but I had to stop nursing the twins. I wouldn't. He got belligerent about it. Said I was still in love with you, that's why I wouldn't stop so we could have sex."

That's what Johanna Wakefield had inferred. "Your mother-in-law…"

"Don't interrupt. This is hard enough to tell. And you wanted to hear it all, so you will."

He watched her, admiring her spunk, even when she was ill.

"Finally, the stress was too much, and I stopped producing enough milk. Even in good times that happens with twins. Then, one night, Derek decided it was his *right* to make love with his wife. He got in bed and told me as much. I was sick about it, but he was my husband. So...I let him try."

"Try?"

"He couldn't. Probably because I was crying." She closed her eyes, as if she was reliving the nightmare. "He never tried again, and it was the beginning of the end. He went back to drugs and alcohol not long after."

"None of that was your fault, Lily."

She shook her head. "Will you let it go now, Simon? This is too hard to talk about, and I'm so tired." She slid down into the bed and pulled up the covers. The cat nestled even closer.

"All right, go to sleep."

"Leave the door open, so I can hear the babies if they wake up. Lock the front one on your way out."

"Just go to sleep, Lily."

Waiting in the hall, he heard her breathing even out, closed the door, checked on the twins and headed to Gil's room, where he stretched out on the bed. He could hear the babies from here if they awoke. He drifted off with one thought occupying his mind, calming his soul. Lily had never made love with Derek after she'd gone back to West-chester.

CHAPTER THIRTEEN

HANK RAISED HIS ARM and slid it across the front seat of his Ford pickup. "You sure you wanna do this, Jen?"

She stared out the window at Grandpa Gil's house. It loomed in the darkness, broken only by a beacon of light from the porch. "Too late now. I promised Katie I'd help her tonight."

Taking a puff of his cigarette, Hank blew smoke out his open window. "Why'd you tell her you'd do it, anyway? You said you hate Lily."

"I do." Though not as much as she wished she did. "But the babies are a different story."

"Does Fran know about this?"

Fran was Jenna's counselor. At their last session, Jenna hadn't told the woman her plans for tonight, because Fran had already hinted that Jenna sounded as if she wanted Lily back in their lives. Fran said it was okay to forgive people. But Jenna wasn't ready to hear that yet.

"Nobody knows but you and Katie." Leaning over, she kissed Hank's cheek. "See you at ten."

Jenna bounded out of the car and made her way up the sidewalk. The air was nippy, but nowhere near as cold as it had been last week at Mr. Martini's birthday party. Grandpa Gil used to joke about the fickleness of upstate New York weather. Jenna stood at the bottom of the steps and felt her heart start to ache. She hadn't been here since he died. All the memories came flooding back...

You're not my flesh and blood, Jenna, but I think of you like that.

Here, let me show you how the clutch works.

We're so proud of you, Jenna. You were terrific in that part onstage.

Grandpa Gil wouldn't be so proud of her these days. She'd been thinking about that a lot. It was one of the reasons she'd changed her hair color from that brutal dye job, and why, tonight, she wore plain jeans, a sweater and one of her old school windbreakers. In the middle of the night, sometimes she admitted she was tired of being bratty Jenna.

The front door opened and Katie peeked out. "What are you doing here, girlfriend?"

"Remembering." *And wishing for things that could never be.*

She climbed the steps. Inside, the images swamped her. She could almost see Grandpa Gil walking around the house, hear him whistling like he used to.

Katie touched her arm. "I'm sorry. You must miss him."

Her throat tight, she nodded. "W-where are they?"

"In the living room. They're so cute, Jenna."

"I know." In the last week, she'd found a ton of excuses to stop by the *Sentinel* after school. Her dad had asked her why she was hanging around there so much, but she'd made things up to avoid the truth—she just couldn't stay away from the babies.

When Jenna walked into the room, she saw Cami on her back, kicking her legs and gnawing on soft rubber blocks. Sitting up, Patrick looked over at them. His eyes widened and he gave her a huge grin, and once again Jenna felt whole. It happened every time she saw them. "Hey, there, buddy, how are you?"

He pumped his arms and made excited sounds.

"He knows you," Katie said.

That wasn't true. He couldn't possibly remember her, but she loved his excitement, anyway, and she rushed to pick him up. She hadn't held him since Lily had come back. "He's so heavy." He batted her cheeks and hit her nose. "How'd you get so big, Patrick? Huh?"

"Lily says he eats a lot. They're about ready for the last bottle, and then they should go to sleep."

"So soon?" Jenna asked. "I couldn't come until the coast was clear."

"I guess we could wait."

With Patrick cuddled close, Jenna sat down on the couch and held him on her lap, unable to look away from his chubby cheeks and blue eyes. "Lily buy the story?"

"Yep, she thinks my cousin's coming to help out."

"Did she say when she'd be back?"

"Around nine or nine-thirty. She's going to a movie with Miss Jameson, and then they're going for dinner. She's freaked about leaving the twins. Made me promise to call, even if it's during the movie. But they're better than any other babies I've ever taken care of."

Katie watched her a minute.

"What?"

"Jen, you don't have to keep this all a secret. Lily would love to know you're here. And your dad? He'd accept it."

"That is *so* not a good idea."

"I'll listen, if you want to talk about your feelings. It's okay if you, you know, kinda want Lily back in your life."

Suddenly Jenna felt like a little girl again, and the truth tumbled out. "She hurt us so much. Dad was so sad it scared me. I don't think I can do it, Katie, even if I wanted to."

"Okay, but I'm here if you need to talk about it."

Patrick tugged at a strand of Jenna's hair and she was glad for the distraction. "You're so strong," she whispered as she kissed his head.

Cami started to whimper, so Katie picked her up and held her close. "Where's your dad think you are?"

"With you at your house." She frowned. "He's got a date with Ms. Priestly tonight."

"They a couple now?"

Jenna shrugged a shoulder. "Who knows? Maybe it'll put him in a good mood for a change. He's been grumpy since Mr. Martini's party."

Something bounded out of the corner. Jenna and Katie both yelped, and the babies tensed. "Shh," Katie said to Cami. "It's just the cat."

"Oh, look at Blackie, Patrick. He's big, too."

When Cami continued to fuss, Katie got up. "Here, sit with her while I get the bottles."

A baby sat on each side of Jenna, and she circled her arms around them. When they nosed into her, she experienced a sense of a peace, of contentment, she hadn't known in a long time. Her dad would be ecstatic about how good she felt, but Katie was wrong. Jenna couldn't risk telling him her feelings about Lily were all jumbled up and crazy. Because she couldn't let Lily hurt either of them again.

AFTER THE MOVIE, Loretta and Lily waited in the foyer area of the Fairview Diner for a table. Loretta's eyes sparkled as she said, "I'd give up all I owned and follow him anywhere, too. Just like Marisa Tomei. Pierce Brosnan just *does* it for me."

"He reminds me of Derek." Which made Lily sad.

Loretta waited a moment. "I'm sorry. I'm sure you're still grieving, despite what happened between you two." One night, Lily had confessed the whole story.

From behind the counter, Mrs. Conklin approached them. "Loretta. Lily." Her tone wasn't as harsh as it had been when Lily'd first returned. For some reason, after the party, people in town were friendlier to her. "Just you two?" She motioned to the far room. "I'm afraid we only have a table in the back."

"That would be fine," Loretta said.

Mrs. Conklin just stared at them.

"Ada? Is something wrong?"

"No." She glanced nervously at Lily. "I guess not." After

another pause, she finally led them to the back. Once there, Lily saw the cause of Ada Conklin's odd behavior.

Cozied up in a booth, sitting together on the same side, were Simon and Ellen Priestly. He wore a beautiful houndstooth sport coat and she had on a silky black dress. Simon was smiling at the woman in a way that Lily hadn't seen him smile since she'd come back to Fairview. Turned fully to face Ellen, his hand covered hers on the table.

For a moment Lily was poleaxed. Self-consciously she tugged at her hair, wishing she'd styled it instead of letting it hang loose. Then she glanced down at her jeans and sweater. Why hadn't she dressed better?

"Lily, here, sit on this side."

"Huh?"

Loretta touched her arm. "Sit over here, so you can't see them."

She stumbled, knocking over a glass. Water spilled across the table and dribbled onto the floor. Oh, great.

When Ada rushed to get a cloth to wipe it up, Simon and Ellen both turned toward them. Simon's eyes widened when he saw Lily, but then his face closed down. Lily simply stared at him, Loretta waved and then they seated themselves.

"Can I get you something to drink?" Ada asked, her tone full of pity. It was almost worse than the town's rancor had been.

"Wine, Lily?" Loretta asked.

They order glasses of merlot, and Lily picked up the menu. But instead of focusing on the specials, she saw in her mind Simon practically making out with his girlfriend in a booth. In a damned public restaurant. Did he think he was sixteen years old again?

Loretta said softly, "It's probably how he felt when you went back to Derek."

She peered over the menu. "Then I feel even more sorry for him than I did before."

Things had been stilted between her and Simon all

week, since her *big confession*—which she'd been furious at herself for making. He hadn't brought it up, either, though he'd stayed all night, damn it. Against her wishes, but what did she have to say about anything anymore? He'd left as soon as she woke up.

After a while Lily managed to pull herself together and made small talk.

"Have you seen your social worker?" Loretta asked.

"She can't come to Fairview until next week. Their office services several towns, but on the phone the woman said the Wakefields can't do anything without her report. She sounds nice, though. Competent."

"I see. Are the Wakefields lying low?"

"Not exactly. They got my e-mail address somehow."

Loretta's brow furrowed. "They've been contacting you?"

"In a way."

She felt again the utter panic she'd experienced when she received the first article from them about grandparents getting custody of their grandchildren. They'd sent her another, a few days later.

"That's mean," Loretta remarked, when Lily told her the story.

"They're trying to scare me into letting them have what they want."

Her friend's gaze drifted over Lily's shoulder, then she leaned forward. "They're leaving, dear."

And going where? To do what? Lily felt a surge of jealousy so strong it made her almost choke on her veal piccata. "Oh, well, good."

"He's headed to our table. With Ellen."

Lily gripped her fork and calmed her breathing.

"Hi, there," he said, when they reached the booth.

"Simon. Ellen."

"Hello," was all Lily managed.

"Out for a night on the town?" Ellen asked.

"Yes, we saw a movie." Lily would be damned if she'd

clam up like some sulking teenager. "Now we're getting a bite to eat."

Loretta added, "I had to drag Lily out with me. This is her first solo flight since she came back."

Lily tried not to notice how formfitting Ellen's slim black dress was and how flat her stomach was. How she linked her arm with Simon's all the while they talked. Under the sport coat, he wore a black silk T-shirt. Lily had always loved that look on him.

"How's Jenna?" she asked, to distract herself.

"Good. She's finally spending more time with her old friends."

Ellen smiled. "She's with Katie Welsh tonight. They've been friends since I had them both in fifth grade."

Loretta shot Lily a surprised look.

"What's wrong?" Simon asked.

"Simon, Katie's babysitting the twins tonight. She told me her cousin was coming over to help out for a few hours."

"Oh, dear. Do you think Jenna's with Hank, instead?" Ellen sounded like a concerned mother.

Simon's shoulders stiffened. "No, I think I know exactly where Jenna is." He slid his arm around Ellen and pulled her close. "If you'll excuse us, we still have the night ahead of us."

Lily watched them walk away like two lovers who couldn't wait to be alone. Her appetite ruined, she put down her fork.

SIMON WAS IN THE RECEPTION area of the *Sentinel* at eight the next morning, snarling down at the ad copy on the desk. Damn it, the pages were a mess. He was going to have to get Lily to take over the design again. Because he was alone, he let loose with several wash-your-mouth-out expletives. Last night had been a disaster, which was why he'd come in to work on a Sunday morning. Nothing had gone right after he'd left the restaurant.

Simon, come in. We'll have a nightcap. Talk...

He'd made the monumental mistake of accepting Ellen's invitation. When she'd inched close to him on her couch, he'd tried to participate. Tried to throw himself into the first kiss, the second. But it was impossible.

Then later, at home...

Why'd you go to Lily's house, Jenna? You must have known it would hurt you.

I miss the babies, Daddy.

He'd been torn. Was it good that Jenna felt that way, or was she setting herself up for another crash, which right now, Simon wasn't sure he could handle? Damn Lily Wakefield for sucking his daughter back in.

And him. After her confession Saturday night, he'd had dreams. But now, instead of Derek sleeping with her, as he'd envisioned before, Simon was making love to Lily. And she'd been so real and so solid, so loving, that he'd awakened to find he'd reacted like a young boy having adolescent wet dreams. Hell, he was forty years old.

Why had he pushed her to tell him what had—or in this case hadn't—happened with Derek? Why had he felt such enormous relief when he'd found out the truth? And why couldn't he stop thinking about the fact that Lily had never gone back to her husband's bed?

Hearing a noise on the porch, he looked over to see someone at the door. He hadn't locked it because no one would come here today. The office was closed. The woman knocked and let herself in.

She seemed vaguely familiar. He could swear he'd seen her before. "Hello, Mr. McCarthy. Nice to see you again."

"I'm sorry, I don't remember..."

"Last year. I came to meet you and Mr. Gardner."

Still, he couldn't place her.

"I'm Liz Gaston. I handle acquisitions for the Heard Corporation."

"Ah, yes, I remember. You came to see Gil and me about selling our shares in the paper to your chain." Her huge, slick chain, which was notorious for gobbling up small local newspapers and morphing them into cookie-cutter rags.

"That's correct." She unbuttoned her light coat. "I'm sorry to bother you on a Sunday, but I got into town a day early for my appointment tomorrow and drove by here. When I saw a car, and the lights, I was thinking maybe I might make contact today."

"I don't understand why you're here at all. Gil and I made it clear thirteen months ago that the paper isn't for sale."

She cocked her head. "I was under the impression that the *Sentinel* might be up for grabs, now that ownership has changed hands."

Simon felt cold dread seep into him. "And how would you know about that?"

"It's public knowledge, Mr. McCarthy. We keep track of the locals. Our department recently flagged the *Sentinel* again as a potential acquisition." She drew a paper out of her purse and squinted at it. "My meeting tomorrow is at four o'clock with a Lily Wakefield. I understand she owns sixty percent of the stock now."

The world dimmed. Then reality bit him in the ass.

Lily was going to sell the newspaper right out from under him.

LILY WAS GLAD the weather had turned mild today. When she'd awakened this morning, the sun was bright and the air had begun to warm up. She'd put on a navy sweat suit, dressed the babies in pink and blue outdoor wear, buckled them into their stroller and headed out. Recently, she'd bought a video about exercising with children, and after seeing Ellen Priestly, she'd decided she needed to build some muscle and get back in shape. She was thinner than before she'd given birth, but still she had flab for the first time in her life.

Welcome to the realities of motherhood.

She refused to think negative thoughts today. She'd had enough of them last night—about the article the Wakefields had sent, the social worker's delay, and most of all, about Ellen and Simon. She couldn't help but wonder what they'd done during their "night ahead." Damn him! When she thought about the suggestive comment he'd made, she got furious, which was a lot better than crying over him. She'd only gone out with Loretta to distract herself from thoughts of him, and it had backfired.

"Forget him," she said aloud as she reached the school. "The creep."

The outdoor track stretched for half a mile and she planned to jog on it. She started slow, checking her watch and increasing speed every five minutes. The wind blew, messing up the braid her hair was long enough for now. The babies laughed at the speed and the feel of the wind on their faces. Lily circled around once before she started to breathe hard. Oh, great, her aerobic capacity was about as good as her muscle tone. She made it around again, and then she had to slow down. Only a mile. How pathetic. She was down to a fast walk when she saw someone coming toward her.

And recognized those wide shoulders and that long-limbed stride. Unfortunately, when he got closer, she also recognized the look on his face. "What the hell are you up to now?"

"Excuse me?" She used the haughty tone she'd learned from Derek's mother. "I'm exercising with my babies." She'd be damned if she'd let on that she felt bad about seeing him last night with the beautiful Ms. Ellen.

His faced reddened. It only made him more handsome in his wine-colored sweatshirt and blue jeans. He closed in on her and grabbed her shoulders roughly. "That's not what I mean and you know it."

"Simon, what…"

He shook her. "What are you trying to do—destroy me?"

Alarm snaked through her. She'd never seen him in this

kind of mood before. "If you're talking about Jenna being at my house last night, I had nothing to do with it."

"I'm not talking about Jenna. She's all right."

His grip tightened and Lily winced. "Simon, you're hurting me."

He let her go so fast, she stumbled backward. "What's gotten into you?"

"I had a visitor at the paper this morning."

"The paper's closed on Sundays."

"Your four o'clock on Monday got into town early and was hoping to conduct business today."

"My what?"

"A certain Liz Gaston."

"Oh. Yeah, I have a meeting with her tomorrow. Why did she come to see *you* today?"

Rage returned in a flash. "So it's true? You're selling the paper?" His hands fisted and Lily wondered briefly what he was going to do with them. She knew how men could turn on you in a heartbeat—but Simon?

"What are you talking about?"

"Ms. Gaston works for Heard Corporation." At her questioning look, he snapped, "The newspaper conglomerate that's been after the *Sentinel* for years."

"There must be some mistake. I got a call from a lawyer's office that someone from New York needed to talk to me about my inheritance. I assumed it was more pressure from the Wakefields. I had no idea who they worked for."

"Why should I believe that?"

"Because it's the truth."

"Do you even know the meaning of the word? And to think how Jenna and I were getting pulled back in."

"Now wait just a minute…" She straightened to her full height and stepped close. "I have *never* lied to you. That's one thing I've never done."

"Oh, yeah, sure." He was wide-eyed now, and fuming. "How about all the times you told me you loved me?"

She waited before she said, quietly, "That was all true."

"You don't go back to another man and break my heart in the process if you love me!"

"I do love you, Simon, even if I did break your heart."

He froze. The fact that she'd used the present tense stood between them like a boulder. His gaze narrowed on her. "Is it true? You didn't make an appointment to sell the paper?"

She nodded, unable to trust her voice.

He swore then. Looked up at the bright blue sky. The sunlight kissed the lighter strands of his hair, turning it blonder. "Regardless, the corporation will try to get you to sell now."

"I'd never sell the paper. I can stand up to any pressure they put on me. I'm stronger than I look, Simon."

"Okay." He gave her one last stare, then turned and walked away.

"Huh," she said to the babies. "That went well."

CHAPTER FOURTEEN

WHEN LILY ARRIVED at work the next day, she marched into Simon's office. It was time to take control of her life, of her dealings with him, with *everybody* who was trying to push her around. He was sitting at his computer, his back to her. His shoulders stretched inside the dark suit he'd worn to Gil's funeral. The whole office smelled like freshly applied men's cologne. "I want to talk to you."

Swiveling around, he said, "Hello to you, too."

She rested her hands on the hips of the plum-colored suit she was wearing today. "Just because you're into pleasantries and aren't swearing at me today, doesn't mean I forgive you."

"Forgive me for what?"

For Ellen. "For your childish tirade yesterday at the track." When he started to speak, she held up her hand. "No. Don't interrupt. I'd like you to come to the meeting with the Heard woman today."

His amber eyes turned flinty. "Why?"

"Because I'm sick of you questioning my every move. Believe me, I *know* what I did to you, and to Jenna and to the town." Briefly she raised her eyes to the ceiling. "How can I forget, when I'm reminded every damned day?"

Was that a quirk of a smile on his face?

"Are you laughing at me?"

"The truth?"

She glared at him.

"You're...daunting when you're fed up." He shook his

head. "Anyway, the townspeople aren't mad anymore. Mr. Martini's party was a bust. Everybody felt guilty for excluding you."

"Really?"

"Uh-huh."

"And Jenna's okay, even if I'm still worried about her getting close to you and the babies."

"Not me. She never speaks to me. Just the babies."

"Be careful with her, Lily. Maybe her relationship with the babies is okay. But I don't want her caring about you again."

That hurt. But she stuffed a response and simply said, "I will, I promise," though the words stuck in her throat.

She waited.

"What?"

Arching a brow, she asked, "What about you?"

"What about me?"

"Do you still hate me?"

"I never hated you. That was part of the problem."

"Okay, good." Why was she disappointed he didn't say more? Why, *why*, did she keep wishing for something from him, some glimmer of forgiveness, when she wasn't going to get it?

"I can see by your face you want more from me. But there is no more, Lily. What you told me—about Derek, about your feelings—makes no difference to what's happened between us."

"I didn't expect it to." She raised her chin. She did have some pride. "You read me wrong."

"Well, it wouldn't be the first time."

"Will you come to the meeting?"

"Why do you want me there?"

"Because I'm not selling my shares and I want you to hear me say it to the Heard Corporation's representative."

"All right. I have a luncheon at the Chamber of Commerce, but I'll be back in plenty of time." He studied her. "I have to leave at five, though, for a date with Ellen."

He wanted to rub her face in it, fine. They'd just get it all out. "Are you serious about Ellen Priestly?"

"Not yet. We dated after you left. We're still at the casual stage."

"I see. Well, she seems like a nice woman, and you deserve happiness."

"I do." Turning from him, she strode to the door. "So do you, Lily," he called after her. But she kept walking.

That afternoon, Lily got another e-mail from the Wakefields. The headline on this one read, Court Says Grandparents Are Better Suited Than Single Mother. The article described a case in Missouri, where the father of the child died and the mother was accused by the grandparents of being unfit. The grandparents were important people in town and they gained custody. The poor mother got visiting rights. For a moment, Lily panicked. It happened every time she thought about losing the twins. She knew she was a good mother, but the Wakefields had power and money. What would she do if they were successful in taking Cami and Patrick away? Her panic turned to stark terror and she had to sit down and put her head between her legs.

Thankfully, she was more composed when Liz Gaston arrived at four on the dot. "Mrs. Wakefield?"

Lily greeted her and they shook hands. "I've asked for Simon McCarthy to sit in on this meeting, Ms. Gaston."

Dressed in a suit—Armani, Lily guessed, just like hers—the woman frowned. "I was hoping to speak to you alone."

"Which I'm assuming was why no one told me exactly who you were when this meeting was scheduled."

"Excuse me?"

"Never mind. Let's go back to the offices."

Simon greeted the woman civilly. He seemed more subdued than when Lily had spoken to him this morning. At the small table in the back of the newsroom, he and Lily sat side by side, facing Liz Gaston. "The ball's in your court," Lily told her.

"I understand you're the new owner of the paper."

"Part owner."

"But you have a majority of shares. Since Mr. McCarthy has refused our offers in the past, we'd settle for obtaining your sixty percent."

"Which means you'd have controlling interest and could run the *Sentinel* however you chose." Simon's tone was laced with barely suppressed anger. His eyes sparked fire.

"Yes, Mr. McCarthy, we would. We just acquired a paper in Western New York under those circumstances and we were able to revamp it according to our long-range plans." She stared at him unflinchingly. "Which is why, if Mrs. Wakefield sells, you should, too."

"I read about the *Buffalo Banner*. You forced the man running it to sell you his shares."

"We make the benefits of selling clear to those involved."

"What did they do, Simon?" Lily asked.

"They brought in a new editor. Gave the old one some menial job, decreasing his salary so he couldn't support himself."

"How horrible."

Gaston's expression was blank. "As I said, it's business."

Lily zeroed in on the woman. "What it is, Ms. Gaston, is a moot point. I'm not selling you my shares."

"Certainly not for five more months. But the deal can be made now, we'll give you a sizable cash advance, and close it after the allotted time."

"No."

Opening a folder, she scanned a paper inside. When she looked up, her expression was smug. "We know about your circumstances."

Lily's hands began to shake and she slid them under the table.

"She's doing just fine now," Simon told the woman.

"Mrs. Wakefield, you're used to the big city. To more than this." Gaston waved her hand around the office.

"Though you have no Wakefield money, we can provide you with enough to live as you're accustomed."

Lily let out a disgusted sound. "I never want to live like I was 'accustomed to' again. And the paper is Simon's."

"I don't understand. Can Mr. McCarthy buy you out anytime soon?"

Lily shook her head. "No, but I don't care how long it takes Simon to purchase the shares. I'll have enough money to take care of my children as he gradually buys in."

"We'll beat his price."

"No."

Liz Gaston shook her head. "I don't get it."

"I'm not selling. As simple as that. Now, if you'll excuse me, I have work to do."

The babies fussed in the back room. Liz Gaston nodded out the door. "Is this what you want for your children, Mrs. Wakefield? To spend their afternoons here? What about a prestigious preschool, better elementary education, a private high school?"

"They're seven months old."

"Can't plan too soon." She waited a beat. "The Wakefields know that."

"So they *are* in on this. I suspected as much." Her voice was raw, full of fear, and under the table, she felt one of Simon's big hands grasp hers. It gave her the strength to say, "I'd like you to leave now. And please, don't bother me again."

After the woman left, Simon let go of Lily's hand and rose.

"The bitch," she said.

Simon chuckled. Then sobered. "Thank you, Lily."

"I made you a promise, Simon, and I intend to keep this one." She nodded to his suit. "Now, you'd better finish up what you were doing, so you don't keep Ellen waiting."

"Lily, I…"

"No, don't say anything. I appreciated the moral support." She turned and went out front before her bravado deserted her.

By THE END OF MARCH, the townspeople had totally forgiven Lily's abandonment, Simon observed, as he watched her across the gym of the high school, sitting behind the bake sale table. This bazaar, to raise funds for more paid firefighters in the department that served Fairview and the surrounding areas, was evidence of their acceptance. Mrs. Billings had asked Lily to help out at her booth and they'd been chatting away since the bazaar had opened at noon.

"Hey, there, handsome." Ellen had come up to the line Simon was standing in to take his turn at the basketball toss. She wore the red T-shirt all the volunteers had on, which read, Fight Fire With Funds.

"Taking a break?" he asked.

Ellen was selling small crafts that she and her students had made in class.

"Yes, some of the older kids are manning the table." She nodded to the basketball toss. "You going to win me a stuffed animal?"

Uh-oh. It was the last thing he wanted to do. After his talk with Lily, when he'd told her he was interested in Ellen, he'd admitted to himself he'd lied in order to distance Lily. "Sure. Okay."

"Great, bring it over when you're done." She kissed him on the cheek and headed across the gym.

Simon watched her, and then his gaze met Lily's. She'd witnessed the kiss and her expression was full of…hurt. Okay, so he was feeling bad, too, and guilty about Ellen. Lily only broke the visual connection when a firefighter approached her.

What was this, the tenth one? The bazaar had started at noon, when the whole town, including the schools, had shut down. The fire department had brought over a truck for the kids to play on outside, but the guys had come inside regularly, to look around, get something to eat and apparently to flirt with Lily. She bestowed a beautiful smile on Ray Lewis, a divorced man with a bit of a reputation.

He wasn't subtle about leering at the nice fit of her jeans and the way her T-shirt stretched across her breasts. God, she did look beautiful.

"Green-eyed monster gettin' to you, boy?" This from Mr. Martini, who'd contributed some of his whittled figurines to the fund-raiser.

"Excuse me?"

"They're sniffing her out. Eddie McPherson, especially. Those smoke eaters are notorious womanizers. Wouldn't trust my girl around them."

"She isn't my girl." But she had been, once. He'd had so many plans. And sometimes, he even wondered if maybe... No, he wouldn't think about a future with Lily. Jenna had to be his primary concern.

Mr. Martini gave him a knowing look. "Anyway, I'm glad to see her here. Felt bad about my party."

"The whole town felt bad. I'm glad they've warmed up to her."

"Your daughter, too?"

"To the babies. She doesn't have much to do with Lily."

Simon's turn at the basketball toss came up, and as Mr. Martini stood by to watch, Simon was hoping he'd lose. But the competitive athlete in him wouldn't allow it and he sank three free throws, snagging a huge white teddy bear with a red bow. Damn.

Might as well get it over with. He crossed to the crafts booth, sensing Lily was watching him. When he gave the prize to Ellen, she hugged him. He barely returned it. This was not working. Simon should have done something about Ellen before now. It was time to put an end to their relationship. Though he couldn't have one with Lily, stringing Ellen along was unfair.

Hank Ferris's appearance at the doorway to the gym distracted Simon. The guy was scanning the area, probably looking for Jenna. He wore his usual jeans and black T-shirt, but at least they were clean and pressed. Jenna noticed him, raced over and gave him a hug. Her counselor had warned Simon that the more he objected to their relationship, the more Jenna would want to see the guy, so he tried not to intervene. Still, he worried about her being with Hank, who was out of high school and worked at Fuzzy's Garage, even if Jenna had at last confided to Simon that Hank wasn't as bad as he appeared. She had also promised that she wasn't drinking or doing drugs with him anymore.

Deciding to get a feel for things himself, Simon intercepted them on their way across the gym. "Hey, there." He kissed Jenna's cheek—she'd had a small unicorn drawn on it at the face-painting booth. "Hank."

"Mr. McCarthy." The guy shook hands with him.

"I'm taking Hank to see the babies, Dad. They just started crawling, did you know that?"

"Um, yes." He'd watched Lily trying to deal with them at the office. First, Patrick would inch away, then Cami. As the week wore on, both got the hang of moving, and eventually Lily was forced to corral them in their playpens.

"You're working with the kids, right?" Hank asked.

"Uh-huh. The child-care room."

Jenna dragged Hank away.

What the hell? Simon followed. On the way, he passed by Lily's booth. He hadn't spoken to her today, so he stopped, "Hi, Lily." Just being close to her made his whole body react. Now that he was over the animosity he'd felt initially at her return, her physical nearness was playing havoc with him. Sometimes, he missed her so much, he could barely stand it.

Her expression was aloof. "Simon. I see you're the big winner today." At his blank look, she added, "The teddy bear. How lucky for Ellen."

Well, she'd certainly stopped being a whipped puppy. Damned if her sauciness didn't turn him on even more.

Another firefighter edged in front of Simon. "Come on, doll. We're taking bets to see who gets the first date with you."

Another jostled him out of the way. "I need the money more, gorgeous."

Then, the ambulance crew appeared. Tom Conklin headed right to her. "Hey there, Lily, how's the hand? Want me to check you out?" he asked suggestively.

Disgusted, and jealous as hell, Simon headed to the child-care room. From the doorway he saw that there were several kids in the play area and over in a corner were Jenna and Hank. His protective feelings warred with what he witnessed. Jenna was on the floor chasing Patrick, whose little butt was in the air as he scooted across the rug. Hank sat in a rocker, holding Cami. The boy knew how to soothe her when she started to fuss. Then, he kissed her head.

"Excuse me. You're blocking the door." Lily stood behind Simon with two bottles in her hands and a big fat scowl on her face.

His gaze softened when he looked at her. "Feeding time?"

She responded in kind. "Always. Patrick's a guzzler."

"And Cami's demure, even when she eats." At her sideways glance, he said, "Yes, I've watched them at the paper." Which only made their loss harder, so he didn't know why he did it.

She smiled sadly, the emotion in her deep blue eyes heartfelt. "You must miss them."

"I do." Lightly squeezing her arm, he stepped aside. "Go ahead."

"This is nice, Simon, the bazaar. Your efforts really do pay off in those editorials."

"We have this fund-raiser every year."

"I know, but the money donated this time around goes to the fire department because of your editorial in the paper."

Had he known the firefighters were going to make fools of themselves over Lily, Simon might have reconsidered writing it. "So, who's gonna win the date?"

She pursed her lips. Her complexion was rosy today, and

the red shirt highlighted it and her dark hair, too. "I don't know yet." She gave him a flirty look again, making him want to kiss her soundly. "I haven't decided." She went over to the babies.

Hank took the bottle as if he'd fed babies all his life and Jenna accepted one, too. Hank greeted Lily warmly, but Jenna didn't speak to her, which was good.

It was also good for Simon to see Jenna's wariness of Lily. Because watching her flirt with the firefighters made him want her to flirt with *him,* and that was a very bad idea.

THE FIREFIGHTERS WERE CUTE, all of them, Lily thought as one brought her a cup of tea. But she had no intention of dating. That was the last thing she needed. Or was it? She watched Simon as he moved from booth to booth with Sammy, taking notes, setting up photographs. He looked so good today in dark jeans and the bazaar T-shirt—she felt the stirrings of arousal just watching him.

"You all right, Lily?" Mrs. Billings asked. "You're flushed."

"Just a bit tired." She glanced at her watch. "And it's only four."

"You can leave if you need to."

"Oh, no, I wouldn't think of it. I'm having fun. And the babies are doing great in child care."

Mrs. Billings nodded across the room. A group of firefighters had just entered the gym. "Oh, my, here's a new bunch." The older woman laughed. "Prepare yourself."

"Shh. It's not funny. It's embarrassing."

"Hmm." Mrs. Billings waved Simon over. "It's our turn, isn't it, Simon?"

He and Sammy reached their booth just as four firefighters made a beeline for it.

Sammy chuckled. She'd warmed up to Lily, too, since that day the staff had excluded her from lunch. The whole staff had, and at least Lily felt better about working with them. "Time for your picture, Lily. Oh, what a good shot. You guys all get around the two women."

"Not me, young lady." Mrs. Billings stepped aside. "You go ahead, Lily."

Before Lily could object, the men engulfed her. Most were big and brawny, dressed in the navy fire department T-shirts and pants. When they were in position, she sniffed. "You guys smell great."

Simon's gaze narrowed on her.

One named Timothy crowded closest. "My aftershave is the best."

"That is *so* not true." Another sidled in. "Mine is."

Lily was laughing when Sammy took the shot. "You're very photogenic, Lily," she said.

"She's gorgeous, that's why." This from Eddie McPherson. "And all mine. Aren't you, sweetheart?"

I think Eddie McPherson's sweet on Lily, but be careful, they call him Fast Eddie.

Lily shook her head, sending her hair flying. "Go away, all of you, I have to get to work." When they left and Mrs. Billings was talking to Mrs. Conklin, Lily looked up at Simon. "Hungry, Simon?"

"What?"

She moistened her lips. "I asked if you were hungry." His eyes focused on her mouth. Did his breath speed up a bit? "We're selling baked goods here." She held up a cookie. "Want one?"

"No," he spat out and stormed away.

But Lily noticed his gaze kept straying back to her as he finished up with Sammy. She shouldn't feel so good about his attention, because nothing was going to happen between them again…but she did.

That good feeling disappeared, though, when a man entered the gym. Mr. Kramer, the Wakefields' social services worker. Earlier this week, Lily had met with the woman assigned to her, and young Gloria Vick had said she didn't see any problems with Lily's ability to care for her children. She'd conduct her own investigation, but she cautioned Lily to watch out for Kramer. He had a reputation for being slick. He spotted Lily and strode over.

"Mr. Kramer? What are you doing here?"

"I've finished my interviews with the townspeople, Mrs. Wakefield."

"I assume they confirmed what I said." *Please, God, let it be true.*

"They did." He drew an envelope out of his inside suit pocket. "This is for you. It was just faxed to me here in Fairview."

"What is it?"

"An official document. In the interim of the custody battle over the two minor children, the Wakefields have obtained visiting rights."

"What?" Lily felt the world spin. She gripped the paper tight and felt the blood drain from her head.

Simon appeared behind Kramer. He must have seen that something was wrong. Lily took strength from him as he circled around Kramer and stood next to her. Without even opening it, she handed him the envelope and watched him take out the paper and read what was inside.

He scowled. "This appears official, Lily. But we need to have Mac take a look."

"I can assure you the papers are in order." Kramer's tone was offended. "As of April 1, the Wakefields are entitled to weekly visits with the twins, and periodic overnights."

"Overnights?" Lily sagged against Simon.

He slid an arm around her. "It's okay. We'll deal with this, Lily."

But Lily's only thought was that this was the first step in the Wakefields getting legal custody of the babies. After all, a case just like it had been the topic of one of the articles they'd sent to her over the Internet.

CHAPTER FIFTEEN

FOR ALMOST A WEEK, Lily fought the panic that threatened her whenever she thought of what was going to happen today. April Fool's Day. Had she been a fool to think she could stand up to the Wakefields, who were powerful people with unlimited funds? Should she have just disappeared with the babies? Her mother had done that successfully.

At the very least, why hadn't she continued breast-feeding? If she was still nursing the babies, the Wakefields wouldn't be able to keep Patrick and Cami all day.

Too late now. For a lot of things. The doorbell rang. A blast of anxiety hit Lily full force. But she smoothed down the pink sweater and tailored slacks she wore, checked her makeup in the hall mirror—she'd be damned if Johanna would catch her looking like a hag again—and answered the door.

"Hello, Liliana." She hadn't seen Bruce Wakefield since Derek's death. He'd always been a handsome man, with a full head of salt-and-pepper hair and a trim build. But now there were lines around his mouth and his blue eyes that hadn't been there before his son died.

"Bruce."

Johanna didn't offer her a greeting. "Are they ready?"

"Yes, except for their coats." She led her in-laws into the living room, where the twins sat in their playpen.

Bruce's face brightened when he saw them. "They're bigger." He crossed to Patrick and picked him up. "My God, he looks so much like Derek."

"He does, Bruce. But he's not Derek."

"What do you mean?" Johanna asked.

"He isn't your son." Lily was shocked that her voice sounded so even. "He's mine, and I'm keeping him."

"Let's not get into this now." Johanna gave her a dismissive wave. "We'll let our lawyers battle it out." Then she added, "Do you know our firm, Liliana? Lawrence, Pollard and Crane from the city?"

"Yes, I know of them. But Mac Madison is a capable attorney. I'm not worried about him going up against them."

"We'll see." Johanna crossed to Cami and lifted her out of the playpen. And right before Lily's eyes, Johanna's facade cracked. Her face softened and her voice took on a mellow quality. "Hello, darling. Aren't you beautiful? Your daddy would be so proud of you."

Cami cooed, and batted at Johanna's face. Lily's mother-in-law laughed out loud at the baby's antics.

Turning away from the sight, Lily crossed to the diaper bags she'd packed. "Their food is in here, along with their schedule for eating and napping. Some clothes and toys."

"Fine. We'll take the children to the Mercedes and Bruce can come back for their things."

"Be careful with them. They just started crawling, and they're into everything."

"We're capable of handling our grandchildren, Liliana." Again, Johanna's tone was shrill. "More than you, I might add."

Lily ignored the jab. "You'll need their car seats."

"No, we've bought our own."

"You bought your own?" Lily's hand went to her mouth. They bought their *own* car seats? That little detail threatened to pull her under.

Bruce frowned. "Johanna, put Cami's jacket on."

Lily stood by and watched the Wakefields dress her babies. At least, they were gentle with them. "Where... Where are you taking them?"

"I don't believe we need to discuss that with you."

"Please, Johanna. I've never been away from them all day."

Instead of answering, the woman carried Cami toward the door. Bruce followed with Patrick and Lily went after them. "At least let me kiss them goodbye."

Bruce stopped, but Johanna didn't. Shaking now, Lily took Patrick's cheeks in her hands. "Goodbye, honey. See you soon."

Patrick grinned, pumped his arms, and said, "Ma ma ma."

For the first time.

Oh, God, she couldn't do this, couldn't let him go. But, she had no choice. Gripping the doorjamb, she watched Bruce take Patrick down the walkway, then both he and Johanna got the babies into their car seats. Bruce strode back up the walk and into the house.

Once inside, he touched Lily's arm. "I'm sorry about all this, Liliana. Johanna's beside herself with grief over Derek." He handed her a slip of paper. "We've rented a suite at the Cornerstone Hotel in Clearhaven. We'll be there most of the day. There's a park across the street, and if the clouds clear away we'll take the babies outdoors."

She just nodded. Her throat felt as if a sock was stuffed into it.

"My cell phone number's on there. If you want, you can call me. Just to check on them."

"Thank you, Bruce."

He scooped up their diaper bags, squeezed Lily's arm again and then left.

Lily stood at the door, watching them drive away. Her whole life was in that car. Nothing else mattered now. After a long time, she finally dragged herself into the living room and saw that Patrick had left his favorite bear on the couch. At the sight of the small stuffed animal, Lily did what she had promised herself she would never do again on the day she realized how badly she'd messed up her life by going back to Derek.

Clutching the bear, she dropped down onto the couch, buried her face in the pillow and sobbed.

"STILL NO ANSWER?" Mr. Martini was standing across from Simon, watching him listen into his phone. The old man was frowning.

Simon shook his head.

"I brought over food," Mrs. Billings said. "She didn't answer when I rang the bell."

Once again, the door to the *Sentinel* opened. This had been going on for two hours. Loretta hurried inside. Simon wondered why she wasn't in school, as it was Tuesday.

"I took the day off," she said without greeting. "I thought I might spend it with Lily. I went over to Gil's, but no one answered the door."

"Maybe she's gone somewhere." Simon didn't think so, but these people were worried. So was he.

Loretta shook her head. "Her car's in the driveway."

"A walk?" Mrs. Billings asked.

Loretta indicated the moisture on her coat. "It's raining."

Sinking down onto the desk chair, Simon rubbed his hand over his face. "Lily's a grown woman. If she doesn't want to see anyone, it's her prerogative."

Three people stared at him as if he'd just confessed to murder.

"She's terrified the Wakefields won't bring the babies back." Loretta raised her chin at Simon. "She shouldn't be alone through this."

"If she's chosen to be alone, then so be it."

"That's cruel," Loretta snapped, turned and walked to the door, where she bumped into Mac on his way inside. "Talk some sense into him," she said loudly enough for Simon to hear. Then she swept out of the office, as if she were exiting stage right.

Mr. Martini and Mrs. Billings just stood there, waiting.

What the hell did they expect him to do? And why did everybody think he could fix this? Should fix this? He wasn't responsible for her or the babies anymore.

"No word?" Mac asked.

"None." He watched her lawyer. "Mac, you assured her the Wakefields would bring the kids back, right?"

"Of course I did, though I guess not enough to counteract those damn e-mails."

"E-mails?"

"Didn't she tell you?"

Simon shook his head.

"The Wakefields have been sending her articles about grandparents getting custody of their grandchildren. Stories from all over the country. I advised her not to open them, but I think it's some kind of morbid fascination."

"Oh, no. That poor dear." Mrs. Billings wrung her hands.

"Why would they do this?"

"To scare her. To make her panic." Mac looked disgusted. "If they could prove she's an overwrought paranoid woman, unable to care for the babies, then they'd stand a good chance of getting custody."

"There's another possibility," Mr. Martini said.

"What?"

"Maybe they think she'll run, like Cameron did."

"Why would they want her to do that?" Mrs. Billings asked.

"They'd find her. It'd be easier today than thirty years ago. Then they'd use it as ammunition."

The thought of Lily on the run alone with the twins made Simon's gut clench. Thunder cracked in the sky and rain pelted the roof, as if to protest the ugly thought. "I'm going over there."

"She won't let you in." This from Mrs. Billings.

"She doesn't have to. I still have a key to Gil's house."

"Go, boy."

"Call us," Mac said.

Simon was out the door before his common sense kicked in and made him change his mind.

LILY LAY ON THE COUCH, spent from her crying jag. Her body felt limp and her head pounded. In the darkened room, she listened to the rain against the side of the house and stared at the ceiling, unable to even think about what she should do. Some mother she was. Maybe the Wakefields were right.

A knock at the door again. She ignored it like all the others. She couldn't see anybody, couldn't let anyone in. Somewhere in her consciousness, she knew she was overreacting, but she couldn't seem to pull herself out of it. And no one could help her. The feeling of loneliness was almost too much to bear.

She heard the jingle of keys. The opening and closing of the front door. What? Who? And there was Simon, in the archway. Still, Lily didn't move, just lay there, her head on a pillow, clutching Patrick's favorite toy close to her heart.

Wordlessly, he came to the couch and peered down at her. Droplets of moisture dotted his head, dampening his hair. After a moment he took off his raincoat, bent over, lifted her into his arms and sat down with her in his lap. Like a child, she let him hold her, cuddled into him, clutched at his shirt. It was damp, too, but she felt warmth emanating from him.

And once again, Lily came apart.

When she calmed, he brushed a hand down her hair and began the litany, the one she'd been unable to recite herself.

"You're a great mother." He gave examples.

"You have the means to support them." He listed her assets.

"They're just trying to scare you into doing something stupid." He talked about the e-mails, the feelings of entitlement that people like the Wakefields took for granted. He told her he believed in justice, as those editorials she loved illustrated, and in the end the babies would stay in their rightful place—with her.

He talked on and on. Lily was lulled by the gentleness of his voice and the rhythmic stroking of his hand on her. Soon, she drifted off.

She roused slightly when she felt herself lifted and settled back on the couch. Covered. She heard the murmur of his voice, soothing her. Later, she heard him talking again.

And later yet, she came awake.

He was sitting in a chair by the window, reading the paper. His hair was dry and a bit curlier. He must have felt her gaze because he looked over. "Hi."

"Hi. How long did I sleep?"

"Two hours. You must have needed it."

"You've been here the whole time?"

"Yeah. I did some work on the computer. Made some calls on my phone."

She pushed herself to a sitting position. "Thank you, Simon."

"It was all true."

"I know. I lost it there for a while and couldn't think straight. After Patrick said *Mama* for the first time, I couldn't keep it in."

"For the first time? Aw, Lily."

"I was so scared."

"You're entitled."

She saw him smile.

"What?"

"You look a bit like a raccoon."

"Oh, my makeup." She rubbed her fingers beneath her eyes.

"You don't usually wear that stuff. And I see you dressed for the occasion."

"I wanted to meet them in full armor."

"I understand. When was the last time you ate?"

She blew out a heavy breath. "I can't remember."

He stood and came to the couch. "Time for some food. Breakfast or lunch?"

"Breakfast."

"I'll make you French toast."

She checked her watch. "I'm going to call Bruce Wakefield." At his questioning look, she told Simon about her father-in-law's kindness.

"There you go. He isn't such a monster."

"No, he never was. But Johanna rules with an iron hand."

"Try to have faith."

Bruce told her that the babies were having a nap. He assured her things were going well and not to worry. Again, he promised to have them back at eight tonight.

Stopping off at the bathroom, Lily caught sight of her face in the mirror. "Oh, wow. I'm a mess."

She scrubbed off the makeup, brushed her teeth and combed her hair away from her brow, securing it with a band. In the kitchen she found Simon lifting the toast out of the frying pan. From the back, his shoulders looked even wider in the dark brown dress shirt he wore with matching pants. At that moment, she missed him so much, she couldn't bear the thought of what she'd had and lost through her own stupidity.

Simon heard her come up behind him and turned around. He gave her a genuine smile. "Well, you look better."

"Wasn't hard."

"Sit." When he got her breakfast on the table, he took the chair opposite her. "You're a beautiful woman, Lily. Almost too beautiful."

That seemed to surprise her. "Why, thank you."

He forked out the toast for each of them. God, he wanted her. It was a physical yearning so great he could barely contain it. So he asked, "How are the firefighters?"

"Still calling." She poured orange juice.

He picked up the maple syrup. "Who won the bet?"

"The truth?"

He grinned at their old exchange. It made him want her even more. "Of course."

She slathered her meal with butter. "Nobody. I'm not in the market."

Oh, thank God. "Ah."

She took a big bite. "How's Ellen?"

He chewed his food. Angled his head. "I lied to you about her. It's not going anywhere."

"No?" Was that pleasure or even hope in her voice?

"Nope. I told her after the bazaar." Very deliberately, he put down his fork. Damn it, he hated this dance. This self-imposed distance. Impulsively, he asked, "What are we doing, Lily?"

"You mean right now?"

"For starters." Crossing his arms over his chest, he held her gaze in a meaningful stare. "I know what I want to do."

"I…I'm hoping it's the same thing I want."

He felt his insides unclench. She wanted what he did. And he'd take it, this one time. But he had to be fair. "I can't make any promises, Lily. Any commitment. Maybe if it was just me, but I can't let you back into my life because of Jenna." He meant that, didn't he? He wasn't using Jenna as an excuse, was he?

"I understand that. And I agree."

He didn't know what he would have done if she'd balked. Leaning over the table, he covered her hand with his. "I want to make love to you."

"I want that, too." She glanced at the clock. "Do you have to go back to the paper?"

"No, I've cleared the whole day. I'll be here till the Wakefields bring the twins back."

"Wow, that's eight hours."

"Hmm." Then, "Do you want me to stay under those circumstances?"

"Under any circumstances."

He stood and stretched out his arm. "All right, then. Let's go upstairs."

She put her hand in his. "Finally."

SIMON BRUSHED HIS LIPS over the curve of Lily's shoulder, down the length of her arm. He kissed her stomach, outlined her rib cage with his tongue. "I couldn't have imagined how your skin felt. How you taste." When he reached her breasts, he closed his mouth around a nipple. It was hot and beaded instantly. "Hmm."

Lily moved restlessly on the bed. "That feels so good. I've wanted this for so long."

Her hands grasped his head, then his shoulders, learning his body as he was learning hers. Her fingers tunneled through his hair, and he felt a pull to look up. The sight of her flushed cheeks, her eyes hazy with desire and the soft perspiration on her face made him granite hard. "Kiss me again," she said.

He took her mouth possessively, increasing the pressure, exploring her with his tongue. His teeth nipped at her, then he soothed her with his lips. Her lower body arched into him.

He grinned. "You're so beautiful when you're aroused."

"Simon…"

Sliding his hand down between them, he covered her. She arched more. And more, into his hand. He rubbed it against her.

She came then, moaning the most beautiful chorus he'd ever heard. Her orgasm lasted a long time, and when she settled, she buried her face against his chest. "I didn't mean to do that."

He kissed her dark hair. "Ah, love, I did." He hadn't removed his hand. Instead, he moved it again, this time sliding a finger inside her, searching with the others until he found what he was looking for. Her body bucked.

"Simon, what…again?"

"Shh, we're making up for lost time."

LILY CURLED HERSELF onto his body, which was stretched out full-length on the bed. He was taut everywhere and beginning to sweat. "I've wanted to do this forever, Simon. *Forever.*" She kissed his neck, gently scraped it with her teeth and took tiny nips along his shoulder.

"Let me touch you."

"No, hold on to the headboard." She ran her tongue around the inside of his ear. He groaned and arched his body upward. Lily reveled in her power to arouse him. "Besides, you've already touched me."

She saw the smile spread across his face.

"Proud of yourself, aren't you?"

"Oh, yeah." Masculine smugness at its best. "Twice for you, love."

He stopped chuckling when she straddled him, her back to his face. She took him into her hands and slowly massaged him. He was hard to begin with, and got even harder. The moans that came from him were long and low and lusty. Leaning over, she touched the tip of his penis with her tongue and his whole body vibrated. "Lily, love…"

She brought him to release then, with her mouth and hands, just as he'd done to her. He gripped her hips and shouted her name, over and over. Her heart swelled and her soul rejoiced.

SIMON SLIPPED INSIDE HER. The feeling was so right, he could barely believe it. Never in his life had he been so connected with a human being. He was facing her now, both of them on their sides. So he saw the moisture in her eyes and trapped a renegade tear between his fingers. "Why, Lily?"

"I just never thought this would happen."

His throat closed, as her words let reality seep in. "Sweetheart, this is only for today."

"Shh, I know. But still…" She moved as close as she could get. "I never thought we'd have the chance to be part of each other."

He kissed her softly at first, then increased the pressure of his mouth on hers. He wanted passion now, not sorrow. And he wanted oblivion, so he didn't have to think about this being only for today. She kissed him back, as if she needed him to breathe.

He began to thrust. Hard. Harder. His head filled with her scent, her taste in his mouth, he let himself go, immersed himself in her, absorbed her. She grasped his shoulders, as if he were all she needed in the world. When she tensed, then cried out, he let himself go. "I love you, Lily," he said, as he emptied himself in her. "I'm sorry. I love you."

LILY GLANCED AT THE CLOCK on the side of the bed. It was 4:00 p.m. Outside, the rain had begun to hit the roof again and cool air trickled in through the crack in the window. "I'm starved."

Simon wound a strand of her hair around his finger. "We worked up quite an appetite."

She sat up. "I'll go get us something to eat."

Crossing his arms behind his head, he sighed. "All right. You can be my personal slave."

"Fine by me." She gave him a sexy wink, trying to stay in the spirit of things. "We have four more hours." She smiled as she pulled on an ice-blue robe and ran her hands through her hair, watching him all the while.

"What?"

"You look like a sultan."

"*You* look like a woman who's been well loved."

"I am."

"Then go get me something to eat."

She reached the door and looked back. "Thank you, Simon."

"Hey, don't thank me, I got as good as I gave."

"No, I mean for everything. I'm not sure I could have gotten through today without you."

"You're welcome."

Lily was a few steps from the bottom of the stairway when the door flew open and someone stalked into the foyer.

Oh, my God.

Her hair dripping, her coat open, keys in her hand, Jenna stood on the hardwood floor and stared at Lily. Her face was a mix of anger and disbelief. "He's here, I know. I saw his car. They said he's been here all day."

"Jenna, let's go into the living room."

She frowned at Lily's robe. "Where is he?"

Lily didn't answer, simply came down the last few steps, hoping to head the girl off.

Jenna stayed where she was and glanced at the steps. "He's up there?"

"Sweetie, look, I was…"

Jenna's eyes widened.

Lily heard, "Yes, honey, I was up there."

Turning, Lily saw Simon on the stairs, dressed, but mussed. It was obvious what they'd been doing.

"How *could* you, Daddy?" Jenna sounded like a wounded child. "After what she did to us?"

"Honey, this is a grown-up thing."

Her face reddened, and Jenna looked like a grown-up, too. She swore at them. "*Both* of you." With that she turned and fled into the rain.

CHAPTER SIXTEEN

JENNA BANGED ON THE DOOR so hard her hand hurt. "Come on, answer, damn it."

Finally, the door creaked open. Hank stood behind it, dressed in boxers. His beard looked scratchy and his eyes were heavy. "Jen, what are you doing here?"

She raked back her wet hair. "I'm sorry, I forgot you were on nights and sleeping in the afternoon. I'll go." She started to turn away, but he drew her around and tugged her inside.

"No, it's okay. What time is it?"

"Just after six."

"I have to get up, anyway." Crossing the room, he lit a cigarette, took a puff and held up the pack. "Want a smoke?"

She shook her head.

"What happened? You look upset."

The images she'd tried to block as she'd walked around in the cold rain for two hours rushed back full force. She shivered. "My father's screwing Lily Wakefield."

Hank lived in a studio apartment, and from the dresser against the wall, he pulled out a pair of jeans and put them on. "How do you know that?"

"The whole freakin' town probably knows. Her in-laws took the twins today, and Dad went over to comfort her." She swore. "That's a new name for what they were doing."

"Jenna, they're adults. Who cares what they do?"

"I care! What if he takes her back? What would I do?"

Pushing off the blanket and pillows, Hank pulled her down onto the couch that he hadn't bothered to unfold into a bed. "I been keepin' my mouth shut about this for a lot of reasons. But if your dad gets back with Lily, you're gonna get exactly what you want. Just don't forget about me, then. Okay?"

Because she was afraid Hank was right, and because she couldn't handle that, she snapped at him. "I don't want them together."

"Yeah, Jen, you do." Suddenly looking older and wiser than nineteen, he brushed a hand down her hair. "Lily made a mistake. Been there. Done that. So have you. But you love her and those babies."

"I love the babies."

He shook his head. "You know, one of the things I always liked about you was that you never bullshitted yourself or me. When you started actin' out, you knew what you were doin'." He leaned over and kissed her forehead. "Don't lose that honesty now."

She closed her eyes, tired and angry and, all right, confused. The gaping hole inside her that had just closed up was there all over again, wide and hollow and scary. And it was because her feelings for Lily were so mixed-up right now.

"What do you wanna do now?" he asked.

Her cell phone rang. Again. "Can I stay here?"

"For what?"

"I *don't* want to go home."

"Think that's a good idea?" The phone kept ringing. "Have you talked to your dad?"

"No. Can I stay or not?"

"All right. But make me a promise. You'll think about what I said."

She promised, but she didn't mean it. She couldn't think about forgiving Lily—she was too much of a coward to try it. Hank was right. Jenna wasn't being honest with anybody.

AT SEVEN O'CLOCK, Simon let himself back into Gil's house. Lily rushed out from the kitchen. "Did you find her?"

He shook his head. "She didn't call here?"

"No."

Lily pointed to his hand, which was still holding his phone. "I'm assuming she's not answering her cell."

"She's not. But she didn't turn it off, either. So she knows I've been trying to reach her." He ran a hand through his hair. "It's like she's trying to torture me."

"Simon, I'm so sorry."

"Me, too." He looked at her face, at her eyes, so full of worry. "Not for what we did. I'm not sorry for that. But for hurting Jenna."

"What you said at breakfast is really true. She's never going to forgive me. We can't ever be together."

The thought was obscene, after what they'd just shared. Being with Lily had eased the gnawing ache that had been eating away at him since she left. But if he'd held any hope that things could be different, Jenna's reaction tonight confirmed what he already knew. He and Lily didn't stand a chance.

"Lily, I…" His phone rang and he checked the ID. "I don't recognize the number. Hello?"

"Mr. McCarthy, this is Hank Ferris."

"Is she with you?" *Please let her be with you.*

"No, I'm at work. But she's at my place."

"Your place?"

"She showed up at my apartment just before I had to leave. She was upset and wanted to stay there. I said it was cool, but I thought you should know she's safe, so I called you as soon as I got to the gas station."

"Give me the address."

A hesitation. "Mr. McCarthy. I don't think going over to my place is such a good idea."

"This is my daughter we're talking about."

"I know. But she's safe and needs time."

"I can't give her that right now."

"She'll sleep in my bed tonight. When I get home, I'll bunk on the floor." Simon heard the boy swear. "I can't believe I'm sayin' this to her father, but I will. I know you don't like me, but I respect Jenna."

"She used alcohol and drugs with you."

"A little weed. Some booze. But only because I knew she'd get it someplace else. And she's finished with that. At least she was before tonight."

"Look, I appreciate your call, but I have to see her."

"Suit yourself." He gave Simon the address. "I left the door unlocked."

"Thanks. And Hank, if I've judged you wrong, I'm sorry. I can't tell you how much you've helped me tonight."

"Whatever." The boy hung up.

After Simon related the information to Lily, he kissed her goodbye and left. He'd hoped to be there when the Wakefields came back with the twins, but that wouldn't happen now. He had his own child to deal with.

Some father he'd been. As the windshield wipers whooshed back and forth, trying to keep up with the downpour, Simon was plagued by guilt all the way over to South Street. But he felt something else, too. Anger.

The whole situation was so goddamned unfair. He'd finally found a woman he could love wholeheartedly and he couldn't have her.

Hank lived in a studio apartment in an old house. Simon pulled up to the curb and recognized the three-story, gray-shingled dwelling as the Jenkins's old place. He climbed the front steps and let himself in. Number three was on the first floor in the back. At the door, he thought about knocking, but instead he simply went inside.

He found his daughter on the couch, blindly staring at the TV with the remote in one had and a glass in the other. Her clothes had dried and her hair had curled from the rain. Ludicrously, Simon remembered how she used to drag him out in a rainstorm when she was little and stomp in the puddles. Recalling her childhood underscored the fact that she was the most important person in his life and it determined what he did now.

Her eyes widened when she looked up at him. "What are you doing here?"

"Are you kidding? I've been searching for you for hours."

"You mean you could tear yourself away from the bitch?"

Up close, the strong scent of liquor in the glass assaulted him. He nodded to it. "I thought you stopped this."

"I did." Her gaze held his and he saw her face was tear-streaked.

"Honey, please, we've got to talk."

She looked away. "That's what Hank said."

Simon removed his raincoat and sat down next to her. "You're right, he's not a bad guy. He called me to tell me where you were."

"I should've known he would." After a moment, she set the glass on the table, and then shocked Simon by throwing herself into his arms. "I hate this."

Thanking God for the break, he clung to his child. Her welfare was on the line and he needed to handle this thing right. "Me, too. You're the most important person in the world to me. I'm sorry I hurt you."

"I hate that you were with her."

He had no words to say.

"Daddy, you can't go back with her."

"I'm not, honey." He wasn't. He couldn't. The living, breathing proof was in his arms.

"Then, why were you with her? Like that?"

"It's complicated." And damned embarrassing to discuss with his daughter. "Truthfully, it's all TMI for you."

She chuckled, as he hoped she would, at the role reversal. "Okay. Just so you aren't going to keep seeing her."

"I'm not."

"Good." She straightened. Wiped her cheeks. "Did the babies go with their grandparents?"

"Yes."

"Mr. Martini said Lily's worried the Wakefields won't bring Cami and Patrick back."

"They will." The constriction in his heart eased as the old Jenna resurfaced. She did love the babies, even if she didn't feel the same about Lily.

"I don't want them to go away."

"Nobody does."

She stood. "Okay, I'll come home now."

Arm in arm, they left Hank's place. Simon's relief that his daughter was safe filled his heart as they got into the car and drove home. But even that knowledge couldn't dilute his pain at the thought of never again being with Lily as he had been today.

TRUE TO HIS WORD, Bruce Wakefield pulled the Mercedes into Lily's driveway at precisely eight o'clock. Lily's emotions had been awhirl, and relief surfaced now that they'd brought the babies back. From the doorway, she watched Bruce and Johanna lift the twins from the car and hold them close to their hearts as they walked up to the house. Suddenly, she felt sympathy for Derek's parents. They'd lost so much. She'd have to think about that and what she could do for them.

Bruce came inside first. "They're asleep." He glanced around. "Where are the cribs?"

"Upstairs. I'll take him." Patrick was a deadweight, but she welcomed it as she climbed the steps. He was back, safe and sound. Maybe this was going to work out after all.

She'd just settled him in when she turned and found Johanna behind her. The woman didn't even look at Lily as she put Cami in her own crib, leaned over and kissed her. "Goodbye, sweetheart. See you soon."

Lily's heart went out to Johanna. Until the woman

rounded on her. She grabbed her arm and dragged her out into the hall, closing the door behind her.

Her mother-in-law's voice was hushed, but her words razor sharp. "You think you're so smart. That you've won Bruce over, like you did Derek."

Fear stirred inside Lily at the wild look in Johanna's eyes. "What are you talking about?"

"Bruce took calls from you. He told me. He thinks we can work out a compromise."

"Oh, Johanna, I'd love to do that. I know you care about the babies."

Johanna's nails dug into Lily's arm. "I'm sure you would. But no deal, Liliana. You've just sealed your own coffin."

"What does that mean?"

"It means that I'm going after you with all I've got. You think getting these townspeople to help you out will appease the courts. By the time I'm done with you and them, you won't know what hit you."

From below, Bruce called out, "Johanna, are you up there? I've brought everything in."

"I'll be right down, Bruce. You won't win, Liliana. I will." She nodded to the room where the twins slept. "Enjoy them while you can. You'll be hearing from me."

Lily gripped the upper banister as she watched Johanna descend the steps. It was obvious the woman had snapped. Just like her son. The thought of what Johanna might do next made Lily's stomach pitch.

ON WEDNESDAY MORNING, Lily had an appointment with Mac before work, so Marta came early, her two kids in tow. The woman was always so amenable and she'd assured Lily her boys would love to spend the time before school with the babies.

Mac greeted her at his office. "Hey, are you okay?"

"The whole town knows I wasn't yesterday. But I am today. And even more determined."

They took seats at a table.

"About the Wakefields?" he asked.

"Yes." She explained how the visit had gone and described its horrible ending. "I feel sorry for Johanna. Derek was her life and she blames me for his downslide. I've become the target of all her bad feelings." She glanced at the framed diplomas on the wall behind Mac. "I thought maybe Bruce could reason with her, but his kindness to me only seemed to enrage her. She's frightening, Mac."

"So I hear. I called one of her lawyers, James Pollard, whom I knew in law school, by the way." Mac himself looked weary today. "I couldn't stand just sitting by when you were so upset. Without betraying any confidence, Pollard intimated that Johanna would stop at nothing to get the babies."

"Those were her exact words. Do you think she'd kidnap them?"

"No, the lawyer did say she wouldn't do anything illegal. Nor does she have to. It's my guess women like Johanna think they have the means to get what they want."

"Hence the threat."

"Yes. I'll keep my feelers out." He leaned over and braced his arms on the desk. "Take heart, Lily. You need to watch your back with the Wakefields, but also remember you're the twins' mother. You have more right to them than anyone else in the world. A court will eventually see that."

As she left the office and drove to the *Sentinel*, Lily forced herself to heed Mac's words. Something had happened to her yesterday, besides finally getting to make love with Simon. For a moment, she let herself remember the touch of his hand, the brush of his beard on her skin, and it gave her strength. His presence, all of his support had made her see reason, and she'd be damned if Johanna Wakefield was going to take that away from her again. If the woman wanted a fight, Lily would give her one.

She reached the office only a few minutes late. Simon's car was in the driveway, and just seeing his blue Taurus made her anxiety calm. Maybe she couldn't have him totally, but at least she'd get to be around him. She'd have to settle for that.

He was at the desk in the front. When he looked up, his face was full of emotion.

I love you, Lily. I'm sorry, I love you.

"Hi."

"Sorry I'm late. I met with Mac this morning."

"Everything okay?"

"No. But first tell me about Jenna." Last night, he'd called to tell her his daughter was home, but he'd said little else. Lily hadn't told him about her latest run-in with Johanna, either.

"She's better this morning. I was worried because she has summer play tryouts this week, and I didn't want her bummed."

"Is she? Bummed?"

"We talked." He rolled his eyes. "Without embarrassing myself, I managed to calm her down by telling her you and I aren't getting back together."

A vise clamped around her heart. "I'm glad you could reassure her."

He stood when she came around the desk and took her face between his hands. "I meant what I said to Jenna. But I want you to know that yesterday was the most incredible experience of my life. And I'm not sorry about it. I just wish things could be different."

How could something hurt so much and at the same time be so piercingly joyful? She almost rocked back with the force of the emotion. But she'd be strong for him. "I understand." Somehow she managed to add, "It was incredible for me, too."

When he went back to his office, Lily sat at the computer and called up her e-mail. There was one from Liz Gaston, reiterating the Heard Corporation's desire to buy her stock and raising the amount they'd pay her. There was something from Mac, Loretta. She read those.

The last e-mail was from Johanna, with another article attached labeled, Mother Proved Unfit.

Lily deleted it. Mac had been right about avoiding these scare tactics. She was done letting the woman intimidate her.

THE WEEK HAD DRAGGED ON as Lily waited to see what the Wakefields were going to do, tried not to think about how she and Simon couldn't be together and wondered what the future held. On Thursday, she received another e-mail article from Johanna, which Lily also deleted without reading. That afternoon, when the babies were up from their naps and playing out front, Lily was working on ad copy when the front door swung open. In walked Jenna. Before she saw Lily, she was smiling, and she looked like the old Jenna in a short khaki skirt and yellow blouse. The good humor disappeared when she got a glimpse of Lily. It was as if she were poison to this girl.

"Hello, Jenna."

"Um, hi."

Simon came out from the back and Jenna's smile bloomed again. She rushed across the room and threw herself at her father. "I got the part, Dad."

As he hugged his daughter, Simon met Lily's gaze over Jenna's shoulder. "Which one?"

"The lead. I'm going to be Fiona in *Brigadoon*."

Lily said, "How wonderful."

When Jenna pulled back, Simon ruffled her hair. "That's my girl."

"I'm so excited. Katie got second lead. Can you believe it, Dad? We're only juniors." She babbled on excitedly about who got other parts, when rehearsals started, what the director said about her audition.

Lily turned away from the sight. As happy as she was for Jenna, this was proof positive that her dad had indeed assured her that his relationship with Lily was over.

On Friday, Lily forced herself to concentrate on the

good things in her life. The babies, of course; the people in town, who'd been kinder and more accepting; seeing Simon happy about Jenna, and Jenna getting back to her old self more and more each day. Even when she received yet another article from the Wakefields, Lily promptly deleted it, and left for the weekend feeling better.

But on Monday, Lily called up her e-mail, and this time she didn't delete anything. Again, there was a note from Johanna. Again, it contained an attachment. But this one wasn't an article; it was a forwarded message, and the subject header read, Reports on Fairview Residents, Eric Barrett Associates, Private Investigator.

When the cover letter came up, Lily's heart started to beat as fast as a racehorse's.

To: Mrs. Johanna Wakefield
From: Eric Barrett
Re: Fairview residents
Enclosed are the results of our background checks on the residents of Fairview, New York. As you requested, a team of five investigators was put on this assignment. Their findings, as well as my comments, are included. Notify me, if I can be of any more assistance.

Report #1
Marta Wilson Kiev
Age: 39
Born: Chicago, Illinois
Education: high school dropout, attended PS #28
Employment: variety of jobs, including waitress, clerk, teller in bank
Highlights: Was a member of the Lizard Ladies, a Chicago girl gang. Questioned in 1997 on suspicion of gang activities and other misdemeanors. Moved to Fairview, New York, in 1999. Met and married Kale Kiev in 2001 and had two children.

Suggested use: Kiev is the twins' nanny. Easy to prove unfitness. Side detail: By all accounts, husband is unaware of her background.

Report #2
Loretta Jameson
Age: 57
Place of Birth: Ellensburg, Ohio
Education: teaching degree at Ohio University; arrived in New York City in early seventies.
Employment: stagehand, ticket sales, chorus girl. Major drama parts in early eighties. Leaves theater in 1985; settles in Fairview, 1987, where she has taught ever since.
Highlights: involved with Joseph Clark, local business-man. Circumstances as to why relationship didn't work out unclear. Subsequent to breakup, subject spent time in Sands Sanitarium; diagnosis, mental issues.
Suggested Use: Mrs. Wakefield's best friend, who helps with children, has history of mental instability.

Report #3
Cameron Gardner Clarkson
Age: deceased, 1991; unsolved case; found dead in alley; suspicion of foul play by man she left work with—a john?
Place of birth: Fairview, New York
Education: high school dropout
Employment: from 1986 through 1991, Clarkson worked at the Cathouse Club in the Village, the Ladies Night in downtown Manhattan and Sassy Gals in New Jersey.
Highlights: Prostitution suspected, never proven.
Suggested Use: May put daughter in bad light; could embarrass her enough to leave town. No evidence Liliana Clarkson followed in mother's footsteps, but innuendo may be effective in discrediting her.

Report #4
Marian McCarthy
Age: deceased, 1996
Place of birth: Ithaca, New York
Education: Ithaca College dropout, 1991, pregnant
Employment: housewife and mother
Highlights: Interviewees from college and hometown
speculate about a shotgun wedding. Before their
deaths, Marian's parents were bitter about her marriage
to Simon McCarthy and subsequent events. Examined
police records of death. Official cause, accident. Fleet-
ing consideration was given to suicide.
Suggested Usage: Simon McCarthy seems to be Mrs.
Wakefield's biggest supporter. Tread lightly in using
innuendo, as you could be sued for slander. The pen,
in this case, is very mighty.

Miscellaneous reports on other townspeople are
included, though they are not as useful: minor incidents
such as children of townspeople picked up for DUI,
possession of marijuana, indecent exposure.
Summary: enough ammunition to discredit Mrs. Wakefield's support system in Fairview.

An eerie calmness filled Lily as she sat motionless at
her desk, staring down at the damaging report. It made one
thing crystal clear: she could bring disaster on the people
she loved, on all those who'd accepted her, supported her
and given her a second chance. Because they wanted to
help her, they could be ruined by Lily remaining in
Fairview.

There was really no question, then, about what to do.

Walking outside so no one would overhear her, Lily
made four phone calls. One was to Mac Madison, one was
to Liz Gaston, another was to Mr. Martini, and finally, she
called reservations at JFK Airport.

CHAPTER SEVENTEEN

ON FRIDAY MORNING, when Lily didn't come to work, Simon was somehow not surprised. In the past couple of days, she'd been acting strangely. First, he'd found her hanging the drawing that he was now staring at on the wall of the outer office....

"What's that?" he'd asked.

Her expression had been so loving, his heart warmed at just the sight of her. "Something I've been working on. I did most of it while I was away in Westchester. I was saving it for the town's centennial celebration this summer." She'd shrugged a shoulder. "I decided not to wait. You shouldn't wait for too much in life, Simon."

He'd studied the artwork. She'd created a big charcoal sketch, framed and matted, of the townspeople. Mr. Martini was there among a circle of five, wearing his fedora and his gruff exterior; there was a small World War II military appliqué in the corner of the hat, indicating his service to his country.

Miss Jameson was stunning in a cape and pants, posing as if she were onstage. A tiny Broadway street sign appeared on the edge of her clothing.

Mrs. Billings was smiling and holding a big apple pie. On its rim were the names of her daughters.

The O'Malley brothers stood behind their bar, scowling at each other. On one corner of the bar was the logo of their pub.

The druggist, the Conklins, as well as other townspeople and even some firefighters added to the composite of the population of Fairview.

"Lily, this is spectacular." Simon had tried to joke. "How come Fast Eddie's in it and I'm not?"

Solemnly, she'd crossed to the desk drawer and taken out another smaller frame. It held a sketch of him at a basketball game. The detail was amazing, and for a brief minute he was simply overjoyed by this evidence of how Lily had viewed him. "When did you do this?"

"One time when I went to a game." Her blue eyes had been filled with emotion. "I never told you this, but that night Jenna said she thought you were in love with me."

He swallowed hard, so moved he couldn't speak for a few seconds. "I was. I still am. More."

Squeezing his arm, she gave him the saddest smile he'd ever seen. "I know. And I feel the same way. Take care of yourself, Simon, okay?"

Before he could respond, they'd been interrupted, but he'd been bothered by her remarks. It was almost as if she was saying goodbye.

The door to the office opened and Jenna walked in. He checked the clock—half past eight. "Hey, honey. Why aren't you at school?"

"I didn't go in yet. I had to see you first." She held a white envelope. "When Hank picked me up to drive me today, he found this letter and Blackie on our doorstep."

"Blackie?"

"Lily's cat."

"Did you read the letter?"

"Yeah. Dad, it's so sad. Lily told me she loved me and I should always think of the twins as my brother and sister. She said you were the most wonderful man in the world and to not be so hard on you." Jenna swallowed hard and her blue eyes were bright with moisture. "It weirded me out, like something bad is going to happen."

It didn't take the next person who entered the office to

tell them what that *bad* thing was. Marta Kiev came inside frowning. "Is Lily here?"

"Isn't she home?" Jenna asked.

"No, and she left me this." She, too, held an envelope.

"What is it?" Simon asked.

"Two weeks' pay. With a note that says she won't need me anymore. I found it waiting for me at her house."

Marta had left the door open, and from the entryway, Mr. Martini spoke to them. "It's not her house anymore. She sold it to me this week. Knew I always wanted it. I only had ten grand to give her, but she said she'd let me know where I could send the rest when I sold my place."

"Why didn't you tell me this before?" Simon was trying to stay calm, but the world was shifting beneath his feet.

"She made me promise not to say anything until today."

"Daddy, what's going on?"

"My best guess, Jen," he said, while his heart was breaking, "is that Lily left town without telling anyone. Just like her mother did all those years ago."

After he got Jenna off to school and ushered Mr. Martini and Marta out the door, Simon booted up the computer. He did everything robotically, trying to block the fear that was hovering on the edges of his mind. Lily had asked him if she could send private e-mail on the machine, and he'd agreed, of course.

He clicked into her server. She'd also told him her password was CamiPat, so with it, he called up her e-mail. She'd wiped the thing clean. No in-box mail waiting to be answered; no deleted items or sent mail. Damn it, everybody saved *something*.

He hit the icon for new messages. There were three incoming.

From Johanna Wakefield, the message read only,

So, are you ready to give them up, Liliana? I told you that you wouldn't like the consequences, if you kept thwarting me.

The second made his heart skip a beat. It was from Liz Gaston.

After your phone call, my partners and I have agreed to double the price we're willing to pay for your stock.

And the last, from Mac:

All the papers are in order, Lily, but please reconsider. There are other ways to deal with the Wakefields.

Simon sat back and mentally put the pieces of the puzzle together. He'd just finished assembling them when his sister walked in and found him sitting there, staring at the screen.

"Simon, what's wrong?"

He shook his head. "You were right, Sara."

"About what?"

"About Lily Wakefield. She's skipped town, but before she left I think she sold my future to the Heard Corporation."

THE EARSPLITTING NOISE of departing flights and the cacophony of weary travelers at JFK bothered Patrick and he started to cry. Lily fished a bottle from the bag, picked him up out of his stroller-car seat and began to feed him. "Shh, sweetheart, it's almost over. We're almost free."

Patrick patted his bottle and smiled at her. It reminded her of why she was here, doing this, and she calmed some. As she fed her child, she refused to think of how Jenna would never see him take his first step or play baseball, or maybe even act in a play. She refused to think of how she'd never see Jenna perform in *Brigadoon,* go to the Junior Prom or graduate from high school. She'd never get to take Jenna to Broadway, either, as she promised she'd do. Though she hadn't really had Jenna in her life for a long time, Lily never forgot those precious months they'd had

together before Lily had screwed up her life by going back
to Derek.

Lily also wouldn't think about never having a long talk
with Loretta, or tasting one of Mrs. Billings's cookies or
seeing the twinkle in Mr. Martini's eyes when she caught
on that inside he was really a cream puff.

And most of all Lily refused to think of never being with
Simon again, never hearing his laugh or feeling his touch.
Her control almost snapped as the knowledge sank in.
Right about now he'd be thinking she betrayed him, and
the reason she was doing things this way wouldn't be clear
until next week when she was safely hidden where the
Wakefields couldn't find her.

She felt a tear run down her cheek at how much the man
she loved must be hurting.

ONE WEEK LATER, Mac strode into Simon's office. When
he saw the lawyer, he tensed. "Are you finally going to tell
me about the *Sentinel?* You said you'd have news today."

"Yes." He handed Simon a manila envelope.

"This is it?"

The lawyer nodded.

Simon stared at the envelope. Then, like tearing off a
bandage from the skin, he ripped open the tab. Out slid
several certificates. It took him a minute to realize what
they were. Stocks in the *Sentinel.* He studied one. "I don't
understand. These are in my name."

"You own the paper, Simon. Free and clear."

"She can't sell the stocks for a few more months."

"That's what Gil's will specified. But it didn't say
anything about giving them away."

"Lily *gave* me the stocks?"

"Yes."

"Why?"

"I think you know the answer to that."

He threw back his chair. "Where is she? I need to see
her."

"I don't know where she is. Nobody does. The only thing I have is a post office box in Manhattan to send her documents. And Mr. Martini has a Swiss bank account number with which to deposit payments for the house." He shook his head. "I can't tell you how bad I feel about all this. I didn't give her enough hope, I guess."

No, damn it. She couldn't have done this. "That's not enough. She could be anywhere. You can vanish without a trace with just a P.O. box and Swiss account."

"I think that was the idea, Simon."

FEELING LIKE POND SCUM, Jenna stared at the house where Grandpa Gil and then Lily had lived. The bright sunshine beat down on her, but she was cold inside. "Why wasn't I nicer to her? Then maybe she wouldn't have left."

From beside her, Katie squeezed her arm. "That's stupid. Everybody knows she's running from the Wakefields. To keep the babies."

"At least they're safe."

"Nobody's heard from her?"

"No, not even Miss Jameson."

"Or your dad?"

"My dad's a basket case." She'd heard him up at night again, just like in the weeks after Lily had left the first time. And he never, ever smiled.

"I loved this house." Jenna dropped down onto the front brick steps. It was late April, and the leaves on the maple trees were out, the crocuses up and the air warmer. "Grandpa Gil loved spring. I miss him so much." Jenna swiped at her eyes. "It's funny, Katie, how you don't know how much you miss somebody until they're gone."

"You mean Lily, too, don't you?"

"I guess. I really screwed everything up."

"I'm sorry." Katie waited. "Let's go do something."

"Like what?"

"Practice our lines for *Brigadoon?*"

"Okay." She wondered if Lily had found her own Brigadoon, a haven from the real world. "She was going to take me to New York, to see Broadway, you know?"

"Yeah?"

"Uh-huh. We were talking about places we wanted to visit, and we both made lists. That was at the top of mine."

"Jenna?" She looked over at Katie. There was an odd expression on her friend's face.

"What?"

"Do you remember Lily's list?"

"Yeah. I think she wanted to go to… Holy shit!" She bolted up. "Come on, hurry. We've got to get to my house quick. Maybe it isn't too late after all."

"Right behind you," Katie called out.

SIMON POUNDED THE BALL HARD on the floor as he ran down the basketball court, hoping to outdistance his demons. He'd asked Coach Carson to let him into the gym this morning because he couldn't stand the emotions battling inside him: the pervasive, ugly guilt over what he'd done to Lily; the hollow regret over what he hadn't done, and spurts of anger that she wouldn't turn to him for help.

She was just trying to protect you.

It didn't work.

She took the only reasonable path.

Well, he understood that, especially after Mac had shown him the reports on the townspeople. There was even one on Marian. He'd been enraged over the lengths to which the Wakefields had gone, but at least he finally understood Lily's panic. And when Bruce Wakefield had shown up at the paper he'd wanted to deck the guy. He might have, too, if the man hadn't been so overwrought….

"We heard she left."

"Did your P.I. try to find her?" He almost hoped the firm was looking for her. Simon himself hadn't hired one because he didn't want to lead the Wakefields to her.

"No. I've put my foot down over this whole thing. I should have done it sooner."

"What do you mean?"

"Johanna's gone away for a while. There's a spalike place, very posh, with all kinds of pampering. But it has a mental health component to it, too. I'm hoping the rest makes her see reason, but in any case, I've called off the dogs myself."

"I'm sorry, but forgive me if I don't feel bad for Johanna."

"Imagine what it would be like if you lost your only child." His eyes had shadowed. "And now lost the only connection with him."

Simon's common decency had overridden his anger and he'd managed to be kind to Bruce...

Swearing at the frustration of it all, he went in for three layups in a row. Damn, damn, damn. If she'd just trusted him.

The gym door burst open and Jenna raced inside and over to him. "Dad, I think I know where Lily went." She gave him a paper.

His heart pummeled his chest as he read Lily's list of places she wanted to travel. "Do you have your cell phone?" He punched in Sara's number. When she answered, he asked, "Sara, are you at the office?"

"Yes. Don't rag on me about working Saturdays."

"Do you still have the information on Lily, from when you investigated her?"

"Um, yes, I do."

"How deep did you go into her college years?"

"Deep enough. I can call it up right now. Tell me what you want."

When he clicked off the phone, he ruffled his daughter's hair. "Come on, Princess, let's go find your passport."

LILY PUSHED THE BABIES back and forth in their stroller. At almost eight months, both were babbling and cooing in appreciation of their surroundings. The café across from the

Louvre wasn't busy this early, so she took her time sipping her latte as she waited for the museum to open. And talked to the babies.

"That's one of the most famous museums in the world, guys. It's huge and you can get lost in it. But I know my way around." She should, as she'd spent a semester studying art in Paris. "There's this beautiful room full of Greek statues, with the *Venus de Milo* in the center. And of course, the *Mona Lisa* is here, but it's behind glass and hard to see."

She kept chattering about the collection, and even mentioned *The Da Vinci Code*. When the babies dozed off, she sat back and breathed in the heady scents of April in Paris. Even if she wasn't here with a sweetheart like the song said, she would try to enjoy the cobblestone walks, the friendly flower vendors and the young waiters who flirted with her.

Basically, Lily was healthy and safe. She'd run every morning, with the twins along, or while Nic and Lois Dubois watched the kids. The couple, who'd been in their thirties when Lily had stayed with them fifteen years earlier for her semester abroad, had welcomed her with open arms when she'd arrived in Paris two weeks ago. She only hoped she didn't bring problems on them while she searched for an apartment of her own up in Montmartre.

At ten o'clock, Lily maneuvered the stroller out of the café and toward the museum; as she walked, she tried to think happy thoughts. But she was distracted by something up ahead, in front of I.M. Pei's striking glass pyramid. Though the sun turned it crystalline and bounced its bright rays off the peak, Lily thought she saw something she recognized. God, was she losing it? Yet when she got closer, the images looked so real, tears came to her eyes. Damn it, the two people standing there looked like Simon and Jenna. This just wasn't fair! It was bad enough that she dreamed about them at night and despite her best efforts, thought about them during the day. Now this…this… mirage.

The man came forward a few steps and said, "Hello, love."

Lily blinked, but they were still there. She gripped the handle of the carriage.

The girl broke away, rushed over and threw herself at Lily. "Oh, Lily, I'm so sorry."

Lily stiffened, but Jenna was solid and full of life in her arms, so she held on tight. Then reality sank in, like a splash of cold water on the face. "How did you find me?" Even she could hear the traces of panic in her own voice.

Simon closed the distance between them. He looked so good, so healthy, even happy. "Don't worry, you're safe. I have a lot to tell you."

Trying to keep her mind clear, she took a deep breath. "I don't understand. I covered my tracks. I never told anybody my connection to this place."

Jenna had dropped down in front of the twins. She peered up at Lily. "Me. You told me you studied at the Sorbonne for a semester in college."

"I forgot about that." She thought a minute. "But Paris is a big city."

Simon told her about Sara's investigation, when Lily had first come to Fairview. "We had enough information to track you here."

And so would the Wakefields. At the horrible thought, Lily began to tremble. Where would she go now?

Simon slid an arm around her, and whispered, "I'll explain everything." Then he said to Jenna, "Honey, want to take the babies for a walk around the square? I'd like to talk to Lily alone."

"Sure." Impulsively, she kissed Lily on the cheek. "It's okay, Lily. Really." Jenna wheeled the babies away.

They took seats on a bench beneath a tree facing the

museum. Simon reached for her hand and she gripped it tightly.

"First, the Wakefields have backed off." He told her about Bruce's visit and gave her the news of what had happened with Johanna.

"Are you sure?" Could this possibly be the answer to her prayers? "Are you sure, Simon?"

"Yes, I talked to him myself. I swear, you're safe."

"I didn't think he had it in him." Still… "What if they change their minds, now that you've found me?"

"They won't."

"I don't believe it." She closed her eyes, tried to think clearly. "It's too much to take in."

"Then think about at it this way. If they did change their minds, it wouldn't matter anyway, because your circumstances will be vastly different." Out of his pocket Simon drew a box.

"Simon, what?"

"Shh." He opened the top and inside the red velvet nestled a beautiful diamond-and-sapphire platinum ring. "Will you marry me, Lily?"

She burst into tears.

"Hmm. Not exactly the reaction I hoped for." He tipped her chin. "What, Lily?"

"You don't know everything, Simon. I can't go back to Fairview and take the chance of the Wakefields ruining the people in town." She touched his beloved face. "You, especially."

"It would be a moot point, even if they wanted to use the reports—which I don't believe they will."

"You know about the reports?"

"Yes, from Mac."

She swiped at her cheeks. "He wasn't supposed to tell you."

"I was beside myself, and he took pity on me."

"So you understand why I can't come back."

"No, *you* don't understand. First, we'll be married, with a stable home and money—thanks for the stock by the way—in a wonderful place to raise the kids. Second, we gave copies of the reports to everyone who was investigated. Even Jenna saw the one about her mother."

"Oh, no."

"Hiding things like this doesn't work out in the long run. Marta had told her husband years ago about her background, and she isn't ashamed of having crawled her way out of a gang. She said she might even use what happened to help kids who are in trouble. Loretta spat out a few choice words, then said the town already thought her odd, so she didn't give a flip about having them know about her problems. And Jenna's cool. We honestly don't think Marian committed suicide. That's all that matters."

Lily looked out at the street before her where people hurried to the museum. "I can't believe this."

With the Louvre as a backdrop, Simon actually slid onto one knee. "So, love, will you marry me? Let Cami and Patrick be my babies, too, and maybe—" his eyes twinkled and he placed a hand on her stomach "—have one more?"

"Oh, God, yes, yes, yes."

He drew her head down and kissed her then, a long, slow kiss. When he pulled back, he met her forehead with his. "Do you have any idea how much I want to make love to you now?"

"Even the Parisians would frown on us doing it right here." Over Simon's shoulder, Lily saw Jenna coming toward them with the babies. "And the kids are back." She chuckled. "You know, Simon, we never have had good luck getting to do this *thingy* thing."

He laughed out loud. It was the best sound in the world. And Lily realized that she did, after all, have her sweetheart, here with her, in April in Paris. And so much more. As she kissed him again, she wondered how she had ever gotten so lucky.

When Jenna reached them, with a wide smile and a too-adult expression in her eyes, she asked, "So, you coming home with us, Lily?"

She looked at the girl then at her babies and finally at the man she loved. "Yes, honey, I'm coming home."

* * * * *

Enjoy a sneak preview of
MATCHMAKING WITH A MISSION
by B.J. Daniels,
part of the **WHITEHORSE, MONTANA** *miniseries.*
Available from Harlequin Intrigue
in April 2008.

Nate Dempsey has returned to Whitehorse to uncover the truth about his past...

Nate sensed someone watching the house and looked out in surprise to see a woman astride a paint horse just on the other side of the fence. He quickly stepped back from the filthy second-floor window, although he doubted she could have seen him. Only a little of the June sun pierced the dirty glass to glow on the dust-coated floor at his feet as he waited a few heartbeats before he looked out again.

The place was so isolated he hadn't expected to see another soul. Like the front yard, the dirt road was waist-high with weeds. When he'd broken the lock on the back door, he'd had to kick aside a pile of rotten leaves that had blown in from last fall.

As he sneaked a look, he saw that she was still there, staring at the house in a way that unnerved him. He shielded his eyes from the glare of the sun off the dirty window and studied her, taking in her head of long blond hair that feathered out in the breeze from under her Western straw hat.

She wore a tan canvas jacket, jeans and boots. But it was the way she sat astride the brown-and-white horse that nudged the memory.

He felt a chill as he realized he'd seen her before. In that very spot. She'd been just a kid then. A kid on a pretty paint horse. Not this one—the markings were different. Anyway, it couldn't have been the same horse, considering the last time he had seen her was more than twenty years ago. That horse would be dead by now.

His mind argued it probably wasn't even the same girl. But he knew better. It was the way she sat on the horse, so at home in a saddle and secure in her world on the other side of that fence.

To the boy he'd been, she and her horse had represented freedom, a freedom he'd known he would never have— even after he escaped this house.

Nate saw her shift in the saddle, and for a moment he feared she planned to dismount and come toward the house. With Ellis Harper in his grave, there would be little to keep her away.

To his relief, she reined her horse around and rode back the way she'd come.

As he watched her ride away, he thought about the way she'd stared at the house—today and years ago. While the smartest thing she could do was to stay clear of this house, he had a feeling she'd be back.

Finding out her name should prove easy, since he figured she must live close by. As for her interest in Harper House... He would just have to make sure it didn't become a problem.

* * * * *

Be sure to look for
MATCHMAKING WITH A MISSION
and other suspenseful Harlequin Intrigue stories,
available in April
wherever books are sold.

HARLEQUIN *Romance.*

presents

Planning perfect weddings... finding happy endings!

Amidst the rustle of satins and silks, the scent of red roses and white lilies and the excited chatter of brides-to-be, six friends from Boston are The Wedding Belles—they make other people's wedding dreams come true....

But are they always the wedding planner...never the bride?

Who will be the next to say "I do"?

In April: Shirley Jump, *Sweetheart Lost and Found*
In May: Myrna Mackenzie, *The Heir's Convenient Wife*
In June: Melissa McClone, *S.O.S. Marry Me*
In July: Linda Goodnight, *Winning the Single Mom's Heart*
In August: Susan Meier, *Millionaire Dad, Nanny Needed!*
In September: Melissa James, *The Bridegroom's Secret*

And don't miss the exciting wedding-planner tips and author reminiscences that accompany each book!

www.eHarlequin.com   HRI7507

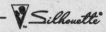

SPECIAL EDITION™

Introducing a brand-new miniseries

Men of Mercy Medical

Gabe Thorne moved to Las Vegas to open a
new branch of his booming construction
business—and escape from a recent tragedy.
But when his teenage sister showed up pregnant
on his doorstep, he really had his hands full.
Luckily, in turning to Dr. Rebecca Hamilton for
the medical care his sister needed, he found
a cure for himself....

Starting with

THE MILLIONAIRE
AND THE M.D.

by *TERESA SOUTHWICK,*

available in April wherever books are sold.

Celebrate the joys of motherhood!
In this collection of touching stories,
three women embrace their maternal
instincts in ways they hadn't expected.
And even more surprising is how true
love finds them.

Mothers of the Year

With stories by
Lori Handeland
Rebecca Winters
Anna DeStefano

*Look for Mothers of the Year,
available in April
wherever books are sold.*

REQUEST YOUR FREE BOOKS!

2 FREE NOVELS PLUS 2 FREE GIFTS!

HARLEQUIN®

Super Romance®

Exciting, emotional, unexpected!

YES! Please send me 2 FREE Harlequin Superromance® novels and my 2 FREE gifts (gifts are worth about $10). After receiving them, if I don't wish to receive any more books, I can return the shipping statement marked "cancel." If I don't cancel, I will receive 6 brand-new novels every month and be billed just $4.69 per book in the U.S. or $5.24 per book in Canada, plus 25¢ shipping and handling per book and applicable taxes, if any*. That's a savings of close to 15% off the cover price! I understand that accepting the 2 free books and gifts places me under no obligation to buy anything. I can always return a shipment and cancel at any time. Even if I never buy another book from Harlequin, the two free books and gifts are mine to keep forever.

135 HDN EEX7   336 HDN EEYK

Name	(PLEASE PRINT)	
Address		Apt. #
City	State/Prov.	Zip/Postal Code

Signature (if under 18, a parent or guardian must sign)

Mail to the Harlequin Reader Service:
IN U.S.A.: P.O. Box 1867, Buffalo, NY 14240-1867
IN CANADA: P.O. Box 609, Fort Erie, Ontario L2A 5X3

Not valid to current subscribers of Harlequin Superromance books.

Want to try two free books from another line?
Call 1-800-873-8635 or visit www.morefreebooks.com.

* Terms and prices subject to change without notice. N.Y. residents add applicable sales tax. Canadian residents will be charged applicable provincial taxes and GST. This offer is limited to one order per household. All orders subject to approval. Credit or debit balances in a customer's account(s) may be offset by any other outstanding balance owed by or to the customer. Please allow 4 to 6 weeks for delivery. Offer available while quantities last.

Your Privacy: Harlequin is committed to protecting your privacy. Our Privacy Policy is available online at www.eHarlequin.com or upon request from the Reader Service. From time to time we make our lists of customers available to reputable third parties who may have a product or service of interest to you. If you would prefer we not share your name and address, please check here. ☐

HSR08

HARLEQUIN

More Than Words

"Jeanne proves that one woman can change the world, with vision, compassion and hard work."

—**Linda Lael Miller**, author

*Linda wrote "Queen of the Rodeo," inspired by Jeanne Greenberg, founder of **SARI Therapeutic Riding**. Since 1978 Jeanne has devoted her life to enriching the lives of disabled children and their families through innovative and exciting therapies on horseback.*

Look for "*Queen of the Rodeo*" in
More Than Words, Vol. 4,
available in April 2008 at eHarlequin.com
or wherever books are sold.

SUPPORTING CAUSES OF CONCERN TO WOMEN ✿ HARLEQUIN

WWW.HARLEQUINMORETHANWORDS.COM

MTW07JG2

HARLEQUIN *Presents*

He's successful, powerful—and extremely sexy....
He also happens to be her boss! Used to getting his
own way, he'll demand what he wants from her—
in the boardroom and the bedroom....

Watch the sparks fly as these couples
work together—and play together!

IN BED WITH
THE BOSS

Don't miss any of the stories in April's collection!

MISTRESS IN PRIVATE
by JULIE COHEN

IN BED WITH HER ITALIAN BOSS
by KATE HARDY

MY TALL DARK GREEK BOSS
by ANNA CLEARY

HOUSEKEEPER TO
THE MILLIONAIRE
by LUCY MONROE

Available April 8
wherever books are sold.

www.eHarlequin.com

HPP0408NEW

HARLEQUIN® Super Romance®

COMING NEXT MONTH

#1482 MOTHERS OF THE YEAR • Lori Handeland, Rebecca Winters, Anna DeStefano

Celebrate the joys of motherhood! In this collection of touching stories three women embrace their maternal instincts in ways they hadn't expected. And even more surprising is how true love finds them.

#1483 RETURN OF THE WILD SON • Cynthia Thomason

Jenna Malloy will never forget the horrible crime she witnessed as a girl. Now the son of her father's killer has come home, reopening old wounds and igniting a passion that could destroy her fragile peace. Unless Nate Shelton can help her let go of the past…

#1484 BABY BE MINE • Eve Gaddy
Marriage of Inconvenience

How can Tucker Jones refuse when his best friend proposes marriage? He can't. Especially when his best friend looks like Maggie Barnes. He wants Maggie to be happy, and that means a fake union so she can foster an abandoned baby girl. As they grow closer, he discovers he wants this marriage to be real.

#1485 A KISS TO REMEMBER • Kimberly Van Meter

Sparks fly when Nora Simmons finds out that the Hollister house is on the market. How dare Ben Hollister come back to Emmett's Mill to sell his late grandparents' home when he never came to visit them when they were alive! Nora intends to let him know exactly what she thinks of him…if she can only forget the kiss they once shared.

#1486 A MAN WORTH KEEPING • Molly O'Keefe
The Mitchells of Riverview Inn

The Riverview Inn is the perfect hiding place for Delia Dupuis and her daughter. They're not here to make personal connections…until Delia meets Max Mitchell. Despite evidence to the contrary, she senses he's one of the good ones—a man worth keeping.

#1487 HEART OF MY HEART • Stella MacLean
Everlasting Love

Olivia Banks and James McElroy were high school sweethearts who believed their love would last forever. But when James succumbed to family pressure to end the relationship, he unknowingly left Olivia pregnant.… Despite that betrayal, they never forgot each other…and they eventually discover that love really *can* last.

HSRCNM0308